FIFTY-FIFTY
NEW HONG KONG WRITING

FIFTY-FIFTY: New Hong Kong Writing

Published in Hong Kong by Haven Books Ltd

www.havenbooksonline.com

Copyright © 2008 by the contributing writers

Cover design by e5

The moral right of the contributing authors has been asserted. All rights reserved.
No part of this book may be reproduced or translated in any form without the express
permission of the publisher or the authors.

ISBN 978-988-98819-7-9

FIFTY-FIFTY
NEW HONG KONG WRITING

Edited by Xu Xi

Haven Books

Photograph by Madeleine Marie Slavick

Contents

The Way We Are, Are, Arguably Are *Preface*	Xu Xi	9

The Personal ...

It Wasn't Supposed To Be Like This *Personal essay*	Keane Shum	15
My City *Poem*	Agnes S. L. Lam	17
Made in Hong Kong? *Poem*	Arthur Leung	20
235 Shanghai Street *Creative non-fiction*	Doris Lau Parry	21
Hong Kong Island Mon Amour *Poem*	Nicholas Y. B. Wong	40
Passing *Meditation*	Edward Rodney Davey	41

Is Possibly Political

The Final Solution: By the One-Country, One-System Think Tank *Satire*	Mani Rao	53
Forty Years To Go *Poem*	Louise Ho	57
What Do You Do *Poem*	Alan Jefferies	58
In Another Ten Years: Some Wanton Thoughts for 2017 *Poem*	Christine Loh	60
A City Passing *Poem*	David Clarke	62
On Visiting Cavafy's House *Poem*	Alan Jefferies	63
Mid-Sentence *Essay*	Lawrence Gray	64

Witness

Exception *Creative non-fiction*	Amy Lee	83
Spring in Hong Kong *Poem*	Agnes S. L. Lam	89
Eyewitness Accounts *Poem*	Ching Yuet May	92
Moths *Poem*	Agnes S. L. Lam	94
Route 99 *Narrative non-fiction*	Keane Shum	96
The Great Wah Fu Public Housing Estate *Poem*	Elbert Siu Ping Lee	99
The Beach of Discovery Bay *Poem*	Woo See-Kow	100

Almost a Love Story

Luke *Short story*	Nicole Wong	105
Shadows of Time *Poem*	Nicholas Y. B. Wong	113
ways to be human *Poem*	Viki Holmes	114
April in Sai Kung *Poem*	Woo See-Kow	116
Triptych *Poem*	Stuart Christie	118
Smog *Short story*	Justin Hill	123

Personal Histories

Two Parallel Motions: Mapping Hong Kong *Prose poem*	Jennifer S. Cheng	139
Supatra's Buddha *Personal essay*	David McKirdy	157
Emotions *Haiku*	Karen Shui-wan Leung	164
Random Fragments From These Years *Prose poem*	Tammy Ho Lai-ming	165

White *Poem*	Alan Jefferies	170
Mirror *Short story*	Viona Au Yeung	171
kinesthesia *Poem*	Viki Holmes	178
Conversations *Poem*	Monica Chan	180
Live It, Love It *Personal essay*	Keane Shum	181

AND A LITTLE REAL HISTORY

Remembering 1967 *Non-fiction*	Jesse Wong	185
Finger, Flower *Poem*	Madeleine Marie Slavick	198
Victoria Park *Poem*	Woo See-Kow	200
Painting Statues Red and Blue *Creative non-fiction*	Peter Gregoire	202
Chine *Poem*	Alan Jefferies	217
The Spoken Word *Narrative non-fiction*	Susan Blumberg-Kason	220
Ten Days of Cholera Epidemic *Poem*	Kwai-Cheung Lo	226

MAPPING MOMENTS

Reinterpretations of Three Poems by Leung Ping Kwan *Poems*	Arthur Leung	231
Penny's Bay *Poem*	Woo See-Kow	234
volar *Poem*	Akin Jeje	235
Ode to the Mass Transit Railway *Poem*	Arthur Leung	236
I for Illness *Short story*	Nicholas Y. B. Wong	238

The Beautiful Game *Sonnet*	Martin Alexander	249
Chung Yeung: Lamma Island 2006 *Poem*	Kate Rogers	250
Once Upon the Lamma Hills *Poem*	Agnes S. L. Lam	252
Petal Beauty *Poem*	Yuen Siu Fung Phoenix	254
Line of Division *Poem*	Shirley Lee	255

APOCALYPSE NOW & THEN

The Mangrove Island *Short story*	Michael Gibb	259
City Chant *Poem*	Elbert Siu Ping Lee	269
Untitled *Poem*	Hatrick Lee Pui-tin	270
Providence *Poem*	John Wu	271
Alarmed by the charm of our own ruin *Villanelle*	Andrew Barker	272
Checkboxes *Short story*	Nicole Wong	273

AMBIVALENT PHILOSOPHIES

I Grew Mushrooms *Poem*	Agnes S. L. Lam	281
the chemistry of fireworks *Prose poem*	Viki Holmes	284
Fish Fillet with Tomato Sauce *Poem*	Cecilia Ying-chai Chan	286
Philosophy of Smoking by an Amateur Smoker *Poem*	Nicholas Y. B. Wong	288
The Prophet Outside the Main Library *Poem*	Christina Chan	289

Preface

The Way We Are, Are, Arguably Are
Xu Xi, Editor

Perch. That's what we do. Like the avian population of our skies and the butterfly lovers who flit around our cultural imagination, we perch, waiting, wondering (some might say waffling), and meanwhile continue to dance till dawn, watching the Hang Seng index dip and rise. To echo one writer from these pages: *It wasn't supposed to be like this!*

This collection of creative writing is not merely a "book about Hong Kong". Such a description would not do justice to the talent between these pages. When I first set out to edit this anthology, the call for submissions read as follows:

> What are the odds on the Special Administrative Region, the S.A.R., beyond 2046? If we were punters, as so many in this city are, would we say it's "fifty-fifty" that China will engulf us or that it will set us free? Or is politics not even the issue on our thoroughly post-modern,

hilly rock, where film, fad and fashion lead, and where the harbor promenade enshrines the footprints of our "stars"? This is a call for submissions to a thinking person's book. What do writers and poets have to say about these times in this city, and how do they choose to say it? Will we, like the poet Agnes S. L. Lam, call Hong Kong "the city/with a history/unforetold"? And even if the odds on our city are fifty-fifty, is this always home, regardless?

What tumbled in over the mostly electronic "transom" was astonishing. Oh, I begged a little, borrowed a little, but mostly, the work that came in was new, shining, and as thoroughly post modern as Hong Kong's 21st-century banknotes, impervious to counterfeit. The Anglophone scribblers out there had plenty to say, in creative non-fiction, personal essays, many, many poems, even prose poems, short stories, narrative non-fiction and even one unusual meditation which is fictional non-fiction. It was heartening to embrace the deluge of submissions, and regrettably, much good writing could not be included. There were simply not enough pages for all the words that flowed across the Internet skies, 2046 be damned. In the end, 63 pieces by 42 writers found their way into the volume. More than half the authors are what we could call "Hong Kong Chinese", and the rest are a mix of cultures, ethnicities, nationalities, some native to the city, many long-time residents or formerly so. Each writer in the book is connected, somehow, to this place, "Hong Kongers" one and all.

Who is this multitude of voices? Here is a briefing on some of the authors.

*There are familiar names—**Agnes S. L. Lam**, **Madeleine Marie Slavick**, **Louise Ho**, **Mani Rao**, **Alan Jefferies**, **Justin Hill**—those writers whose books sneak onto the shelves of bookshops here and around the world, and of course, in cyberspace as well. We do live in cyberspace these days, do we not? But what most delights me is the opportunity to introduce, in these ravishingly old-fashioned printed pages, the new writers whose works you may not yet know,* but should. In particular, meet **Nicole Wong, Keane Shum** and **Viki Holmes**, three talented young scribblers, three "typical" Hong Kongers who are, naturally, completely atypical. They are, respectively, a fiction writer, an essayist and a poet: could a city's literature ask for more to light its future path?

Where do all these writers come from? The Writers' Circle was most prolific and sent several contributors to this volume, notably **Lawrence Gray**, its founder, as well as newer voices, for example, **Tammy Ho Lai-ming**. A call for submissions also brings in the unexpected, from those who labor in solitude as writers will and remain invisible: **Woo See-Kow, Ching Yuet Ming, Nicholas Y. B. Wong** are three such scribes whose work demonstrates vastly contrasting styles—lyrical, classical, edgy—a testament to the rich diversity of voices from these shores. Lurking around the halls of the local academy, where creative writing is now at least indulged and even taught a little, although not a lot, both professors and students: **Amy Lai, Monica Chan, Viona Au Yeung** and **Arthur Leung**, among several others, sent work from Baptist, Lingnan, Chinese and Hong Kong universities, respectively.

Further afield, from the University of Iowa's prestigious MFA writing program, **Jennifer S. Cheng** "comes home" after an absence to investigate the perennial question of identity informed by multiple languages, dialects and cultures via a finely honed sensibility. As well, from OutLoud and Joyce Is Not Here, two regular reading series, several voices made themselves heard, including one of OutLoud's faithful organizers, **David McKirdy**.

Women in Publishing also sent several submissions which we were privileged to consider. No Anglophone anthology of this city would be complete without those writers who are current and former resident expatriates, such as **Martin Alexander** and **Edward Rodney Davey**; our history, lest we forget, is inextricably bound to both a colonial past as well as the modern, globalized economy.

The concerns of these writers were varied and broad, since the human experience insists we immerse ourselves in just about everything. (Literature, after all, is one of the "humanities".) Given the deliberately ambivalent topic—"fifty-fifty"—they responded with both the personal and political, as well as a plethora of other observations. Writers bear witness to the heroic as well as the shameful, pour out love and almost-love stories, mine the universal out of personal histories, and naturally pay enormous attention to the siren songs of real history, heard and unheard. What do we know of Hong Kong's communist party, one that has existed here for years? **Jesse Wong**, a former staff journalist for The Asian Wall Street Journal, offers a compelling narrative with personal characteristics, while political activist and author **Christine Loh** weighs in with "some wanton thoughts for 2017".

What, too, of those moments that capture this compulsively manmade yet surprisingly natural geographical space? A Lan Kwai Fong club is **Akin Jeje's** moment, while **Kate Rogers** casts her gaze on the day of the dead on Lamma Island. And an apocalyptic vision, now and then, worries its way into print before the volume closes on "ambivalent philosophies", reflecting the wild and whacky world we live in, of which our city is a protean piece.

So let me invite you to suspend disbelief and enter into the realm of imagination, because that is what good writing does, takes you to another space, another dimension, another level of being. Above all, do not be too literal in your reading. To be literal is the province of bureaucracy, not art. Instead, enter these pages with an open mind and a willingness to gamble at least a little—if not a lot. Perhaps by the time you close this volume, 50-50 may tilt towards more favorable odds for our collective voice, one that speaks for the S.A.R. of the nation to which we belong.

Stockholm, November 2007

The personal. . .

It Wasn't Supposed To Be Like This
Keane Shum

I told someone the other day that I have lived in Hong Kong for eleven years, and it sounded deceivingly constant.

It is eleven years spread across four occasions and six apartments, sometimes with all my family members, sometimes with each of them individually, and sometimes with none—hanging out with different sets of friends, while studying and while working, under British rule and under Chinese rule, even sometimes under the influence of democratic rule.

What is it to be constant in this city, anyway? The fading relics of my past disappear with such speed, with so little pageantry, that I have to luck upon a walk down Queen's Road East to spot the expiry of Wing Wah, the world's biggest couple-hundred square feet of true toy heaven, or accidentally take a bus that routes through Ocean Park on the weekends to rediscover the slides of Water World, crumbling plastic tunnels that, invaded by vines, no longer reach the pools because, of course, there are none.

So I hold fast to the rare ties that bind my many lives here, the precious few places that thread through all my years. Hong Kong International School. The Country Club. The Big TV. Dags.

And, until half a year ago, the Star Ferry.

This one hurts. You can take my toy store, or my water park, but go easy on adolescent romances and childhood flights of fancy. I don't need my G.I. Joes or slippery summertime adventures anymore, but I still want to take my kids to the $1 weight scale with views of the harbour and tell them I once stood there with the whole world at my feet. When the day comes that I've resorted to calm and open spaces, I want to trek up and down those red loading ramps, shoulder to shoulder with humanity, and see if my shoes are big enough to fill the gaps between the mini-speedbumps. And when I'm old and jaded, I want to rewalk those waterfront paths of teenage angst and love, hand in hand with naivete.

But I won't, and it hurts.

It's gone. And as if the government wanted to say an extra fuck-you to nostalgia, all that remains are the ghosts of protest, so that I can't forget the life but all I can picture is the wake. The echoes of Tiananmen are stunning: the posters on walls, the hunger strike, the ribbons, the banners, the slogans, even the faux funeral. And once again, I was late to mourn.

As we grow up, for whatever reason, we feel more mortal. We more desperately seek to preserve what will one day be irretrievable. We start to peek out the curtains of a youth spent accumulating life and realize that loss happens, too. But this one, this day, came too fast. It wasn't supposed to be like this. This haunting, permanent absence. This lack of sympathy for sentimentality. This absurd reality.

My City
Agnes S. L. Lam

This is a city
where a village boy could become a movie star of
  Hollywood renown,
where film stars demonstrated against nude photos of
  an actress taken against her will.
The death of an artist could draw thousands to the streets,
a white rose each in torrents of rain.

This is your city
where men are charmed by women intelligent and supple,
  skin
moisturized by humidity most months of the year. One
  married a Danish prince,
others are wooed with diamonds by neon waters and some
  still single fly
weekends to play golf.

This is our city
where vegetable sellers, taxi drivers, people in their seventies
  feel proud
a Hong Kong girl dreamt their dream, brought home Olympic
  gold surfing the winds
and waters off Cheung Chau, an island even smaller
than Hong Kong.

This is the city
which alerted the world to the deadly virus
named Sars, the city of researchers, working round the clock
  with scientists

in eight other countries, breaking its genetic code
in just three weeks.

This is a city
of people who donate money for flood victims in China.
Personal tragedies in newspapers attract immediate support
   from strangers.
A city where young people volunteer to clean old people's homes
and orphans are not left alone.

This is your city
where most young men do not get drunk on Friday nights.
Most teenagers do not do drugs, few swear at their teachers and
most parents, however poor, still make sacrifices
for their children.

This is our city
with more mobile phones per square foot than anywhere else.
People do not tire of communication, with their friends,
   families, colleagues,
stockbrokers, estate agents, slimming consultants,
fortune tellers, yoga trainers, image makers.

This is the city
with an award-winning airport
and glass castles where willowy shadows work long hours and
   the night
begins at nine in designer style,
sparkling with wine.

This is a city
of Chinese silk, Belgian chocolate, French wine, German cars,
   Swiss watches.
Scottish mountains in fog give way to Mediterranean sun and
   laughter. Foreigners
come for a year or two, attend concerts, watch fireworks by the
   harbour,
stay a lifetime.

This is your city
with measures against corruption ranking high.
Politicians attack each other only in words. Bombs are not found

on the underground and no one is imprisoned for what they say
as the whole world watches.

This is our city
where spies abound, masquerading as journalists,
   photographers, researchers,
art dealers, bartenders, restaurant owners, events organizers,
innocuous schoolteachers, honourable schoolboys and what else
I do not know.

This is the city
with a history
unforetold.

This is Hong Kong—
my city
of poetry.

*Hong Kong, in spite of severe acute respiratory syndrome (Sars),
20 April 2003*

Made in Hong Kong?
Arthur Leung

We're loud in public, mean and callous;
no wonder we're looked down on.
No good, you think of us Hongkongers!

And the Cantonese dialect sounds indecent
tim, compared to English, Mandarin
and Japanese (so you've taken one lesson).

You distance yourself in every foreign land:
you aren't one of the Hongkong men *gah!*
They speak Cantonese you pretend not to understand.

When people ask your nationality
you say you're Chinese but never add
"Hong Kong", that essential quality.

You know it's a shame, being a Hongkonger,
a shame for you. And Hong Kong's a heaven,
the number-one city in South China!

Instead you wish you were an American
or (*choy!*) a Japanese. Or you're jealous
that among us you're a less lucky one?

Aiya, Hongkongers like you—many others!

235 Shanghai Street
Doris Lau Parry

Please forgive me if I upset you, Ma, when I suggested on my departure from Hong Kong that you should not leave Grandma alone at home; I did not mean to offend you or to dictate how you should live your life. I should be more sensitive to your feelings—about being trapped as Grandma's caregiver. But ever since Grandma's latest visit to the doctor, I have been filled with apprehension—she is 95 years old after all. This does not mean we only care about Grandma. I know you are 75 years old and could use being taken care of yourself. What can I say, Ma? We are indebted to you, forever, for what you have done and are still doing for this family. Please do not think for a moment that I, or any of your children, love Grandma more than we love you.

You don't really begrudge us, I hope, for being concerned about her; you of all people must appreciate that she is such a big part of our lives. Perhaps you resent being the one saddled with looking after her, day in-day out, and now in her fragile state, with the responsibility of keeping her alive. You often mumble, as if to yourself, that it is unfair for you to shoulder this onerous task of caring for a sickly old woman who is not even your mother. Once you start down that road, what follows inevitably is another tirade against Father, the man who has failed you so miserably, and who won't or can't even look after his own mother, expecting you to continue to make sacrifices for him and to keep his mother safe at home. You often say, "I had to send my father to an old-age home and have him suffer the indignity of being treated like a prisoner in that filthy place. If we didn't put him there he might still be alive today."

It's natural for you to feel that way but please don't torment yourself with guilt. You had little choice when Gung-Gung began to show signs of dementia since neither you nor any of your brothers or sisters had the means to take care of him at home. You cannot blame yourself either that he slipped and fell in the bath at the nursing home. They sent him to the hospital where they operated on his knee and he died from complications after surgery. The fall could have happened even if he were living at home. He was ninety-one, and he had lived a full life. It wasn't anything you did or didn't do.

And while Grandma is your mother-in-law, has she not been like a mother to you all these years? Do you not know that she is so profoundly sorry for and ashamed of her son's behaviour? Have you not heard her say the worst part of her fate is having her only son turn out exactly like her bad husband? I think you also know why Grandma stuck with her marriage to Grandpa, the abusive brute with four concubines, when you often told us, "I would have left that bastard a long time ago." She didn't leave him, like three of his four concubines, because Grandma knew she had the responsibility of Father's young family on her hands.

It was you who told us that Grandma apparently gave a solemn undertaking to your paternal grandmother, when she went to propose marriage on behalf of her son, that she personally would make sure that you would be well taken care of, and that you would never suffer a bad day with the Laus. No matter how much you were wronged in this marriage, looking back, don't you agree Grandma has done her absolute damnedest and been totally honourable in keeping her promise to your grandmother? If not for her meagre earnings as a maid—sometimes holding down two jobs at once—you and the six of us would never have had food on the table, a roof over our heads, clothes on our backs and we would never have received the education that we did. The commitment by her to your grandmother has cost her an entire life. Grandma has done nothing short of lived *for* us.

∞ ∞ ∞

We all say things we don't mean when we are angry. Sometimes you say that what Grandma did for us was no sacrifice at all, that it was her penance for not bringing up her son properly. "If she had been a good mother, your father would not be so useless and irresponsible!" At times you transferred your anger and resentment for Father to Grandma because you felt she was too protective and indulgent of her son. But Father is her only son, and with Grandma's upbringing and background, she did not know any other way. When you have a bad day, Ma, you would say Grandma's promise to your grandmother was all but empty because the marriage proposal was made on false pretenses. The Yips only accepted the Laus' proposal on the strength that they were an established merchant with a "nice little business" in Hong Kong, far away from the trouble and poverty of Dongguan and what was brewing elsewhere in China at the time. You were only 12 when your mother died from tuberculosis and never became close to your stepmother, so Second Grandmother, your favourite among your three grandmothers, took it upon herself to find you a good husband to safeguard your future. When Father sent Grandma to ask for your hand in marriage, your Second Grandmother thought she had found just the man.

It was too late by the time you realised that the man and your new family were not what Second Grandmother believed them to be; all that caché associated with having a Hong Kong business was pure façade. Until you married into the Laus, you like to tell us, you lived a life of luxury, with servants, cooks and maids, and the Yips maintained residences in Guangzhou City, Huang Tsuen and Sai Kau. You knew Hong Kong way before Father did. The Yips took off for the Colony when the Japanese invaded China and food was scarce, first settling in a rear cubicle on the first floor of the tenement building behind Hong Kong Cinema on Spring Garden Road in Wanchai, before moving round the corner to occupy the entire second floor of the building where Spring Garden Road joins

Queen's Road East. "We returned to Guangzhou when the Japanese occupied Hong Kong; but we had fun living in Wanchai," you told us many times; you were obviously fond of living in the Colony.

Your grandfather, a *daoshi*, was a cultivated and decent man. I loved the story of how he joined the Taoist order in adulthood: he fell critically ill shortly after he got married at 21. No conventional medicine helped so the family took him to the Taoist temple in the village. After performing the necessary rites, the *daoshi* diagnosed the problem: it was his dead elder sister who had possessed him because she was upset that he married while she was still single in the underworld. He had violated a taboo by marrying ahead of a senior sibling. The *daoshi* saved his life and told him to join the order as a working priest for the remainder of his life. Gung-Gung was his only son; educated at home by a private tutor, he read Chinese classics, and he learned English, although with little success, at Stone Room, the most exclusive English language school in Guangzhou then. You used to tell us your father was too lazy and he was often scolded by your grandfather for playing truant; when he should have been at Stone Room he was really window-shopping at the Tai Sun Department Store. You were fond of repeating this story, and that all of the Yip children, including the girls, went to school in Guangzhou City. Your family was well-heeled and cultivated. Contrast that with the Laus you married into, and no wonder you felt sorry for yourself.

The Laus were butchers and small-time merchants, with little education to speak of. Grandpa was adopted as a child because his parents were too poor to keep him. He had a hard life growing up, being used as cheap labor rather than loved by his adopted family, which probably explained his abusive behaviour. He had four concubines in addition to his wife, but that didn't stop him from going to prostitutes, drinking parlours and gambling dens. He had no interest in any of his three children—Father and Fat Aunt by his wife and, after their arrival in Hong Kong, his only remaining concubine gave birth to a girl, Small Kiu. I guess the Lau men are never destined to be responsible husbands and fathers. Grandpa never paid any attention to Father, hence Father became who he is. In his youth, he was a lay-about. Even after he married you, he would hang around his father's butchery, where Grandma also worked, not doing very much except drinking and gambling with the guys. Like Grandpa, he was also a philanderer even if he couldn't keep concubines openly. We could almost say he's a carbon copy of his father, in aspirations, behaviour and ultimately, in destiny—they weren't liked very much by their families.

In your predicament you found your guardian angel in Grandma. From day one she shielded you from hurt at the hands of the Lau men. When Grandpa's butchery business fell apart and Father showing no sign of growing up and taking responsibility, Grandma went to work as a live-in amah for a wealthy family in Kowloon City. She knew she had to earn money to avoid having you and your children beholden to Grandpa who was never known for his kindness or generosity. When Grandpa's remaining concubine, Ah Cheung, gave birth to Small Kiu, Grandma and you were relieved that Ah Cheung wanted the three of them to move out of our middle cubicle on the third floor at 235 Shanghai Street, diagonally across from the old Yau Ma Tei Market, where Grandpa's butchery had been. The three of them rented bed-space on the verandah on the second floor of a tong-lau on Battery Street, a five-minute walk from us on Shanghai Street. So Grandpa moved out and saved us his abuse for only when he visited, which was still too often for your liking, I am sure.

My first home, 235 Shanghai Street, is a place I will never forget and a place I often dream about since I left Hong Kong. I don't understand why; the place is only a hovel, barely a step-up from the squatter huts that were so common on hillsides in Hong Kong then. Grandpa rented two cubicles on the third floor in partnership with Mak, another butcher from Shek Lung, a nearby village, when both of them owned a meat stall selling pork in the old Yau Ma Tei

Market in Yung Shu Tau. Both had expanding families to feed and house, so it was logical that they should look for space for the family near work.

Our building was typical of the pre-war tenement blocks: three-storey high, two street numbers sharing a wooden staircase, each number representing an apartment of about five hundred square feet. We shared the stairs with number 233. On the ground floor, both 233 and 235 were goldsmith shops. I can still recall faces and people living in the many cubicles on either side of each floor, but not as well as our neighbours on the third floor of 233 Shanghai Street. Ma, I have a small confession to make here: Remember you once caught me writing letters to "strangers" when I was still in primary school? You were so upset that you gave me a good thrashing with the cane—our routine punishment. Well, I continued to write to my pen pals after that but only used a pen name and changed my return address to the third floor of 233 Shanghai Street! When I got home from school I would check their mailbox, which was banged up with all the others against the wall in one corner at the bottom of the stairs, and should I find a letter addressed to my pen name in our neighbor's mailbox I would hide it in my schoolbag. Mailboxes were not locked up like they are now, in fact few things seemed to be locked up, or private, in those days.

I envied our neighbours across the stairwell at 233 Shanghai Street because they had more space; there were only four families sharing the third floor at 233. We seemed a lot more jam-packed on our side, with the communal kitchen always full of people, cooking or washing—even bathing. My siblings and I loved bathing in the tin basin in our middle cubicle; but the women had to bathe from basins in the kitchen, even when other families were cooking or doing other chores in there. They only kept the men out by half closing the kitchen door, and strangely, all the men seemed to only bathe late at night when all women were done with cooking and chores in the kitchen. Or perhaps it was not so strange, how else were they able to bathe otherwise? When I became too big to bathe in the basin inside our cubicle, I, too, had to suffer the humiliation of bathing in "public", in the kitchen. Also humiliating for me was often running into the man we called Uncle, naked and having a wash on the roof whenever I was up there to collect or to hang out the laundry for you. He was a distant relative of Sixth Auntie in the rear cubicle. Sixth Auntie was a Tangka widow and shared the cubicle next to the communal kitchen with her mother and a teenage son whom we called Brother Sum. When Uncle arrived from China he had nowhere to stay so Sixth Auntie took him in and rented out her hut on the roof to him. She also introduced him to the foreman at the construction site where she worked and he became a construction worker, too.

I hated being in the kitchen, especially when someone was bathing. It's embarrassing but also difficult to pretend to ignore a naked body. The women would urinate in the kitchen, too, straight on the kitchen floor—I presume that is why in those days everyone wore those clunky, platform wooden clogs that would keep our feet dry and clean. At meal times, the kitchen would be choking with smoke from the wood-burning stoves of four, five families, all going at the same time. On a rainy day, the soot that had accumulated on the ceiling of the kitchen would drip down like sticky, black glue, so before going into the kitchen everyone had to wrap up their hair with a sheet of plastic, which they tied up under the chin and could be kept folded up like a concertina fan. The worst thing about the kitchen was the wooden barrel of faeces, sitting in a corner right next to the stone bench where we prepared food and kept our chopping boards and small wooden basins for washing the dishes. The very thought of the close proximity of food and faeces disgusted me. The barrel was emptied by a woman ironically called "Night Fragrance", who would come to each apartment, empty the content into one that she brought on a bamboo pole, every other night at around one or two o'clock in the morning. On cold winter days, everybody would pretend not to hear her call on the staircase because no one wanted to leave their warm bed to go and open the door of the apartment for her.

FIFTY-FIFTY

Aside from the Maks in the front and us in the middle cubicle, our landlady, an elderly widow everybody called Toothless Lady, lived in a bed-space in the corridor, close to the verandah; and for a few years, another family had the loft right outside the kitchen. They did not stay there long. The smoke and heat, not to mention the soot, made that space unlivable even by our very low standards then. Toothless Lady was stingy and would raise hell as soon as we were late with the rent, but she was very kind and helpful to you, particularly after Grandma began to work and live in Kowloon City and left you alone most of the time in the middle cubicle. We are fond of Toothless Lady; you often repeat this story as you remember her: You were by yourself when you went into labour with me in the middle of the night. Toothless Lady was the one who took you—in a taxi, no less—to Kowloon Hospital. Taking a taxi was a major expense then, especially for someone as careful with money as she. After I was born, Toothless Lady sat outside the hospital waiting for the bus service to start at 6 a.m. before she would go home.

Father was never at home; you, barely 20 when you were married, had to manage on your own. It was hard enough that you had no experience in housework or raising children, but you also had no money or resources. Father didn't have a regular job and would spend what little money he made from the itinerant work on drinking with the guys or sometimes extravagances like a radio and then, a gramophone player. You had to make do with Grandma's meagre salary. In a bad month when Grandpa lost more than usual on gambling, he would take some of that whether Grandma liked it or not. Father, just as bad, would not think twice about swiping whatever was in your wallet as his own. That's why we had seen so many fights between you and Father: for our sake you guarded your housekeeping money fiercely. Toothless Lady was always there to console you when you lost a fight, suffered bruises on your face and failed to keep the money away from your husband. "Younger Sister, don't cry; children grow up very fast. Before you know it, they are adults and they will keep you in luxury," she used to say to you.

Madam Big—Mak's wife in the front cubicle—often assumed a superior, condescending attitude whenever she talked to us. While Grandpa lost all his money and sold his butchery, Mak's was so successful that he expanded his and went on to operate a much bigger butchery in Kwun Chung Market near the Jordan Road Ferry Terminal. I know you didn't like Madam Big much, even when you tried to get along with her superficially, you kept her at a distance. And you were always pained when faced with the dilemma of going hungry or borrowing rice from Madam Big. Not having enough rice to last till the end of the month when Grandma would come home with her salary was a regular occurrence. I can still see that look on your face, Ma, as if it were yesterday. That look of agony, not knowing whether you should let your children go hungry one more day or whether you should swallow your pride and go, once again, to Madam Big and suffer her condescension while you asked to borrow two cups of rice. "Oh, Younger Sister, you are a poor dear! You know, the worst fate that befalls a woman is marrying the wrong man. You have eyes, but no pupils to see, what a pity!" Madam Big would say before she obliged.

Ma, you must have put up with this more than you cared to remember, because I don't recall us starving much in those days. Rarely did we have to go to bed hungry, but often we would only have a bowl of rice each. No meat, no fish, no vegetables, just plain, steamed rice. You would cook the rice with a pinch of salt and a drop of oil, to give it a little taste—we had a name for it, I remember, we called it "oil and salt rice". Even oil was scarce in those days. We used lard a lot when Grandma still worked at Grandpa's butchery; we couldn't afford peanut oil. I was always the one who, as you ran out of oil, would be charged with going downstairs to buy two or four taels—depending on how much money you had. I was also the one who had to go across the road to Woo Heung to buy five cents worth of Tofu Fa when my siblings and I cleaned out the only dish of meat or fish on the table before you even came out of the kitchen for your meal. Tofu Fa, with a little soy sauce, makes the otherwise plain rice tasty and easy to swallow.

I sometimes think of you, Ma, carrying water for the family when Hong Kong only had four hours of supply every four days, so bad was the water shortage that summer. One day coming home from school, I saw you, in clothes more than half-drenched, heavily pregnant with Wing Tsai, queuing up at the hydrant among the chaos of people and water tins and buckets, in front of the ceramic shop at the corner of Shanghai Street and Kansu Street. Your turn came and you filled the two old kerosene tins, which had a wooden stick across the top; then you quickly attached each tin to either end of the bamboo pole, under which you deftly put your right shoulder by lowering your body and your bulging stomach. You raised your legs gingerly at first, with the bamboo pole balancing on your left shoulder and the two bucketful of water swaying slightly at either end of the pole. You were walking as briskly as you could with that rotund body of yours, while trying hard—with little success—not to let too much water spill out from the kerosene tins, from the hydrant at the street corner all the way to Sang Cheung Goldsmith Shop on the ground floor of 235 Shanghai Street, and then up three flights of stairs, to fill our two water vessels at one end of the communal kitchen.

Perhaps the reason I remember this so well is because of Wing Tsai: the next time you had to carry water after the day I saw you in the street—four days later—you had to be sent to hospital in the middle of it. I was wondering why I didn't see you in the queue at the street corner when I walked past after school. Climbing up the wet and slippery, wooden staircase, I bumped into Madam Big with her water tins. "Hey, you know where your mother is? She's in the hospital! And I heard it's a boy! Thank Wong Tai Sin, finally, a boy!" Madam Big was right; we all thanked Wong Tai Sin. Grandma had been going to this temple for years while you kept on giving birth to girls—three girls after me—and then finally, the Laus were blessed with another boy, 12 years after the first one died.

I can imagine how you and Grandma must have been devastated when my elder brother Lum Tsai died. He was your first-born and by all accounts, he was good-looking, bright and a charmer. I wish you had kept a picture of him. Apparently you and Grandma were crying so much that Ah Shiu, the son of Second Auntie, living in the rear cubicle across the stairwell at 233, took away the only picture we had of our elder brother, to save you two from grieving. But I made up my own pictures of Elder Brother that I never knew or saw, from what you told me about him. He was a happy and easy-going child. He fell ill when a typhoon hit Hong Kong; his condition worsened during the night but you had no money to take him to a private doctor. It was typhoon signal number ten and all public transport stopped running, so you and Grandma walked, shielding him from howling winds and rain, to Kowloon Hospital three miles away. When you reached the emergency room of the hospital, you found no doctor on duty because of the typhoon. When doctors came after the typhoon passed the next morning, it was too late for Elder Brother.

I'll always remember what you told me about Elder Brother in the hospital: "He was so clever, right up to the end. He was barely two years old, but he seemed to understand he was dying. He smiled, held our hands, and looked right at us with those doleful eyes..." After he died Grandma cried for a week, sitting on the floor in our middle cubicle. "Not eating or drinking, for days, she just thrashed about on the floor, like a child throwing a terrible tantrum, completely out of control," you told us. When I came into the family, Grandma was so afraid that I would be taken away by the gods, like Elder Brother, she nicknamed me "pig" because lowly beasts like pigs were not worthy and wouldn't be the envy of gods, whereas all my friends thought I earned my nickname for being a glutton. She also gave me my formal name *Kwan Cheung*, which means bringing lots of boys. Yet I failed her miserably by bringing three sisters.

∞ ∞ ∞

Hong Kong is booming, the China market is hot, hot, hot—whichever business one is in. The stock markets in both places are going like gang-busters; new millionaires are made every day. Before my annual summer visit, emails and phone calls from my siblings arrived fast and furious, all telling me how my baby brother Wah Tsai is now an entrepreneur with a huge business empire and to consider returning to Hong Kong to join his business. I know you well, Father, you identify most with money and the brand names it can buy; you have always wanted one of your sons to become another Li Ka Shing. Since Wing Tsai had already made a name for himself as a professional, you pinned all your hopes on Wah Tsai. You must feel your dream has come true finally. But even if Wah Tsai is successful and rich now, why should that benefit you? You weren't even there for him when he was born. In fact, you deserted him—and us—for three whole years.

I have always accepted that I have to love you regardless of who you are—the father who never provided, the father who never was—until you sold our ancestral home, without consulting anyone in the family, a few years ago. You might think I was born in Hong Kong; I never even lived in Dongguan, so why would I bother with a decrepit, old house that was taken over by migrant workers for so many years that only the shell remained, anything worth taking away had been chopped and taken away. You might even argue that if none of us, the male heirs included, ever has any intention of returning to Dongguan or to the ancestral village of Huang Tsuen to live, what then is the point of keeping the disintegrating house, only for the benefit of squatters.

Well, I can't speak for the others in the family but I'm very angry that you sold our house in Huang Tsuen. Don't you remember how excited I was the first time I went to see the house with you, Grandma and Ma? That must be some fifteen years ago, we took a taxi from Dongguan City centre to Huang Tsuen. I could feel the palpitations in my heart when the name "Huang Tsuen" first appeared—in the name of a petrol station on the main road—through the taxi window. We drove past Hou Street—I never knew Hou Street really existed. I had heard the name a thousand times when Ma or Grandma sang the same lullaby to get the baby to sleep: *Let me rock you good baby/When you grow up you'll marry someone from Hou Street/But what do they sell in Hou Street* ... And the moment I first saw the house was bittersweet: so broken and filthy, nothing like what I had imagined and yet at the same time so familiar that it was as if I could see Grandma cooking in the corner that was once the kitchen or getting water from the well—now dried up—outside the house. We could see clothes and rags hung up on poles whichever way inside the black walls of the house, all the doors and windows were gone, and so were the beds and other furniture that Grandma and Grandpa left behind when they went to Hong Kong with the Lau contingent in 1949.

Grandma pointed to an empty space which was obviously a bedroom in its former life now strewn with makeshift cooking stoves and other utensils, and said to me: "That used to be our bedroom. I gave birth to your father in that room. Nobody went to hospitals in those days; giving birth was just like hens dropping eggs and everyone did it at home." As I took photograph after photograph of everything in sight, Ma was amused. "What kind of a photo will this make? It's all grime and dirt! You are wasting the film ..." You and Ma practically had to drag me away as I lingered among the remains of what used to be the Laus' main residence for at least three generations. Years later I would take my own family, my *gweiloh* husband and our three children, to Huang Tsuen and show them our house, our roots. Now that you have sold it, Father, what links do we have with Huang Tsuen and Dongguan? How can my children show their children where their great-grandfather was born, and how can they show them that the Hou Street in the lullaby really does exist? Have you thought of that?

I wish Grandma were not so indulgent of your every whim and did not consent to the sale. And I wish she had not confided in me; I would rather that she kept this a secret between the two of you.

And I still don't dare to tell Ma—if she knew she would consider this the final act of betrayal by both you and Grandma. She might be so angry she would throw Grandma out ... What was worse was when I confronted you and wanted to know what you had done with the proceeds from the sale, you showed not the slightest bit of remorse. "It was no big deal; I only received two hundred thousand dollars for it, just small change." I said what about Ma? You should at least have shared the money with her, if not equally at least some of it would be good. "No way, why should I? Hasn't she made my life miserable enough? Besides, she doesn't need the money." Do you know how shocked I was when I heard you say that to my face? Did you even have a conscience? I was absolutely stunned—it was not the money, it was the ungratefulness behind that indictment against Ma that shook me to the core and that will forever drive a wedge between you and me. I keep thinking about this statement of yours and asking myself: did you mean Ma tied you to a family you didn't want, or what did you mean?

Being the eldest of your six children, I have seen—and I remember—more than any of my siblings the fights you and Ma had, whether over money, or rather the lack of it, or over your many infidelities. For you to accuse Ma of making your life miserable is like calling the deer a horse. You have completely turned the truth on its head. I can forgive you for not supporting the family, leaving that onerous duty to Grandma; I can even forgive you for loving other women while you were married to Ma. But I cannot, and will never, forgive you for accusing Ma of making your life miserable—she who has borne you seven children and raised six of them, with the little money Grandma made as an amah; she who has put up with your philandering and desertion and never once kicked you out; she who at the age of 75 is still looking after your mother at home while you live separately, free to enjoy your days with whomever and in whichever way you see fit. Without Ma—and Grandma of course—you wouldn't have your six children today who pay your bills and keep you in comfort, if not the luxury, that you wanted. Have you ever thought of that?

Father, I tried very hard to put the past behind me, behind us. But I don't think it's ever going to be possible; I feel its dark shadow constantly over us so much that I, in fact, avoid seeing you these days during my visits to Hong Kong. And I'm most offended now that you think Wah Tsai has struck gold, you are going to sweet-talk all of us that we are really one big, happy family. Without Ma or Grandma, I don't think any of us really want to have anything to do with you. Sad and most unfilial of us, but you deserve what you get from your unwanted family.

I recognised your ugly, money-grabbing behaviour when we met Wah Tsai for dinner on the Sunday after I got home from America. The waitresses made a beeline for Wah Tsai as he walked into the restaurant—he is clearly a big-spending regular. If he's as successful as everyone in the family says he is, Wah Tsai still looks and dresses the same way he always has. With a non-branded cotton polo shirt over a pair of sandy-colored Bermuda shorts, he looked a little younger than his years. But I worry about what all this newfound wealth is doing to him. He looked tired and washed out—at 7 pm on a Sunday when he was supposed to have spent the day relaxing. In the short ten or fifteen minutes while we waited for him, you did not stop talking about how well your youngest son was doing now, the influence he yields in the marketplace, the connections he has in the highest echelons of Beijing politics—and of course, how nice it is for us to be dining with him in this "Hall of Fame" Chinese restaurant. You even implied that I should count myself lucky that my baby brother, busy, successful entrepreneur that he is, managed to find time to dine with me so soon after I arrived in Hong Kong.

You kept pushing the most expensive dishes to me and Ma, "Braised Giant Grouper Fins *a la Ancienne*", "Dry-fried Shark's Fin with Crabmeat, Accompanied by Organic Chicken Consommé", and what about the *de rigueur* steamed fish? Pointing to the exquisite groupers and other deep-sea varieties swimming vigorously in the floor-to-ceiling fish tank taking up almost an entire wall on one side of the restaurant, you sounded as if you were the restaurant owner trying to sell his most expensive fare to boost sales. I sat there in glum resentment, completely tuned out of what you were saying. I looked at you and the way you were grinning from ear to ear, talking with your large hand gestures, looking like a slimy second-hand car salesman that cannot be trusted in any circumstances—you seemed like a total stranger to me. As Wah Tsai walked toward our table, the captain and other staff in the buzzing restaurant came over, as well as the waitresses who led him to the table; by now everyone was swooning over him: one was pulling the chair out, another pouring tea, yet another gave him a hot face cloth. The grin on your face was even more exaggerated now, you gave Wah Tsai a gentle slap on the back as he sat down next to you, as if to announce not only to the restaurant contingent but also to the other diners around us, "This is my son, everyone, my son who has struck it rich!" There can be no mistake that my baby brother has arrived—and no mistake either , Father, that though we may be related by blood, I wish I had never known you.

I did not choose you for a father; I had no choice in the matter. But you, Father, you had choices. Your choices led to what and who we are as a family today. Would you have chosen differently knowing what you do now? Until quite recently, we—your children—had been under the impression that you and Ma had a typical, arranged marriage instigated by elders on both sides, when neither party knew each other before the wedding. But that was not the case. According to Ma, she said another girl in the village had already been arranged for you when you stumbled upon Ma, who was taken to Huang Tsuen by her elder brother to visit their Second Grandmother. At the time Ma had been living in Guangzhou City with her grandfather and her parents. We could say it was fate that brought you and Ma together, but you decided to renege on the arranged marriage with the other girl after you set eyes on Ma. It was clearly your choice. You told Grandma to approach the Yip family and ask for Ma's birth date and times. When Grandma presented those to the fortune teller, he told her that marriage would be a disaster because Ma's and yours were not compatible. But you refused to accept that and insisted on proceeding with the marriage proposal. You, not fate, chose Ma.

So what was it that attracted you to Ma on that fateful day? Was it her good looks? A photo of Ma in her early thirties shows her to be a classic South Country beauty, like the movie star Lok Tei. I can imagine how stunningly beautiful Ma must have been at 18. Or were you so perceptive that you saw the perfect life partner in Ma, that grim determination to do her absolute best through good times and bad? Could you have known then that this shy, teenage girl from Guangzhou would raise six children for you, through the harshest of circumstances, and in her old age she would still be of service to you looking after your frail mother?

Call it love at first sight or puppy love. Whatever it was, it did not stand the test of time. Ma believes that even while the marriage proposal was in progress you were unfaithful to her. She thinks it was in your blood, you coming from a long line of philanderers in the family. I don't know if behaviour can be inherited; but I'm doubtful that you and Ma ever loved each other. As far back as I can remember, there were only ever tears and fights. You were never around much, for Ma or for your growing family. On the odd occasion you were home, you would sleep in our shed on the roof, leaving that dark, stuffy middle cubicle to Ma and us kids. At first the fights seemed to be always about money; as I went to secondary school, I began to realise it was not always money that caused the fights.

We used to call her Bad Woman, a name that was given by Ma when we asked her where you were. "With Bad Woman," Ma would say, her face dark and grim. The only time I saw how hurt she must have been was not long after Wah Tsai was born. When, after four girls, Ma finally gave birth to a boy, Wing Tsai, everyone was relieved. "Thank god, your Ma does not have to be a baby-machine any more," Madam Big in the front cubicle would say to us. So we were all surprised when she became pregnant again, especially given your constant bickering and you never being home much. Ma said, "I didn't want another child; I didn't want any of you lot if it had been up to me. But your Grandma begged me. She said 'only one boy in the family is too risky, look at what happened to our Lum Tsai'. Grandma said Wong Tai Sin promised her two grandsons so the one after Wing Tsai would most definitely be a boy, too." Grandma told Ma she could stop after one more baby. Well, it was true; the baby was another boy: Wah Tsai came 18 months after Wing Tsai. But Father, by then you had practically disappeared from our lives, having moved in with Bad Woman while Ma was pregnant with your last child. One day when Ma was still "sitting out the month" after she gave birth to Wah Tsai, I came home from school to find her sitting up in bed, tears streaming down her face while nursing the baby; that silent, vacant stare was at once scary and heart-breaking. I was so frightened that I fled that dark, dingy cubicle like a shot.

I was never fully aware that you had left us for three years, since you were rarely at home at any one time. If Ma didn't bring that up at the Laus' Chinese New Year Lunch I would still be ignorant. She didn't mean to embarrass you, I'm sure—after all, it was New Year and you get together with your two sisters and their families only during Chinese New Year and Grandma's birthday. It was my fault for asking your younger half-sister, Small Kiu, why her husband didn't show up, when everyone in the family already knew the answer. Grandma has always treated Small Kiu like her own. Aunt Small Kiu and I were very close when we were little, since we're only four years apart in age. I loved going to visit her at her school on Chatham Road in Tsim Sha Tsui, instead of going home after school. It was another escape from the middle cubicle and Ma's long face and crying babies. I felt a little guilty that I had not kept in close touch with her, but when she broke down in tears at my innocent question I knew something was wrong. Ma came to my rescue by consoling my aunt: "Don't be silly! It's really not worth crying over! Look, your children are all grown up and on your side. Even your youngest is thirty years old. Wah Tsai was only just born when your brother left me for Bad Woman. Three years he was away, I never shed a tear."

When you heard this, Father, the look on your face was hard to describe. I could see you shifting uncomfortably in your chair across that large round table at Maxim's Restaurant. I was embarrassed for you, I have to admit, I wish Ma didn't raise that. But she did not make it up, even if her claim of "not shedding a tear" was pure bravado. But what went through your mind, Father, when Ma said that? Did you have any regrets, either for abandoning us for three years, or for leaving Bad Woman and coming back to the family? I could see you were relieved when Fat Aunt piped in, "Of course he'll be back, like so many of these Hong Kong men with mainland mistresses. These *dai luk muis* don't hang around for long, you know. They are only after the money. As soon as she finds out your *lo-gung* is no business tycoon from Hong Kong, she'll dump him for someone else." Bad Woman may not be a mainlander, but she didn't hang around for long either. Or did it hurt you to leave her to return to the family? The answer does not matter much, Father. Not to me, not to Ma.

Hong Kong Island Mon Amour
Nicholas Y. B. Wong

in 1945, someone died in hiroshima.
temples devastated, the ladder to god
turned upside down, human bodies
severed apart. flesh and blood
blended with soil, became a motherly
part of the cruel nature. since then,
i imagined: japan wound sink.
gozilla and power rangers were born
to guard the graves of disquieting deaths.

in 2007, everyone survives in hong kong.
the fortuneless remains fortuneless,
the fortunate still stays fortunate.
sweat and hope depreciates to a
currency called money. living below
the poverty line, yet hovering above
the horizon of fate. scanty feet
firmly on the postcolonial land, a
wrinkled bankbook in angry hands.
since then, i stop imagining.

Passing
Edward Rodney Davey

Has it ever occurred to you how fateful the departure of a boat can be? For a while, after the engines have started, you cannot be sure whether the vessel is leaving or whether the swell has just lifted it momentarily from the quayside and will return it, with a sigh, to its former berth; whether you still belong to the land, or have already been delivered up to the sea and its uncertainties.

I used to experience this as a moment of release. The seamen casting off the mooring ropes cast off the bonds which tied us to the shore. We were free on the water. When, after an hour and several calls at nearby islands, the ferry came alongside the ramshackle jetty at the end of its voyage, that freedom seemed complete. It was as though we had moved to another country.

I remember there the abandoned paddy-fields where the rich grass was cropped by small brown cows, and where the path took one for a short distance under an arch of old magnolia, after which the walls lining the path inland were dressed with great lobes of purple bougainvillea, straggling and varied hibiscus flowers, and the ever dusty mallow which I never saw in bloom. The shallow ditches were clogged with water-pepper. Further on, the sabre-like, bright red flowers of the coral-bean grew in the shelter of a low, bare escarpment which prohibited a quicker climb to the promontory above. And when one finally emerged at the top, there below (invisible before reaching this point) was a whole hedgerow of brilliant yellow allamanda marking the village limits on its western edge. The mauve ipomoea climbed the trees and peeped curiously out from among the shadows, like the eyes of wise but sickly children.

Of course, there was no overlooking the rubbish tips, the dusty football pitches, the blackened and stinking village incinerators, the public toilets exhaling a smell of urine (much concentrated in the heat), which greeted the visitor soon after leaving the pier, and no overlooking, either, the debris of old baskets and nets, and all the other detritus of village life in these parts. It is with an effort that I remember them, however. To me this island is still (and perversely, it would not surprise me to hear you say) the island of flowers.

One part of it had a special place in my affections. It was the five or six graves in the middle of nowhere which overlooked the secluded and, from the land, almost unapproachable strip of sand some hundred feet below. Set into one of the neatly cemented crescents was the vitrified photograph of an old woman gazing patiently out to sea.

From here, seated on the warm stonework, one had a view, over the stubby hawthorn shrubs, over the wild grasses trembling in the wind, to the hills beyond where centuries of storms have torn away the soil and bared huge, many-shaped boulders that look ready to topple down the slope. Once, I recall, a butterfly settled on the tip of my shoe. The tiny creature opened and closed its wings in ecstasy. My desire that it should remain (like an elaborately coloured bow) chased it away. It had a blue dash on each wing of mottled orange. As blue as the horizon.

These brief memories exercise over me a strong fascination. They stir in me a desire to return. But something holds me back, and because I am not certain quite what it is, I tell myself it is not the season for such adventures and that I can always go another day. Spring storms have blown in, you see. The papers have begun to speak of disasters if it does not stop raining soon. I imagine that we shall all be washed into the sea in one great, last mudslide—a modern-day Atlantis—the electric cables flashing and hissing as the grey-brown waters close over us! So I have stayed here to write to you and watch the rain.

In spite of it, I have twice walked down into the city. Each time, all the lights but the street lamps shone (and even some of these were lit, undecided whether it was dusk or dawn). It seemed, when I glanced ahead from under my umbrella, that we walked on sheets of glass. For suddenly the city is laid flat in its own reflection. You walk through light and windows. From above, the pedestrians under their umbrellas resemble a huge, multi-coloured pangolin. In dim corners, which would otherwise have gone unnoticed, a bulb shines, relit in the dirty shimmer of a puddle and reflected a million times in the falling drops of water. Signs come to life, casting onto the damp air around them a glimmer of red, of yellow, orange, blue, emerald.

Once, I headed down the steps where Old Alexander still keeps his antiquarian bookshop. There I felt an immediate kinship with the dusty volumes on their sagging shelves, and with the gusts of fetid disintegration exhaled through the ever open doorway. I went in. I fetched down a horribly mildewed copy of Leonardo Da Vinci's *Anatomical Drawings* and decided to buy it, as much for the drawing themselves as for the fact that its spine was broken and its pages hung on lengths of brittle thread. It suited my humour. It suited the weather. Thunder, following a strangely invisible lightning, roared amongst the traffic noise.

I let my eye wander over the sectional views of dissected tongues, necks, thorax and genitalia. *Mors sola fatetur ...,* I remembered vaguely from Juvenal: "Death alone shows what little things are the bodies of men"!

While I unstuck and delicately turned the pages of the 'da Vinci book' (as Old Alexander called it) I must have looked very melancholy. Thinking I had caught a chill, he recommended a mixture in hot water of brandy, lemon-juice and honey—"So good for the voice, sir, so beneficial for the chest!" Then, perhaps because of some intuition, he went on in his asthmatic, confidential whisper, his breath smelling like the decaying books in whose midst he must have spent the best part of his life: "Cinnamon water, sir, mixed with Jamaica Pepper-water, compound spirit of lavender, syrup of orange peel and a volatile aromatic spirit ... Ah, sir, now then, there's a cordial sure to revive a despondent soul!"

Old Alexander must live on it; I have never seen anyone more cheerful who has greater reason to be miserable.

It sets me thinking, suddenly, of an occasion some years back, while on one of my then infrequent walks, when I came across a footprint clearly outlined in the hardened earth beside a small stream. Idly fitting my shoe into it, I recognized the footprint as my own made the last time I had passed that way, nearly a fortnight earlier. I marvelled at the coincidences which had ensured its preservation. It made me pause to consider the passage of time which separated the man who stood there now from the man who had walked that way so and so many days earlier.

I do not really believe in signs—or perhaps, I do, but somehow not seriously (so I tell myself); and yet, if ever there were a reason to believe in them, here it was in my footprint. It made me think, not very originally, how insecure our lives are, how suddenly we can meet our ends, and how little we leave behind which is intimately ours. What we forfeit at death is not just our power of speech and motion; more simply, more dismayingly, it is the space we occupied and the impact our bodies have on the things around us. While we live, they must make way for us; they must bear our weight, resist us, obey us. It is this casual, unavoidable contact with things, and the marks we leave on them, which attest most directly to our existence.

One afternoon (and this really is a long time ago) we sat astride a cannon which jutted out from the crenulations of the old colonial fort overlooking that other city, its islands, estuary, boats and steamers, its crumbling rooftops where here and there a small tree had flourished, its washing, its smoke and its flags. The city noises, made faint by the hot, offshore breeze, scarcely disturbed the quietness.

Cleansed by wind and sun and the just discernible fragrance of the overhanging acacias, but most of all by the distance, I had the distinct impression of being dissociated from the life that went on below. For a while, it was as if we had been granted a dispensation from the toil of ordinary mortals, as if we gazed down on hell from a garden sanctuary whose battlements were built to enclose us for the rest of time. I thought I understood how it might feel to be redeemed.

So strong was this impression that it accompanied me down to the Protestant chapel and, more remarkably, into the pretty cemetery behind it with its frangipanis, all superbly in bloom, which filled the air with their scent and decorated the grass and the gravestones with the flowers torn off by an earlier storm.

We walked among the graves reading the names of those buried there—sea-captains, merchants, parsons, young lads who had boarded their first ship for far-off lands and never returned; above all (although not the most numerous) the infants struck down by disease when scarcely a few weeks old, and their mothers who had not survived, in this unkind climate, the labours of childbirth. All sincerely loved, sadly missed, respected, remembered for their honourable service—but to us, to you and me, my dear, wandering that afternoon under the countless white and yellow blossoms, just the dead, those whom it was impossible to imagine ourselves following because their lives were as remote from us in nature as they were in time.

They had lived in closer contact with the objects, with the *tackle* of human existence—the cloth, pots, crockery, dust—which had corrupted them, made their flesh more perishable. Whereas we believed ourselves secure from such things and destined for immortality.

Afterwards, after we had left the church and its cemetery, we stood in the hot, still square outside, undecided what to do next, whether to seek a cooler spot at the water's edge, or to suffer the atrocious heat in the lanes and alleyways made picturesque, in their way, by the vestiges of a bygone age they clung to.

Nearby there was a small, grubby shop—not even a shop, actually; a sort of stall set into the doorway of a flaking tenement—where an old man in black sold incense sticks. I bought two of them. They fizzled brightly away in the gathering dusk and spread a faint, alabaster light onto our hands and faces. They broke the spell the afternoon had cast over us.

Then yesterday evening it happened that I was sorting out one of those anonymous boxes into which we are in the habit of tossing the odd photograph. Over the years, these cartons and their like occupy so much space in the cupboard they have been stored in that they have to be removed to make room for the next item on its way to oblivion. I tipped one of these boxes onto the floor and scattered its contents with my hand. There among the photographs was one of you, so young, so fresh, so charmingly at ease with your youthfulness. So remote.

I knew it intimately. I have no idea how it got into this pile of casually assembled snapshots dating back, I discovered, almost thirty years. It ought to have been enlarged and framed and taken its legitimate place beside our other photographs and keepsakes. But there it was, half lost. There you were, and there, too, were the impressions associated with this particular photograph which I had never quite forgotten, either.

You sit on a large, granite boulder in the shade of a casuarina, your weight on one arm, face raised, wearing the marks of a faint smile while you stare down at the camera. Neither too bright, nor too dark, the light reveals very clearly each of your features, which together produce the idea of someone elevated, both physically and spiritually, from the dusty realm we, your devotees, inhabit. The huge bulk of the stone forbids our approaching you. The sky, visible through the thin branchlets of the tree, makes its claim upon you as if you were a phantom sent among us in acknowledgement of our devotion. You look calm and self-sufficient. There is even a little mockery in your gaze. You have nothing in common with us, wretched creatures that we are.

The photograph brought to mind an occasion (it embarrasses me to this day) when I was reduced to utter misery, so much so that I sank into a morose, bad-tempered silence, from which it took you a good deal of coaxing to rouse me. 'Look here ...!', 'Look there...!', you said, laughingly, pointing out this or that feature of the landscape and its vegetation. But I was not in a proper frame of mind to look anywhere, except at my feet.

We had been eating fish in that seafood restaurant which overlooked the shallow inlet on the northern shores of the 'island of flowers'. An ugly enough spot, what with the great quarry on the farther side, its grimy water and floating fishponds. I had deliberately turned my back on that depressing sight. The little, white-walled courtyard where we sat had a certain charm, though, in spite of the garish green, corrugated glass-fibre sheeting which served to protect some of the tables from the sun, and the lunatic flickering of a neon strip over a tank of unsuspecting fish. One of these, gasping and heaving on a wet plate, was later brought to us for our gastronomic approval.

We sat at a table whose shade was provided by a mulberry tree and a wandering branch of pomegranate which, out of curiosity I suppose, had clambered over the wall from the adjacent garden and hung in full blossom above our heads. The sunlight cast a shade of vermilion from the pomegranate blossom across your hair and shoulders. It made you both real and intangible. I had only to stretch out my hand to touch you, but there was something beyond my fingertips which could not be touched, which did not belong to me, and belonged perhaps to neither of us. This accidental ornament of sunlight was short-lived, fading and reviving as the clouds moved quite briskly across the sky. In my overwrought, mournful mood it seemed that across your face a dream face had passed, identical to your own and yet not yours either, impassive, remote, vaguely hostile.

When, in a gesture of companionship, I laid my hand on yours and you turned it over so that I should touch the more sensitive part of it, I had the impression that I reached out to hold what was passing, or to grasp what lay motionless and scarcely perceptible beyond it. There were no words to express my helplessness. There was nothing to be said; there was nothing to be done but sit in silence and eat our fish.

Proposing afterwards to walk to the island's western end, we were surprised—do you remember?—by a flurry of raindrops which made us look up into the sky in fear of an unexpected and unforecast storm. We sheltered beneath the great, twisted banyan at the spot where the path turns sharply to the left and descends into the village. This is the tree which nourishes itself from the moist air and, by means of its aerial roots, anchors itself again and again to the earth in recognition of the element to which it owes its existence. No tree conducts more obsessive a love affair with the soil it grows from.

We waited a while. In the meantime, the wind came off the water and could be seen climbing swiftly up the hillside through the grass and leaves. Far away, boats crossed on the brilliant afternoon sea.

Those few drops were all, as it turned out. But we were already descending the path to the village, and, having no wish to climb the slope a second time, we strolled along the causeway to the ferry pier. Through the slats one could see the water, thick with flotsam and spangles of diesel oil. Overhead, in their usual rage, the gulls screamed at one another, chased their reflections through the waves, or bobbed about in the scattering debris hoping for a titbit. From the quarry there was a rumble of machinery. Now and again an explosion set off a small landslide.

Arriving much too early for the ferry, we had—the expression pops into my head—we had time to kill. I smile. *What is time?* Augustine asked himself in great perplexity. If no one asks me, I know: if I wish to explain...I know not. But one thing we might say of it is that time appears to kill itself. It is none of our doing; it lies in the nature of the instant. We do not even have to wait for it to happen. It was enough to sit on the rim of the pier, our legs dangling like four erratic pendulums, until the sight of the grimy little ferry steaming blackly around the headland reminded us that the hour to leave was almost upon us.

I wonder if in fact it is this recollection which is at the heart of my reluctance to set out again across the five or six miles which separate us here from that island. After all, I could dress for the rains, and it is not cold. I could steel myself against the inevitable disappointments, too. The topography will not have changed. The graves and the old lady will still be there in their shallow dip, the toppling boulders will not have toppled, yet, and dampness often makes a flower's perfume more intense. In that, and in things like that, I am sure I could find a measure of consolation. Who knows, perhaps the anglers and their buckets still line the pier. They were never deterred by the weather.

No, I truly believe now that it is recollection of the old ferry which detains me in the city. *Why?* I hear you ask. I know what you are thinking. You think that the pastures and spacious palaces of...memory (that is Augustine again, fruitlessly mulling over the problem of time) should be enough in themselves to make the journey unnecessary, never mind the weather. Anyway, the old ferry has gone to scrap.

That is right, I am sure. But let me say this by way of explanation and valediction: once on board, I buried myself in the ship's innards where the engine-room could be seen and most powerfully smelt through an open companionway. I watched the fly-wheel, pistons, valves, tappets and drive-shafts slowly gather speed—a bright, oily, curiously primitive spectacle—as the vessel backed away from the pier and turned towards the open sea.

Is possibly political

The Final Solution:
By the One-Country, One-System Think Tank
Mani Rao

The disturbance from Hong Kong persists, and seems to involve those interested in "prosperity", and those interested in "democracy". While an economy that is dependent on China for its health is plausible, the idea of "democracy" is absurd for Hong Kong—can democracy dawn upon just one street in town, in just one province of a nation?

We have considered the option that China could choose to ignore this absurdity and permit full elections in due course. China's cities are now in full bloom and Hong Kong is like a limp bauhinia in comparison. Moreover, Hong Kong's Chief Executive will report to the President and execute the orders of the central government; the local council will be run by subordinates who collect taxes, maintain law and order, and assign workloads to other subordinates; and the heady air of freedom in making petty decisions will keep them all sedate. There is no political risk in allowing them their so-called democracy ... but it will mean that we have forgotten history.

Let China never forget the intrusion of foreigners. We gave them permission to carry on commerce and even to practice their own religion. They took advantage of our generosity and ransacked us. Riding on flimsy excuses and pretended self-indignation, they demanded indemnities, which we generously conceded.

As a result, we now have an anomaly at our doorstep. An asylum for people too weak to take on the work of building a glorious China, absconders who have sold themselves to superficial freedoms and been polluted by foreign ways. Today, their understanding of history is so shallow that they get agitated when some rock pile or ferry terminal is merely touched, but they feel nothing for real losses, like the looting of our palaces and the wanton destruction of our treasures—things without age or price.

The question, then, is not an economic, political or administrative one; it is about the restoration of our national honour—even if it may only be a mere scratch upon our honour. Hong Kong is not just a last colony, but a foreign civilisation, and a symbol of foreign arrogance.

Imposing straightforward military rule in Hong Kong would be the quickest solution, as Hong Kong has no army, navy or airforce. But the foreign pest press will make a lot of noise. It will be a headache.

A conservative alternative would be to ignore today's troublemakers—they will be too old in 2047 AD to be of any real threat—and to target our attention at Hong Kong's angst-free generation, those born after 1989, minds that will be easier to mould. The key area for attack should be derived from the observation that Hong Kong people believe they are different from people in the rest of China. They (think "they") dress elegantly, drive on a different side of the road, use British electrical plugs and have their own ISD code. We cannot revise so many pesky details at this juncture, so we will simply superimpose the China way of life upon the Hong Kong way of life. We will flood Hong Kong with inexpensive China novels and China television programmes, have magazines attribute the success of Hong Kong role-models to their China connections, and get Hong Kong movie stars and pop stars to set the trends. We will make it more cultured to take a holiday in China, more sensible to marry someone from China and more fashionable not to speak Cantonese. Our phonetic approximations of international fashion brands will proliferate—this won't be piracy—and we will devalue the Hong Kong shopping experience. Our re-education campaign will purge Hong Kong people of foreign-mindedness. Our protective surveillance will cover every aspect of their life, purifying them (although unknown to themselves) and getting them ready to welcome us, when we can repossess Hong Kong in a more satisfying manner. This is a slow process and it will be expensive—but we have the time.

The third option would be to intervene in a justifiable context. We would escalate an existing source of tension and then resolve it advantageously. Taking a cue from the fact that most wars are based on religious differences, our think tank has explored the enemy's churches for objectionable behaviour. The Vatican has canonized saints and missionaries in China as "freedom fighters who died defending their religious faith". Further, they have issued a condemnation of the Chinese Catholic Church and excommunicated its independently-appointed Bishops. Let us retaliate by canonizing our own saints and missionaries in China. The Pope is sure to call upon Christian nations to intervene. We can then retaliate by asserting our secularism and ban Christian places of worship across China—Hong Kong included. Hong Kong councillors, breast-fed by devout Filipina maids and unable to conceive of life without them, will refuse to comply and appeal to the world-at-large to intervene. The U.S. army will land in Hong Kong, ostensibly to guard Hong Kong's churches. Hong Kong will become a U.S. colony, hate it, and turn to China for help. We will oust the U.S. Army, take back a subdued Hong Kong, and in an act of magnanimity, lift the ban on Hong Kong churches provided they conduct their services in Mandarin. Hong Kong will finally celebrate China. The risk in this solution is that if the reactions are not forthcoming, if the Pope is not provoked, if the U.S. cannot be bothered, we will have invested a disproportionate amount of energy for nothing.

A fourth direction is speedy, efficient, and yet, cannot be traced back to us. Developed by our team after weeks of brainstorming, here is a method so natural that it is absurd, and so absurd, it could not have been unnatural; a strategy that will amaze future historians.

The concept will need to be unleashed on Hong Kong's Lamma island. We will send out our illegal immigrants (IIs) in larger numbers to disembark on an unpoliced wharf at the northern part of the island. One by one, the dogs on Lamma will begin to disappear as our hardy IIs live in the wild, kidnap dogs and feast upon them. Revolted, Lamma residents will evacuate the island. Deciding to change with the times and the tastes of its new clientele, Lamma's seafood restaurants will feature a new item on the menu. The smell of dog-barbecues in the air will put off visitors to Lamma, including those only visiting graves. Peng Chau, Cheung Chau, Lantau ... island after island will fall ever faster to our dog-eating squads. Fearing the spread of this menace into Hong Kong and Kowloon, and unable to remain inside their cramped flats, Hong Kong dogs and their owners will evacuate the region in a hurry. When we next celebrate reunification day in Hong Kong, not one Hong Kong dog will bark at our firecrackers.

We believe that this is the final solution for the Hong Kong question. A display of our invisible hand and consummate authority in guiding the spirit of Hong Kong back to where it belongs—in China. A detailed implementation plan is available for your perusal.

This is a fictional narrative. The real author is a dog-lover.

Forty Years to Go
Louise Ho

Long before the event
Two parties agreed
The structure in place
Must not be altered

(Contractual terms
Try to fix what in time
Time changes anyway)

This frenetic dynamo of a place
Protean as ever
Stretching this way and that
In multiple dimensions—
Who is to say
This dense matter of a beast
Would not stretch the next ten
To sixty or more
Or reduce forty
To a mere twenty
Or less?

What Do You Do
Alan Jefferies

What do you do
with all those things
all those things
you meant to say
and never did and
now it's too late
cuz

Do you save them up
or do you cash them in

All those things
you meant to say and
never did and now
it's too late cuz

What do you do with
promises never kept
things you meant to do
and never did and now
it's too late cuz

Is there a place called
never too late?

Is possibly political

where all those things
you meant to say
and all those things
you meant to do
are done and said

where it's never too late
cuz

In Another Ten Years:
Some Wanton Thoughts for 2017
Christine Loh

In another ten years
Life will be cramped
Every way we turn
We see large walls
Some tycoons
Made fortunes
Pouring concrete here
In another ten years
We will
Be ready
Be brave
Enough
To tear them down
A new city
Will be born
In another ten years

In another ten years
The leaders will be no more
Forgotten, displaced
Achievements erased
Perhaps even
Remembered for
What they are
Small-minded
Visionless
Temporarily in power

Pouring concrete
We no longer
Want to see
Time will have passed
In another ten years

In another ten years
We will
Be mightier still
We will
Be more carefree
Yet full of memories
We will
Be stronger in body
Freer in spirit
In another ten years
We, the people,
Will be mightier still

A City Passing
David Clarke

When suddenly, a little before daybreak,
an invisible procession passing by,
you are woken to exquisite music,
don't mourn for what you've never gained,
or bathe in the sweetness of melancholy.
The city had been dying for a long time,
and there's no room for the weakness of nostalgia.
Nothing should be printed in sepia.
Don't say it was a dream,
that your ears deceive you,
but have the grace to live
where the present is,
accepting with an open heart
the music that is given you now:
a final delectation, new to all ears.
As someone long prepared for this to happen,
don't degrade yourself with empty hopes.
Go firmly to the window. Drink it in.
Listen with emotion,
but don't make the pleas of a coward.
And say goodbye to the city you are losing.

*(After Constantine P. Cavafy's 'The god forsakes Antony'
and Leonard Cohen's 'Alexandra Leaving')*

Hong Kong, July 2007

On Visiting Cavafy's House
Alan Jefferies

In Hong Kong I built a small
audience for my poems.
In Alexandria, the Arab poets
hoisted me onto their shoulders
and marched me through the streets.

Yet in my own country
my work is invisible, and so am I.
When I see other poets,
people I have known for years,
they look right through me
like I'm dead already;
but their indifference is wasted on me.
They can hate me all they like.

I am poet—
transparent as sunshine.
There is nowhere for their
hostility to settle.

I scatter my verses across the planet.

Alexandria, 2007

64 | Mid-Sentence
Lawrence Gray

What's the story? I've been asking this for years. It's how I deal with the world. What's the story, I say, and have to conclude most of the time that there is no story. Life sort of happens in a messy mix of accidents and processes beyond one's control, though all your own fault. It happens, whatever you do, and the story is just not there, though you might want it to be. Is a story a beginning, a middle and an end? But there's something lacking; a moral mostly. A story means intentions and obstacles and triumphs and failures. Where's the story in just being born and dropping off the end of the conveyor belt? Where's the story in getting up and going to work? Where's the story in getting by, having a drink, toasting a sandwich, having a chat on the phone and cashing a cheque? Stuff happens, intentionally sometimes, in reaction to other stuff mostly, and largely in accordance with a logic not of our own making, unlike in fiction where we can choose everything and make the story work.

The lack of story could be a story, I suppose, in a post-modern, or is that post-post-modern, sense. Make what you will of that. Critical discourse long ago became about counting consonants and kicking the author out of the equation rather than trying to work out why something was better than something else. Coolness perhaps became as good as it got. But, we all know that it's the story, stupid!

And that's the case with history and our grasp of the future. If history is reduced to statistics and processes, we aren't interested. But find a love story, find a struggle between good and evil, a great warrior who believes in their destiny, or a prophet trying to live life according to some fiction, and our attention is grabbed. And our money taken. The story is a commodity. The reality of history, like wars, is statistics, or perhaps music—though it can be pretty ugly music. And you concoct a story to make people willing to play a role in it. Nobody wants to be just a note on the stave, a cog in the wheel, a number in the statistics, and so how can an entire society exist and flourish that has no myth, just a set of numbers? Or is it that it could exist, only nobody would care or notice? Which brings me (in a very roundabout way that all the naff books on how to write essays tell you is wrong) to Hong Kong: the point! And that is the point, because the point of anything is a fiction and the fiction of Hong Kong has a strange and pointless nature. If the myths of the communist motherland are not to be swallowed, then nothing else can be! And if they are, then whatever that story is, it won't be Hong Kong's.

So what's the no-story of Hong Kong? It was born, it grew and maybe there will be an end. Cities do end; some abruptly. And some evolve into other cities. Climates change, rivers run dry, economies collapse, and fashions start coming from elsewhere rather than one's own creative dynamic. Cool turns to naff. And Hong Kong one day will be either too naff to live in, or under six feet of water and the playground of monsters or midgets as yet not evolved. So when people ask what has changed in Hong Kong after ten years under Chinese rule, one searches for a story to tell them, an illustration of change, of moral intent, a point of departure, an end, a beginning, a hero. But one has to manufacture it, falsify, fictionalise and in effect make a primitive judgement just to please an audience. The truth is just statistics, though one can romanticise and start looking for the tune.

So has the tune changed? Have we slipped out of the incessant march music and eight-tone scales of the West into something less rhythmic, more pentatonic, more shrill and operatic? I even have difficulty in pinpointing any change in tone. What you get are statistics and processes and complexity and the certain knowledge that, come 2045, the assigned date for the death of the Hong Kong SAR, a forgotten component of the agreement between the UK and China, that one is still going to have exactly what one has, though maybe some fantasy-history will have emerged that, in this town where nobody gives a damn about history, history will make not the slightest bit of difference. Any discussion about Hong Kong turns into an infinite regression into parentheses.

Hong Kong used to have a crowd-pleasing story. Hong Kong was founded by drug dealers, so the story goes, though if you want to be pernickety you can look a little more closely and discover it was not quite as cut-and-dried as that. There was even a Hong Kong before the British came, for a start, and the Hong Kong history museum now likes to present all that and portray the English bit as just a blip.

The Convention of Chuenpeh 1841 ceded the island of Hong Kong to the British and if we think of Hong Kong beginning when the British came, maybe it ended when they left. But then, who has left? The British government left, but they more or less had little to do with the running of the place from the time the Japanese invaded. And it can be argued that much the same people run the place now that Beijing has in theory taken over. And in some respects they are much the same people, some of them direct descendants of the Chinese who threw their lot in with the British when they first started doing business in the region. Though that starts making the story very complicated and the story begins to fall apart and turn into this unheroic, unspiritual, amoral, progression of stuff that just happens when lots of different individuals with certain drives and needs come together in the pursuit of those things.

But let's get back to the story. Was the founding of Hong Kong a noble, outrageous, piece of adventurism? Hardly. It didn't even warrant much of a Boy's Own Spin at the time. Everyone involved got sacked, reprimanded, stabbed in the back by someone who either thought it should never have happened or was too pathetic a reward for so much effort. Charles Elliott, who signed the Convention of Chuenpeh, was made chargé d'affairs in Texas, which was very much a punishment appointment, if you consider how he would have had to host dinner parties for the dismal bunch of drunks and slave owners who had seized power there. And for that matter the Chinese Mandarin, Lin Tse-Hsu, who set his sights on destroying the opium trade, also lost his job for, in effect, doing his job! The escalation into war had more to do with Beijing's inertia and inability to support its own administrators. Lin was, after all, a man of humble origins who had worked his way up, and the aristocracy were not inclined to communicate with the likes of him. Too clever by half, and suspiciously logical and hard working, he was sent off to the newly annexed Illi basin in Xinjiang, to host dinners for Kazakh opium addicts and slave owners—a little bit of Chinese imperial adventurism conveniently forgotten in all but the name of the province: the New Territories.

It was a mix of misunderstandings, double-dealing, bribery and corruption all in the service of the needs of the time's level of technology. To trade with the East you needed a base to fuel your steamers. And to deal with complex commercial regulations you needed laws that recognised the concepts used to organise the economies of the West. Chinese law could not handle it and the Chinese quite sensibly regarded steam engines as dirty, noisy affairs that frightened the cows. There is the story told of Chinese backwardness where the ignorant Mandarins tore up the railway lines to Guangzhou because they disturbed the countryside. In my youth the history books used that as an example of why the British Imperial mission, morally dubious in many aspects, was also justifiable. We modernised the world. Nowadays one can look upon those Mandarins and think them perfectly sensible people. They would weep at the polluted state of China's cities and point out how not just China is destroyed but the whole world. Bad *feng shui*! That's what Global Warming is ... and now I've lost the story again. Other stories seem potentially available, if we find it useful to pick them out of the noise. What, we may ask, is politically useful? Which, we may well ask, is the most lucrative commercial story? How can I serve my own purposes? Or should I just be cool and knowing and enigmatic, hinting I know secrets that you do not know and have powers and connections that you do not have? Us Brits can be inscrutable when we want to be.

And so, 1842 and all that! History reduced to the best bits—only, in Hong Kong well, there is an awful lot of noise in Hong Kong, a lot of selves to be served and not many good bits. So after 1842 and all that, the official founding of the city of Victoria, a name that never quite caught on though officially it still is the Hong Kong Island part of the city—much as the City of Hull is officially called Kingston, though nobody much cared for the King and thus the locals called it Hull, after the river—I digress.

Where am I?

Ah, yes, 1842 and all that!

So we find Hong Kong history to be a list of squabbles, infighting, bewildered moments where the place sought a role for itself and much about drainage and sanitation. The story then became China and not Hong Kong. Though Hong Kong did produce the Taai Ping, a murderous, free-loving Christian sect with socialistic leanings that in the end frightened the Westerners as much as the ruling Qing Dynasty. Could the Falun Gong of 2007, much given to large drum-beating processions through Hong Kong (mysteriously without any media coverage whatsoever), be a modern descendant of such enigmatic forces in the Chinese soul? They ooze a boxerish vibe and Taai Pingish religiosity. To paraphrase Basil Fawlty, "Don't mention the Falun Gong!"

And to paraphrase Jiang Zemin, to rid us of this evil cult, the Taai Ping that is, Chinese Gordon, eventually of Khartoum, led the Qing to victory and the next thing we know, a rather dull little medical student at Hong Kong University started thinking China needed to get rid of its Emperors and institute modern institutions of Government. Sun Yat Sen goes on to be possibly the dullest revolutionary ever recorded in history, but undoubtedly the founder of modern China.

And here is something curious about Chinese history: it so often is a sweep of processes rather than great heroes. The individual is buried in the waves of history. Or at least that is how Chinese history is studied. Its popular variant is a confused mess of stories without much care for chronology or accurate depictions of the era they come from. And the stories are often wild and woolly, with gods and demons thrown in for good measure. It is all opera! And as everyone knows, you can never really follow the story in an opera: you are supposed to know it somehow, but you never do, not all of it and often not the same story. And perhaps, since all history is just this mess of stuff, the Chinese are right. Collect lots of boring records and annotate them and let the popular imagination create wild stories and call it history, while the real history is the number of bricks in a great wall and how many man years it took to build it.

Somewhere in all that is a lingering idea of the good man, versed in literature, arts and good taste in general, but where the West came in and destroyed the lingering remnants of the Chinese story, came the idea that man is only as good as the system makes him. Power without check inevitably destroys virtue. The game is everything and what makes for a good game? Good rules that everyone understands and can, if they produce boring results or unjust ones, be changed. And so Cricket arrived in Hong Kong but would the Chinese play it? No!

How come the Chinese never cottoned onto the one game that could shame the colonialists and prove themselves as more than equals? One has a sneaky suspicion that most Chinese who emigrated to Hong Kong either did not notice the British were there or were glad they were there instead of the Qing. But essentially they ignored them, as they pretty much do today. Donald Tsang recently announced, if my reading of the *South China Morning Post* in April 2007 was correct, that "the opinions of ex-pats" are of little importance. Maybe they misquoted him. But probably not.

What changed the rules of Hong Kong's game rather abruptly was Hong Kong's falling into the hands of the Japanese. It has its stories, its moments of tragedy and high farce: the Japanese were slaughtering and raping nurses while the Australian forces, idiotically dumped in Stanley as a futile attempt to bolster up a pointless defensive stance, broke into the bars and got drunk. And as the British propaganda machine got into gear portraying the Japanese as sub-human devils, British officers entertained their counterparts in the Japanese army at banquets with plenty of wine, as a prelude to their dismal internment. This is perhaps where the Hong Kong of the British Empire died and what was born afterwards was an afterthought, a misalignment of historical forces. The Americans did not want it.

And they, more than the Japanese, were the enemy then. They wanted Hong Kong handed over to Chiang Kai Shek but the Brits in the internment camp of Stanley had other plans and reclaimed the colony. Nobody here argued with them and the British swiftly sent the navy to make sure they got there before the Americans. If the Americans had been quicker, if Chiang Kai Shek had not been mired in organisational chaos, and the Brits in no mood to compromise, Hong Kong would have died then and there, becoming a windswept backwater, pillaged by the communists, and left to rot. What a story the place would have had then! Its pivotal role in the modernisation of China would have been dismissed as a joke, a desperate imperialist conceit confined to a few footnotes referencing obscure academic papers that once bothered to argue the point. Instead, it became the refuge of Shanghainese businessmen, retreating Kuomingtang and Cantonese refugees, and the modern Hong Kong of sweatshop labour and plastics factories. Suzy Wong grew up amidst all this and started writing stories about The Miracle of Hong Kong.

By the time the Handover came it was as though the rest of China had caught up, but was still an unknown quantity. With the Soviets collapsing, China looked set for regime change of some sort and Hong Kong would thus, so some said, take over China! Perhaps it already had. The blunt use of the military to suppress unarmed student protestors in Tiananmen Square in 1989 put paid to that and conjured up images of old China, Stalinist policies, and Maoist excesses. Hong Kong shook and for a moment the story of the Handover began to look interesting, for annihilation does produce a sense that they deserved it and a moral makes a story. Would it be a case of People's Liberation Army troops rampaging, blowing up shopping malls and arresting dissidents? Was one a fool for hanging around waiting for the internment camps and mass executions? Would there be daring escapes? Would there be heroic encounters? Would there be a song and a poster image of a banker beating off a retreating tank with his briefcase?

And the press flew in, hoping for a story, desperate for a story, and all they could come up with was the revelation that White Men actually do labouring jobs in Hong Kong. Or at least, the couple of white guys they found doing a bit of furniture removal for a Chinese boss were held up as a sign that White Supremacy no longer ruled, forgetting the rather blue-collar origins of the sailors and soldiers that propped up the bars of Hong Kong since its inception. One wonders how much money the man who concocted that piece of copy got from the syndication rights. The best image was of a kilted squaddy at the War Memorial caught in a gust of wind revealing that nothing was worn beneath his kilt and all was in perfect condition. This was perhaps the antidote to the labouring white men, for it proved that the devils in skirts were still to be feared, if the film *Carry on Up The Khyber*, voted best British movie of all time, is anything to go by. Private Widdle would no doubt have approved. (I implore you to see the film, as it explains everything there is to know about the English.) And there was something Widdlish about the whole Handover ceremony in which both sides managed to out-kitsch each other in a display of pomp and circumstance and Gay Soldiery that proved that the plot had long ago been lost and everyone really knew the concept of national sovereignty was draining away in the face of globalisation.

And so, what the press found was rain and a t-shirt featuring the Union Jack being painted Red. The icon was perhaps more prescient than it was intended. The flag was not so much changed as merely painted over—for beneath Hong Kong remained, well, jacked, and not unlike Hawaii, with its Union Jack vaguely protesting its annexation by the monster next door. Now that is an odd story that lingers in the footnotes of history, why the Union Jack should represent Hawaii and why Sun Yat-sen conducted much revolutionary activity in Hawaii. Rich ex-patriot Chinese with American passports hover in the shadows of the founding of modern China, and now—with American MBAs in hand and newly acquired Putonghua—their grandchildren head for Shanghai and its business opportunities. And curiously, the seemingly conservative emblem of Imperial Power presides over a rather bolshy stick-it-to-the-man attitude, capable of giving anyone claiming the mandate of heaven in all its forms a headache.

To continue the great and glorious history of Hong Kong and its Miracle...

In the lead up to the 1997 Handover, the Brits half-heartedly tried to keep rioters from the streets by allowing for greater democracy and boosting up the economy with great works like the Airport. But afterwards, the Chinese returned the government to the old bureaucracy, though they kept the airport. It looked nice.

There seemed to be a story brewing: here was the disastrous economic downturn and the even more disastrous new Chief Executive, Mr Tung, hell-bent on producing a Singaporean-style benevolent dictatorship, which turned into more of a re-enactment of Ferdinand and Imelda Marcos's last days when he managed to get half a million people protesting on the streets against him. But underlying it, Hong Kong was much the same. There had been riots before. There had been strikes before. There had been upturns and downturns and indecisive governments before and anyone who had been in Hong Kong long enough would know, the very pulse of the place, the music if you like, assumes what goes up, comes down and sometimes you get lucky and sometimes not.

It was all taken in its stride. The heart of Hong Kong beat much the same as ever, even when the Plague, a much loved depleter of Hong Kong's 19th-century population, returned, in the form of SARS, and the old Hong Kong politics of drains and sanitation resurfaced. There was even a tragic fire, the Garley Building, like many other tragic fires: from the Happy Valley Racecourse fire of the early part of the last century to the Shek Kip Mei Squatter Camp in the middle part of the century. Fires, plagues, street demonstrations, bureaucratic paralysis, rapacious tycoons sewing up monopolies of property, service industries backed by dodgy money from gun runners, drug dealers, gambling syndicates, corrupt officials, crazy *feng shui* masters etc. etc. etc. etc. and etc.—these are the everyday fibre of Hong Kong's way of life. Anyone who enters Hong Kong throws themselves upon the rough waters and hopes some wreckage comes along with a handy bit of gold hanging onto it. And in this messy, piratical world enough luck is generated to keep everyone hoping for their turn. Nobody is rewarded for hard work, for brilliance, for exceptional abilities. You either get lucky or you do not and that is all there is, and Hong Kong would like to think that this tune is its very own, but one finds it hummed throughout the world if one does not live in a fantasy.

Though to say that Hong Kong people do not live in a fantasy is perhaps overstating the case. People literally do get sold magic beans on the street. Little old ladies have their savings prised out of their bank accounts by unscrupulous flim-flam artists peddling magic beans that restore good health, good fortune, and full heads of hair. They have been known to tragically blind babies by rubbing magic incense ashes into their eyes.

In a world in which policemen have gun battles with each other and write poetry about the meaninglessness of existence, if the evidence presented in a 2007 court case featuring Officer Tsui who was given to robbing banks and taking his mother on exotic holidays is anything to go by, there is no moral to the events of Hong Kong; thus no story. If the case of one of the richest men in Hong Kong being kidnapped and scolding his wife for paying the ransom without negotiating it down and then being kidnapped again and disappearing (rumour has it, over the side of the boat speeding him to Taiwan as it was intercepted by the Chinese navy) is anything to go by, nothing happens without an element of absurdity. The now very rich wife took to sporting pigtales, wearing mini-skirts, and queuing up for cake coupons while the money languished in probate. Then there was a lawsuit from the aging father who already was rich enough. Then, on her winning all the money, she quickly dies a premature death and a mysterious *feng shui* master lays claim to it all. And then hefty doses of media management crank into gear as questions start surfacing suggesting that all of this saga might be the tip of a very iffy set of circumstances. Follow the money, one might say, but it could be very dangerous to actually do so. And so ...

Where was I in this absurd soap opera?

Nowhere!

The facts of Hong Kong lack moral content, let alone the fictions. Hong Kongers prefer spectacle and absurdity to coherent story telling. *Mo lei tau*—nonsense—has been perfected and art has never made much headway, perhaps because reality has outstripped it and similarly not made much headway. So what is the story? There is no story, there is film director and comic actor Chow Sin Chi turning out live action cartoons with a deft use of the non-linear editing suite. There is process and the process continues, repeating, recycling, reforming and eventually, one assumes, dying. It is a piece by Philip Glass endlessly cycling through the circle of twelfths, and fading out in a clatter of Chinese gongs.

Has the Handover changed anything? It does not look like it.

Have the Brits finally gone and the whole place reverted to the sleepy Chinese fishing village it once was? No. But then the whole of China has changed. Has Hong Kong joined the rest of China? Not quite. It drives on the left-hand side of the road, for a start. It does not arrest government opponents; it rather invites them to endless lunches and onto endless committees. Has the English language disappeared? It was never there in the first place. The Chinese slept one side of the bed and the English, the other. But the English were never here in large numbers and although there are fewer Europeans here, an awful lot of the Chinese are not exactly Chinese nationals, but rather products of overseas education if not nations. The ABC, BBC, CBC—American-Born, British-Born, Canadian-Born Chinese—are everywhere and some of those are more American, more British, more Canadian than the Westerners who arrive with their dreams of exploring oriental culture.

Globalisation has changed the world, but not Hong Kong, for Hong Kong was a product of the globalisation process, is the epitome of globalisation. The market made Hong Kong. Trade routes made it. And although the steamers do not need a fuelling stop any more, the airport is one of the largest in the world and the container terminals shipping goods in and out of Hong Kong are still there. Economics drives the place, not personalities, and it remains a first-rate place for third-rate people. Talent is scarce and business opportunities are many. Buy cheap, sell high. That's it! That's the story. A city that struggles to be a city instead of a workers' dormitory! That's not a story. A city that was never quite a city, but more a depot! A city that has no soul! A city that lacks culture and taste! A city that is hot and happening and ever changing and never changing! An exciting city! A city of dullards and dimwits and dickheads! The ignorant rule. Nobody rules. No story. Just stuff. A lucky place to be in! Especially if you like dancing and horse-racing.

Mimi Wong, an HSBC banker, paid US$15 million for tango

lessons! And quite rightly got most of it back when her instructor called her a lazy cow. Only in Hong Kong could US$15 million fail to impress upon someone the need to be at least politely diplomatic when confronted with an idiot.

Maybe Hong Kong *is* learning diplomacy. It's learning about China. It is gathering more information about the new China and finding it not the monolithic evil force in the backyard, but rather a mess of bits and pieces, some with good investment prospects and others, as ever, rife with warlords and corrupt officials. Beijing has become nicer, in as much as the men are younger, though not young enough to forgo dying their hair an alarming jet black to keep looking vigorous. But the age is sixty-something rather than eighty-something nowadays and the men are professionals, engineers, economists, political-science graduates, experts and general managers who create focus groups and committees and study papers. China has no crusade. It struggles to replace the irrational with the rational and provide the framework for everyone to play the competitive game and not exploit those who have not as yet got the message.

Hong Kong might not be learning to love Beijing, but it is losing its fear and learning that there is a game to play that might have some harsh rules, but all one needs to do is accept certain principles—the primacy of the communist party for a start—and then everything else is negotiable. And even what actually constitutes the Communist Party seems to be negotiable. Membership has been thrown open to all the "Advanced" social groupings, meaning technocrats and businessmen can be "Communists" now without having to accept Marx as the last word in Economic Theory. Meaning, if you pay your money, you get into the good seats at the Olympics reserved for important officials.

But that is assuming too much. Hong Kongers are a little gauche, a bit naïve, a little cosseted by the good times, and products of bizarre devilish deals. Mainlanders hardened to the ways of the Mainland come in two forms: ignorant peasants out to grab whatever they can and smart, well-educated graduates out to grab whatever they can. And the notion of the communist is lacking in Hong Kong discourse, unlike the every day of China. There is government, authoritarian yes, but as was always the case in China, the Emperor is but one man and is a long way away playing with his concubines and communing with the forces of heaven. Everyone else is putting their bets on which horse will win, and sometimes if the recently excavated radio controlled drugs dispensers planted at the starting rail of the Happy Valley Race Course are anything to go by, working on elaborate means of cheating the whole system. And the suspects were mainlanders, as they always are. So the love and trust of China, of Beijing, is but a sycophantic hope for someone to protect them from the rapacious hordes.

The Chineseness of Hong Kong is a throwback, called upon from folk memory, half forgotten and barely relevant to modern China, but that does not matter! And that is the odd thing. Whether one can conclude that this has changed anything in Hong Kong is a moot point. The story is a mystery, a chaotic soap opera with no end, except when the Aliens land and inform the entire cast that it was all a dream.

What Hong Kong means is that stuff happens and one can turn a story on it if one likes, but the story is a fabrication, a piece of propaganda, and indicates a need to manipulate, to gain control, to establish an order, and in Hong Kong one finds that this is remarkably lacking. And so a coherent Noble Lie for those who vie for power here and do not really want it that much. There are no great leaders. They all follow in the wake of Sun Yat Sen, in being dull professionals who somehow get assigned the role in whatever the system is churning up. We have an 800-strong committee to vote for the Chief Executive and since only the man Beijing thinks suitable will win, it seems pointless opposing him. But recently opponents have somehow emerged. A sort of Loyal Opposition has been sanctioned. And, so the argument goes, since it is pointless, maybe someone should run in opposition to expose the pointlessness and it will at least make the chosen winner explain their policies. And this is ideal for people who actually do not want the job very much to at least show that they think policy decisions by the government matter, even if the ones announced and discussed in public are not actually ones that the government really does much about. The point, though, is to create a fiction that some can believe in, that there is a mandate, and that the elected Chief Executive has addressed the public, whose opinions matter to the eight hundred electors. But as the desire is not really there, there is no story, just a fragmentary drama with a few good scenes, and ultimately nobody suspends their disbelief for long.

Since the Handover there have been no riots, and arrogant officials have a habit of ending up in the courts exposing their arrogance to the public who find them all rather embarrassing. Whether it is contempt for the ignorance of the general public, or even the "stupidity of Hong Kong teachers", as discussed in another recent court case concerning government interference in academic freedom, it all smacks of a uniquely Hong Kong muddle brought on by uncertain powers and the ever-levelling effects of backstabbing and envy. There is no prize left unscorned and it is just far better to keep your head down, avoid conspicuous displays of idiocy and wealth, and definitely side-step ambitions in public areas, and muddle on in a very British way that sits very well with the natural anarchy of the Cantonese. Render unto Caesar what is Caesar's and get on with your own business, especially if you happen to have some nice offshore earnings and property in various places around the world.

How can I conclude this overview of the Handover?

I feel I should just end in mid-sentence, like most conversations in Hong Kong. Nothing is concluded. Everything is talked away in lunches and pointless meetings. Decisions do not get made, but things happen and we all live reasonably well, some a lot more reasonably than others, but they do such stupid stuff with their money as to make one realise that one actually can have too much money. Or at least Hong Kong can. They prefer to horde it for a rainy day, for a future ancestor, for HSBC bank, or buy a bag of magic beans, or a pack of Tom.com shares from Richard Li.

If one wants to look for a great pronouncement, to find something the Western newspapers want to write about, or the historians even, the story must be about democracy and its failure to be implemented. The story, though, is the non-story, for only when democracy happens will the British colonial legacy finally die, except that it died a long time ago with the Japanese invasion, so whatever ran the place, made the place, was the place, had nothing to do with democracy (which would be the end, or beginning), but somehow the hunger for democracy does not motivate anything much...well, not much more than a sharp intake of breath.

The dynamic that fuelled Hong Kong was the isolation of China under the revolutionary period, and now China's embracing of the market economy drives Hong Kong. External forces rather than internal take the lead and a democratic Hong Kong will probably find itself in much the same situation, with everyone moaning about how useless and indecisive the democratic government is. Democracy is a brave attempt to create a moral and make a story. Freedom, democracy, and the opening up of the Hong Kong society and thus a cultural renascence, a flowering of many blooms, a resurgence of the film industry, a gathering of creative literati and visual artists, are all possible, if enough actually care. History will have progressed. The story has a happy ending. Or it just goes on. And who says the place wasn't democratic in the first place, because essentially, everyone does exactly as they please and those with the most money get to buy more than those who have less, but so it goes, that's not going to change in this world, in this lifetime, anywhere!

Another gasp of polluted air, devoid of oxygen and packed full of toxins ...

So Hong Kong the cool, forever! And that is it. Hong Kong does what it does, is what it is, and languishes as a footnote, and does not give a damn. And the non-story of the British is, what a success the Handover is! And the non-story of Beijing is, what a success the Handover is! And the non-story of the Chinese is, how clever we are, and the non-story of the ex-pats is, hey, here we still are! So it's a happy ending. So how cool can you get?

Witness

Exception
Amy Lee

I ... How should I begin to talk about myself? Should I start with my disappearance? Well, the trouble is, no one was curious about my disappearance. No one even noticed that in the operations of their daily routine, something, or someone, was suddenly not there. My disappearance was not a disappearance because no one had registered a missing relationship with me—my absence had not left a noticeable void in anyone's life. You see, I disappeared together with my son. If my son had been alive, and had he been crying and asking for help, strangers might have taken note and started a search. A boy had lost his guardian; a highly organized society such as Hong Kong would have noticed a crying boy with no mother. Unfortunately though, my boy was with me when we both disappeared. And thus, I was not missed. At least not enough to start people asking questions and trying to find me.

I was found finally, not because people had wanted to, but because an unlucky new tenant had moved into a flat and was in the process of redecorating it. Workmen were doing something in the kitchen. The new tenant had given instructions to have the kitchen remodelled; something needed to be especially done with the huge cement block beneath the cooker. The new tenant was puzzled over the previous owner's bad design; there was no space to store gas or kerosene cylinders. When the workmen started to strike the block to break it down, a human hand—my hand—was exposed, scaring the daylights out of them. They stopped everything and called the

police. Officers arrived and took over the job of shattering the block, and discovered me and my young son. Obviously, bodies dead from natural causes do not get buried under cookers in residential flats, and this discovery immediately turned a redecoration project into a major crime investigation.

So I was found, and that made the headlines. While no one ever gave me a second glance in my life, and no one cared enough to notice that I was missing, the discovery of my body became a major news distraction in the daily lives of most Hong Kong citizens. Stories were told about the workman's shock when he saw my hand protruding from the mass of concrete he was removing. Reporters made up their own accounts about the cooker, the flat, and the idea of hiding dead bodies in peaceful, ordinary residential areas. Policemen were quoted as saying that never had they encountered such a gruesome case before. After months of intense international tracking and investigation, they finally got hold of my murderer in Indonesia. During the investigation, whenever a new clue or connection was discovered, it went into the newspapers, and became the core around which all plausible theories were woven. The newspaper articles became almost like a serialized novel—and our pictures appeared whenever they could push them into the paper. Thus we got more than just 15 minutes of fame during the relatively quiet, banal Hong Kong of the late 1960s; practically all literate people knew about us and our story.

Or so they thought.

They thought they knew us because many of them had not only read the papers, but also watched *The Criminals*. Should I consider that my personal moment of glory? An ordinary woman like me, single and with a child, struggling to survive in a busy city such as Hong Kong, and yet managing to get onto the big screen—that's something, right? They called it one of the ten most horrendous crimes in Hong Kong's colonial history. I'm not surprised, given the media's efforts to stop people forgetting. But of course, what they remember today may not be me, or my son, but the movie. In many people's minds my face has been merged with the pretty face of Si Si, the actress who played my character. Well, imagine having her be me! The long hair, the delicate face and the slender body—star quality in any era! But my poor son got transformed into a dumb girl in the film, played by a plump little girl with a look helpless enough to melt hearts.

They just loved seeing the weak and voiceless (in this case, a literally voiceless little girl) being victimized, didn't they? The sight of a pretty, young single mother struggling alone in one of the most materialistic places in the world, with the little child as an extra burden, really got to their heart? To exist in this place was bad enough, but to meet a man who promised to take care of mother and daughter and who turned out to be the worst of all was so bad that it could only happen in a miracle—or a movie. The man in the movie only wanted to use my body for his financial benefit, and did not care about me or my child at all. Finally, on a stormy night (it had to be stormy, given the tragedy of our fictional life), he made it very clear that I should start earning, to justify my existence. A struggle followed and he killed me accidentally. My child escaped and went down to the night watchman for help. But of course, she could not say what the matter was, and the fiend grabbed her and took her back to the flat and drowned her.

That was the crime. But the movie was not over. My friends came to visit and could have discovered our death right there and then. But the fiend's evil made them scared and uncomfortable. They left the very place we were murdered and did not notice anything. Although the movie ended with the police arresting the fiend in Indonesia, the arrest was added almost as an afterthought to the movie. The point was the beautiful face of the actress and the helplessness of such beauty in a place like Hong Kong. That was what made it a Hong Kong crime, an event which would define the place and some of its people.

But who cares that the public memory of one of the most horrible crimes in the history of Hong Kong, was constituted not from facts but from a fictional intervention almost a decade afterwards? Who cares that my son and I became a beautiful single mother and a literally voiceless girl? Public interest in us lies not with our lives, and certainly not what we would have to say. Only with our deaths did our stories become anything of interest to the movie-makers, the story-tellers and the general citizens. Stories were told not just about us, but also about the flat where we were found. All of a sudden, everybody was saying different things about us, the place, and anything they could relate us to.

But I have been silent, and silenced, by the proliferation of news articles and other narratives constructed about us. I have turned in frustration in my grave. The impossibility of saying: "Hey, what about me? Have you thought about me? The human being, not the picture, not the victim, and the hand buried in the solid stove."

I am very aware that voices from the deep void of death are not always welcome, and this was echoed in another, more recent case of undetermined cause of death. This case was reopened following an appeal by the deceased's family. In 1999, a female body was found in an almost empty Hong Kong flat. It was a skeleton filled with maggots; the head was found detached, in a dustbin near the bedside table. The state of decomposition meant it was no longer possible to test for the cause of death. The only trace found from the skeleton was traces of heroin in the hair. There was an investigation, but obviously the body and the scene of discovery did not provide much information for the police. The traumatized family had wanted to link the death to the rich boyfriend of the deceased, who owned the flat. I am sad to say it, but what have we learned about this poor sister who died quietly in a flat and whose family wanted to know the truth? News reports showed pictures taken during her life—some were professional pictures during her modeling career. Together with these portrayals of beautiful smiles and beautiful clothes in a stylish setting, however, were stories, hearsays and fantastic speculations which did not go beyond her face and her body. For the thirty-something beautiful years she had lived in this world, what was left was a lot of noise around the dark void of her silence. The visual images on the celluloid provided all the information people needed to call forth a being who had existed in the world for more than three decades. She had a loose life, it was said; she took drugs, it was said; she was a gold-digger, it was said—because the photos were the proof that she was the beautiful girl who must have enjoyed her beautiful body hoping for a beautiful life.

Well, I don't know her either. But when the media printed these photos and stories, had they considered how much this beautiful person had meant to her sisters, to her parents and to all those people who had worked with her? Had they ever thought of asking whether she was competent in her professional practice? Had they considered whether she was a loving daughter to her parents? Or whether she had been a good emotional support to her sisters in the difficult path of growing up together?

Oh, but those things are beside the point, some will say; those things are not the rightful realm of newspapers and magazines; they do not help the sales a bit! Well, that, unfortunately, is the case. The bright metropolitan city of Hong Kong has just celebrated the tenth anniversary of its return to the motherland, and a big reason for celebrating is its still very much valid claim of being a metropolitan hub, something it has been proud of since the 1970s. Ten years under the protective wings of the motherland and Hong Kong is no less; if anything, it is even more of a metropolis. This is surely a cause for fireworks.

But lo and behold, the festive fireworks have gotten under our skin. The display of cracking brilliance and cacophony has seeped into the pores of the city, deep into its blood, so that display has become a mentality. The everyday blossoming of colourful news photos on the newsstands, over the show windows of the convenience stores, on the LCD screens in the public transport systems, on the intimate small screens of our private mobile phones... It is all a big show—with nothing inside.

I am confident that Hong Kong will continue to be a metropolis, the fireworks will continue to cause wonder and applause. Everywhere, captivating images will continue to be displayed, and silent women's faces and bodies will continue to be part of the exhibition which is called Hong Kong. My photo beside the news headlines is almost 40 years old now, but it looks not much different from current photos of current women in Hong Kong. They are equally silent, equally on display, equally deprived.

I know and we all know that the world is not always kind to women, dead or alive, young or old. This place is, fortunately or unfortunately, no exception.

But I have spoken. I will not be silenced.

Spring in Hong Kong
Agnes S. L. Lam

Spring in Hong Kong—
people complain
about walls sweating with humidity,
leather soles going mouldy,
budget cuts all round,
a mysterious pneumonia affecting tourism,
another Gulf war dragging markets down ...

But these few mornings,
I see the cotton tree
red with fleshy petals
holding bowls of spring rain
against a blue sky,
white clouds.

As a child, I used to want
to eat the petals,
drink the rain,
there being nothing much to eat
at home.

Last night,
I dreamt the cotton tree
had grown a few hundred feet
from sea level at Sai Wan
to Pokfulam Road

from a time before memory ...

FIFTY-FIFTY

Bauhinia trees are in blossom too—
purple, pink and white as usual.

The only time
I saw the bauhinia
outside Hong Kong
was in Xiamen
one December on a field trip.
'That is the flower of the Hong Kong SAR.'
I pointed it out to my mainland hosts.
They did not know. No wonder
the Golden Bauhinia given by Beijing
to Hong Kong for the Handover
looks nothing like our flower.
Do not look a gift flower in the petals.

There are of course other spring
flowers in Hong Kong
but I won't tell you about them.
This is not a botanical lesson.

Instead
if you happen to be
on Pokfulam Road,
on the stretch between Bisney Road and Mount Davis,
watch out for the new
street lamps with shades in light
sapphire blue and glass bowls so delicate,
almost precarious,
I hope they will not fall
onto cars or passers-by
one typhoon in summer.

Even if they do,
it will not be a disaster—

nothing compared to bombs
ordered by Bush and Companies
in the name of security ...

Tomorrow
war will destroy
these sapphire lamps.

Tomorrow
the world will not be
the same again.

So tonight
I claim
Lamp 38941
by the ancient cotton tree
in my dream

for this spring,
this last night of poetry.

Hong Kong Literary Festival, 19 March 2003, the night before America's attack on Iraq without a United Nations resolution

Eyewitness Accounts
Ching Yuet May

I

Prince of Wales Hospital, main corridor on the ground floor, 13 March 2003

An empty vault of a hospital
With Sars, yet unnamed,
Hovering in the air.

The busy paddle of feet,
The clinking of IV poles sticking out from mobile hospital beds
    ceased.
Fear spoke loud
Hemmed in by the silent, white-washed walls.

People knew,
    before their government confessed.
They tried to flee from death,
    feet mired in the lies of their rulers.

II

Star Ferry, 11 November 2006

Stronger than the flood,
Streams of people flowed in and
Out of the wave-green pier,
Their cameras shooting the clock tower

doomed to an untimely death.

Coils of cable unwound,
      boat drifting apart.
One young man, on the lower deck,
      hands free of camera,
          touched the rough surface of a wood post
Rising from the water.

A touch of dreams,
A touch of history,
A touch in my heart.

With all these, the rulers are out of touch.

Moths
Agnes S. L. Lam

3 new cases today,
4 dead, 1 a private doctor,
cumulative death toll, 278.
Every afternoon at 4.30,
everyone waits
for these Sars statistics to decide
to wear or not to wear
a mask the next day.

278 dead,
in this hospital or that.
Before Sars, people used to die too
but no one gave you statistics
every day ...

As the record rises
these few weeks,
moths have been appearing
as if from nowhere
in my home.
I do not remember seeing
them in previous years.
Flakes of cocoa powder
half an inch wide, almost
one and the same,
they perch on the edges
of our beige leather sofa,
on the white window sill

next to the toilet seat
watching as you sit.

Every time I bother to count,
there are three or four nearby.
They do not fly about.
They do not flap their wings.
They do not seem to feed
but on light and air.
They do not stare.
They just appear,
linger in silence,
disappear.

Have there been 278 of them?

Rodrigues Court, 31 May 2003

Route 99
Keane Shum

Apart from a momentary glimpse of the sun setting against the Hong Kong skyline before heading south, there is nothing particularly special about going home after work on Citybus route 99. You go straight down King's Road from Shau Kei Wan, through the Aberdeen Tunnel, then pass Wong Chuk Hang before making the rounds on Ap Lei Chau. The just-full crowd is made up of disengaged passengers, tuning out the day at the office with their earphones or literally nodding off, their sleeping heads swaying back and forth with the turns of the bus. Nothing particularly special.

But one week in July, instead of showing up in the hundreds of thousands at Victoria Park, Hong Kong's people power made a cameo appearance the day before on Citybus route 99. It was a nondescript affair, largely unnoticed except perhaps in the minds of those of us sitting on the bus at that moment. There were no reporters milling around searching for quotes, and no photographers looking for good crowd shots. No one even whipped out a camera phone. Which is why I feel obligated to make sure, in writing, that what happened on that bus doesn't get forgotten and that its hero, Citybus driver Chiu King Hong, gets his proper due.

While trotting his bus along the Fortress Hill section of King's Road, Mr. Chiu realized that a handicapped passenger sitting at the back of the lower deck was in need of help. He stopped the bus at a convenient location so that traffic would not be blocked, then asked the passenger what she needed. Though she was unable to articulate what exactly was wrong, Mr. Chiu had the good judgment to decide she needed an ambulance and so he called 999 to ask for one.

But as he was the individual who had made the call, Mr. Chiu was also responsible for receiving the ambulance. He let the rest of us passengers know as much, opened the doors of the bus, and assured us that we could transfer to the next bus when it arrived. In the meantime, a kind man sitting in front of me had taken the ill passenger by her arm and found her a bench on the sidewalk where she could wait for the ambulance.

No one on the bus seemed to mind the wait. Those in a rush quietly got off the bus to look for alternative transportation, and those of us that weren't sat patiently, understanding Mr. Chiu's inability— and admirable unwillingness—to abandon his sick passenger.

Until, that is, a grumpy middle-aged man stormed down from the upper deck, demanding to know why the bus hadn't started moving yet. Mr. Chiu calmly explained the situation to him, only to receive a dose of verbal abuse in return. The man raised his voice and scolded Mr. Chiu for leaving a whole busload of passengers stranded, under the assumption he was speaking on behalf of the entire bus.

He wasn't. Instantly, without hesitation, several passengers began berating the man, raising their own voices to drown his out, rightfully telling him that Mr. Chiu was hardly at fault and lecturing him on what it means to actually care for others in need. They told him to just get on another bus if he was so desperately pressed for time, and to not be so stingy that he couldn't afford to pay an extra $7 fare when someone's health was in danger. In a move that brought quiet smiles to the faces of observing passengers, the man shut up and, defeated, dipped his head to avoid making eye contact with anyone. Several moments later, he wordlessly stepped off the bus.

Soon enough, the ambulance arrived, the ill woman was sent safely on her way, and Mr. Chiu returned to the driver's seat, taking all of us home safely as well, if slightly later than planned. In all likelihood, he went home that night without fanfare, only to spend the next day, July 1, reading in the newspapers about the disappointing turnout at this year's protest march. He would have read about how the people power that was so evident the last two years was now in decline, or how Hong Kong people have lost their edge.

But as my hero for that week, Mr. Chiu was the clearest reminder to me, even as I walked with 20,000 others to Central Government Offices that Friday, that Hong Kong people had not lost their edge. I don't mean their money-hungry, need-for-speed, burning-Tung-Chee-Hwa-in-effigy edge. I'm talking about the edge of humanity, of caring for others and respecting everyone's right to health and safety and general well-being, which is really what we all ultimately want. Universal suffrage, among other things, is but the necessary means.

After the grouch who yelled at Mr. Chiu had gotten off the bus, one passenger declared, "He doesn't understand how Hong Kong works." No, and neither do you if you think this town has lost its zeal for democracy just because "only" 20,000 people get on the streets to ask for it.

The Great Wah Fu Public Housing Estate
Elbert Siu Ping Lee

There it is,
an unmistakable extension of
the autumn sky,
a back chamber to nurse those
who have lost their pride.

Hiding in the recesses of the southern heights,
your not-so-fair complexion fails
to catch the eyes of passers-by.

Winding corridors,
made treacherously longer by ever-dimming lights,
harbour the playground for children in plight.

Lone stairways,
stretched ever steeper,
form the challenge,
for early-retiring adults without insight.

Where are you leading us
you great monument of urban decadence?

Keep us warm,
keep us in,
keep us from the nuisance
of metropolitan life.

Salvation and damnation,
together you paint the face of this raw urban delight.

The Beach of Discovery Bay
Woo See-Kow

The sandy beach
looked so beautifully natural
yet it's man-made

Acres of sands
were a nuisance somewhere else
that needed solid level ground
for a new town

Now the sands
are here on their second life
a playground for
the affluents
and the movers-and-shakers
of a bygone era

A little girl
playing in the sand
wearing her Sunday best
with a plastic matching set of
bucket and shovel
in pleasant neon-pink

Her Chinese parents nearby
each carried a swollen backpack
as if they were prepared
to scale the Himalayas
acting every bit the shy tourists

sightseeing in
a foreign land

The child
visiting here
for a day
felt happily
at home
busy
building sand castles
on what
is truly
her ancestral soil
laid
beneath
the new sands

Almost a love story

Luke
Nicole Wong

I made many false starts by imagining the ad I would place in magazines and papers: "Looking for Luke who grew up in France. Came back to Hong Kong in 1994. Met you at Berlin Lan Kwai Fong. Last saw you at your shop in 1999." The placement does not matter; I will the wandering eyes of the readers' to stop at the small rectangular box. But my words are meaningless: none of the readers will know Luke; Luke himself will never see the ad.

"Give it a try," a friend said to me.

"Slight chance it'll work."

"It'll make a good story."

"Expensive way of getting one."

Local papers are out of the question, since Luke cannot read Chinese. Entertainment magazines in English are the rage these days, but Luke has never been a reader. The ad might—by some miracle—catch the attention of a friend or colleague, but how much they know about Luke is another matter. I don't remember Luke talking about his life with others, or I don't see him having friends who would listen.

It was twelve years ago when that stranger knocked the glass over. Broken glass glittered in the dark; the faces of my peers became indistinguishable at the end of the bar. I escaped to the dance floor, where a slender woman in a black bra-top entangled herself with me. I was fifteen and did not know if I should touch her or scream.

"C'mon, Sandra."

A young man pulled Sandra away and took my hand. I studied the way he turned his head and the collar of his linen shirt, as if they were clues to what I was doing with myself. The dance continued with a French couple and their friends at the club called 1997, a fashionable name before the Handover. Intoxicated by the freshness of things, I whirled around in a circle of strangers and a dazzling mixture of scents and colors. "Tequila time!" A handsome Spaniard dragged me away and passed me salt and lemon. The French couple performed their kiss to anticipated applause. The one between Luke and me lasted too long, to everyone's laughter.

At 5 a.m. Luke and I finished a dozen bottles of Corona at the Wan Chai harbor, threw empty bottles into the sea and ran away from screaming police. With too much sun in my eyes, I saw the world turn into an alien space outside the cab's windows: trees and hills made furious brushstrokes, crossing out the housing estate that was my home. I woke up on Luke's shoulder with vague terror.

"I'll pick you up for lunch later."

The image of Luke and me kissing goodbye still cuts through the morning mist. And his words to the driver: "Give me a free ride back to Hong Kong Island, will ya?"

I still feel there's too much sun in my eyes when I remember Luke leading me through the Women's Street market or a crowded temple. In the throngs, Luke turned around and reached for my hand, his short, dark eyelashes leaving their mark in my memory. His hair gel smelled of watermelon; his white shirts, always wrinkled, smelled of fresh laundry and hugged his muscular body. Luke seemed to have more clothes than any other nineteen-year-old I knew, or he looked more exotic to me in the endless white shirts he had brought back from France.

Most typical Hong Kong stuff fascinated Luke, such as an ad on a streetlamp. "What does it say?" "Room for rent. Can blow." "A room with a prostitute?!" "The word 'blow' means 'cook' in classical

Chinese. It means there's a kitchen." In a cheap Chinese restaurant, Luke noted the pencil above the waiter's ear. "I thought you only see that in old Cantonese soaps." The waiter pretended he had not heard it, in the way most strangers avoided Luke after taking a second look at his handsome face. In the food court of a shopping mall, Luke rolled up his sleeve to expose his upper arm and show me his scar. "From my granddad's rivals. He was the head of a gang." "Not a glamorous story." "I like hanging around with you, but you don't always have to be a smart ass," he smiled and recollected the discos he went to and the girls he screwed in France. On the phone he asked me what I had done in that department. I told him the truth.

"That doesn't sound like you."

"Why not?"

"You're not seeing me coz you're scared."

"You don't know me."

I ceased to know myself as well. On any Saturday night I would be sitting on the steps outside Berlin, running my fingers on an ugly scar on a cute guy's arm, or watching him raise money for alcohol and drugs. One night I let go of Luke's hand on the dance floor and a man took me in his arms. The music did not stop as the crowd dispersed; the security guards appeared and shepherded me outside. Luke and his friends were yelling at his attacker, who apologized to me with a sheepish smile from the other side of the road. I stood on the pavement and watched them in silence. Luke turned to look at me; he looked stunned.

He gave me his necklace in a park in Wan Chai. It was a platinum box chain.

"It's from my late granddad. I want you to always keep it."

At 6 a.m. an elderly man was practicing tai-chi in front of us. The moment I realized the beautiful morning mist was actually air pollution, I woke Luke up and told him it was time to catch the first train.

Luke looked older when I saw him half a year later: longer hair, unshaven face, thicker around the waist. I stared at the table; he drank and talked.

"There're many things I would have liked to share with you."

The light was flashing as we got out of the pub. I strode across the road, only stopping in between cars. My ears hurt, my hair being shorter than ever that winter. Luke and I stopped in front of a fashion boutique, laughed at dummies with heavy make-up and big grins. I lost balance and half stumbled.

"I should teach you how to walk properly."

"We'll see."

It became a running joke: that Luke would start a modeling class for me, which meant walking around his place with a dictionary on my head or a coin between my knees. Luke liked to mimic the way I walked in front of Jenny and Siu Ming: he jerked, knocked down a file of clothes, turned around and saw me sitting on his bed, savoring one of his porn magazines.

I stayed at Luke's place whenever we hung out. Luke's childhood friend, Jenny, had lived next door with Siu Ming. Luke had told me Siu Ming moved into Jenny's place when she was thirteen, and I had not believed it until we met Jenny's mother one Sunday. She'd heard that Jenny was married to some guy who had got her pregnant, and avoiding her creditors by dancing at various clubs. Siu Ming, with thick furrowed brows and a sad smile, continued to pay off some of Jenny's debts and had no clue where she was. Luke whined about how Jenny "couldn't do without a man" and "got herself all screwed up at twenty-three", not saying he himself had lost sleep over it.

I was invited to Luke's family gathering another Sunday afternoon, where his mother pointed at his suede jacket before we I even said hello. "My son can make soup with this $5,000 jacket when he's broke," she laughed. Luke's uncles shook my hands and giggled. I saw them a few more times and remained a topic of gossip, especially when they had to lie to Luke's girlfriends.

Luke and I laughed at those lies in the same bed in different apartments, when his girlfriends thought he had gone camping in the mountains. We stayed up to watch weirdoes gobble live octopuses and insects on Japanese reality shows, in an apartment where there was no bathroom door but only a plastic shower curtain. On his bed, Luke spread photos of himself practicing Thai boxing and letters from his sister in Paris, exchanges of love in a foreign language, anecdotes of longing and loss. There were tales about his departure from Hong Kong at the age of eight: taken away from home, sent off to the airport, landing in Paris the next day; stories about his reunion with his mother after eight years of separation, about his half-sister's daily dose of bird-nest as a cure for skin allergy. "They have the money," Luke motioned me to turn over for a back rub. I spent my sixteenth birthday at his next place, a two-storied house he rented from a relative for practically nothing. At 2 a.m. Luke put an open can of sausages outside the store across the street. Luke took a few shots from his window; I never saw the mice and only laughed. Deep into the night, I would feel Luke's arms around me and I would reach out for them, out from the realm of heaviness or lightness, the two having merged. I never made it; I fell back into troubled sleep. Some other times I woke up and looked at myself in the mirror in the bathroom, trying to grasp the world Luke had made me enter: things he used to love, colleagues he did not like, characters and settings I could only imagine. I could not see why Luke wanted to see me or why I stayed, or if we would have nothing to say to each other one day. I never understood why some people wanted to keep me in their life, why they could not let go and walk away.

"You listen to people and their life stories," Luke said. Some took my silence as a sign of understanding, which was true in most cases. Luke knew I never explained myself to anyone. "You should learn," Luke hushed me, "To Love Somebody—this song is for you." I did not say that I could sing that song at twelve. At seventeen I saw that many things were an illusion, such as Luke's moving houses in pursuit of a better home.

I was eighteen when Luke had a fight with his regular girlfriend, a rich girl who had a luxurious house on the Peak. She had heard too much about my presence at Luke's place, and called to order him to send me home.

"I told you. I never slept with her!"

He hung up. I asked her what his girlfriend said.

"She said, 'That's even worse.'"

"True," I laughed.

"One day you'll turn out an exceptional person. I look forward to seeing that," Luke lay down beside me, played with my hair on the pillow, fell asleep. I followed his breathing and the shadows on the ceiling; I knew his thoughts were with mine, or mine with his, at abrupt moments when he awoke and nestled against me. The playfulness that carried him through his waking life remained on his lips, and made me think of a cat that had killed a possum and come home to sleep. I studied his features for the first time in a long time, details I had absorbed in the last three years. I stayed in that familiar space for some time before I grew tired from lying too still.

It was the first time I could not sleep beside Luke.

The second time was when I checked out his new apartment in Sheung Wan, after I had lived in seclusion for months before my last public exam. The truth was I had fallen into depression, become ill and lost twenty pounds in a month. Luke bounced across the road in a cream-colored Armani suit, looking sleeker than ever as he greeted me with a big smile. Siu Ming looked even more comical with the same furrowed brows and grin, as he talked about his "fresh start" in life, his new job. We went dancing at an executive club of which Luke was a member. He had split with the jealous girlfriend. On the mini-bus Luke talked about how he liked his new place, a spacious studio apartment that overlooked the highway and the sea. "Come over any time," Luke said. "You know I care for you like a sister." I leant on his shoulder and pretended one could be happy with someone without complications, and my future could be a reliving of that moment.

I opened the windows once I got inside.

"You've grown taller since I last saw you."

"I'm nineteen."

"Some people keep growing into their mid-twenties. You're taller than me now. Quit those high heels or you'll stumble when you run from people."

I was returning to the lure of the sea and the noise of the cars, but Luke sat me down on the couch.

"Tell me what you've been up to."

I talked about my summer jobs: how I switched from one to another and did what I hated.

"And yourself?"

"I'm happy to see you."

"You aren't talking to me anymore."

"I don't know what you're talking about."

"You know you have an irregular heartbeat?"

"No.".

"I do. I held you when you were sleeping. You're tense even in your sleep—you keep things from people no matter how much they love you. Do you ever love them back?"

"I do."

"I've never seen it. I know where your heart is, but it isn't there." He took his hand off my left breast and slid down the couch. "Where is it," he touched my knees, "is it here?" He sat up on the floor, took my fingers and put them on my cheeks, "Is it here?" He ran our hands through my hair, his forehead pressing mine, "Is it here?"

I waited before I pulled my hands out of his.

"Let me go."

"You only have to ask. I've never said no to you."

I covered my face so Luke would not see me cry.

"I'm sorry. Let's go to bed."

I left in the morning after Luke had fallen asleep.

Luke got me on the phone a year later.

"Promise me you'll come."

With that familiar gleam in his eyes, Luke introduced me as the girl he cared about "like a sister". "I've heard lots about you," a fellow shopkeeper said. I loitered and pretended to check out some clothes, when Luke tried to ask me about my life. I talked about university and avoided anything personal. He told me why he quit his job and how he came up with his designs. "Here's one for you." He put a white knitted top into a paper bag. "And something else. Turn around."

It was a soft silver chain with a moon pendant.

"I'm afraid I'll break it."

"Come back for a new one if you do. I've missed you."

He smiled at me in the mirror.

"You're looking great. A young woman now."

His shop was gone by the time I changed my mind. The fellow shopkeeper was still around, but I could not bring myself to ask. My landline no longer worked and neither did Luke's. I wore that necklace several times. It fell apart.

I don't write about people in my journal unless it's the first draft of a story, or memoirs about my closest friends. I devoted one entry to Luke over three years ago, which ended with me getting my phone line reconnected.

The call never came.

I saw Luke in that shopping mall, a year after I had changed my mind. Luke was still Luke: handsome face, stylish shirt, walking up the stairs with two girls. For a moment I wondered if one of the girls might get upset, if I put my hand on his arm and smiled as he saw me, his eyes gleaming, expecting a hug. The moment passed; I watched Luke walk away and disappear from my sight.

Shadows of Time
Nicholas Y. B. Wong

You removed your ring and embarked
on the tram. The dim light at the bed still
cast a shadow on the disclaimed silver. I
pondered on the mattress and let its softness
bear my anger. Silence is not gold,

but deadly dismay.

You uttered some words before you left:

Objects have shadows. Time doesn't.
Especially ours.

I looked around the room and ransacked for a trace
of time's shadow. You were right.

I failed. We both failed.

The tram was crawling dully and predictably
on the lubricated rails. Its slowness mocked at our
derailed love. I opened the shutter of my eyes and
shut down my senses to catch the last continuing
moment of your departure.

The image blurred.

There's no sign of you, but I could see
The mourning shadow on the metallic
body of the distancing vehicle.

ways to be human
Viki Holmes

there are worse things than being kind
there are many ways to eagle peak and,
as the sun looms low over the only
policeman's bicycle on lamma, we
are making a way. there are many,
as i say, there are worse things
by far than learning how to face
the anger. we each hold a flame
in our open palms and watch
how the other's flickers at
the wind's hum. there are worse
things by far than moving
along the path, it is all ascent,
after all and you may not find
heaven in the living world at
every peak, but this one does
its job. the flames wobble, as
we do time and again, talking
of worlds and words and making
the same mistakes, but every
time is a little more
graceful than the last, and every
time we have someone with us:
sometimes tracing our steps
as the rice dries, other times
we are the ones to lag and
see our friend move smoothly

forward up the mountain's
side, their flame maintaining
for all their movements back
and forth. we move
together, up the path and
there are worse things,
by far, than this saha world,
this glowing sphere, these
rocky paths we never walk
alone.

(for Alan Jefferies)

April in Sai Kung
Woo See-Kow

Pitch black
in the narrow plaza

Candlelights
flickering dimly
on the tables out at
the sidewalk cafes

Slowing the night

A Paris night off the back
of Sai Kung's main street

Silver moon over San Francisco Bay
at the crest of springtime

Cherry blossoms at sunset
in a Kyoto park

Vancouver by the waterfront

All those sentimental places
came to me
at the same time

Across the table
your fingers stroking
a cup of tea lovingly

Almost a love story

I caught
your sparkling eyes

Wherever we may be

Anywhere is Hong Kong
anytime is the month of April
every time
when
I see
your face
shine so invitingly
in
misty
light

Triptych
Stuart Christie

I. New Jordan Temple

You sit on the heat of the roof,
legs splayed beneath a bicolor tarpaulin
reclaiming bricks
from shattered masonry.

The chisel in your hand,
ancient cement and still white
moulding are driven off, like locusts

so that these bricks
or even
angled one-thirds of them
may be used again.

Here at the new temple,
jackhammers driving,
incense burns on an old card table
and ripening fruit rots.

The *sih fu* keeps the dust down
with a lazy hose
his brown robe limp about
sweaty calves.

All of this is, and will be, his.

The report of the lift,
arrived!
rings precisely with a mobile phone
in this clamoring
   faith zone.
It used to be a cheap hotel,
faux fleur-de-lis tilework at my feet
   in neatly conical piles

Another monk takes the debris away,
wipes the veil of dust from her glasses,
urges a cart into the lift and descends.

Out on the *tin toi* (quite simply the roof terrace,
but, to me, seeing
you there,
it is just what you say it is—
a sky platform)

the ropes of the blue and white tarpaulin
seemed attached to nothing
except heaven
and you.

You drive the hammer capably,
it speaks regularly
into the warm summer afternoon.

Stray sparks burn into well past three
as the pile of reclaimed moments,
these bricks for the new Jordan temple
rises around you.

I crossed over here.
I came all this way to find you.

Ten stories up, the weight of sheetrock on my back.
And here, my love.
Here, my love, you are.

FIFTY-FIFTY

II. Alchemy

1.

Your arches grip sea stones,
rocks pare my cuticles,
the golden moon

Is it Mars?

drops into kelp
at the base
of the swimmers' buoy.

Sand in my hair
waits until the ferry
to mistake my pocket
for sea spume and grit.

Your arches grip sea stones,
turning to a familiar
sound, responding,

Yes it is.

My ankles ache.
St. Francis carried the rock
on his shoulder,
 the pope shuddered bull.

Do you remember?
Carrying the weight of
translucent birds' bones,
water cresting,
saline floating.

It isn't so, alchemy.

You drink my marrow
and smile.

Fretwork and scaffolding
splinter. We came here,
believers in diffusion.
We depart mystics.

2.

The poet ordered single malt in
a hotel room in Duluth,
and shuddered.

He recognized
a face in the wallpaper
and smiled.

He reached for an ashtray
and died.

A cigarette burning down,
his carbon elegy.
Ashes for the police,
arson and soul.

Agape.

Another wormhole:
his moth-eaten waistcoat
worn ritually
since 1929.

Our world is so
much earth and fire.

Do you remember?
The planet you urged

yellow

was my gold?

III. At the Tsinghua Lotus Pond

Here at dusk
in your other China
worry settles on you
like a mantle.

The frog-killers
cast their lights
arcing into the ponds
a surveillance of
lotus leaves.

'Do not face the moon
With an empty jar,'
you said.

So I filled ours up with light.

They spear each filigreed surface
each pool bubbling
the hope of pain, a burst night flower.

You recited Li Bai
by the light of the red moon:
'Do not wait for life,'
you said he wrote.

I looked into your eyes.
I will not wait.

(for Priscilla)

Smog
Justin Hill

When the cool north wind blew, Meili stood on the top of Victoria Peak and looked across the bay to the distant peaks behind Kowloon, imagined she could smell Hunan again—the kebab stalls spicing the night markets, the hiss of chillis in oil—and she held that thought for as long as she could before the impatient crowds pressed in on her again: yabbling and pulling and nagging for attention, and she took in a deep breath, like a swimmer breaking the waves and called out, "Oil paintings! Skyline paintings!"

It was the kind of voice that used to call out "Candied crab-apples!", Wen Jun thought as he painted. He painted and she sold, that was how it worked. Wen Jun was Meili's husband. The description still amused her. Husband. It still felt like putting adult words to a childish thing. She didn't feel old enough to marry, or be married, but it had been necessary for her to get the resident permit.

They'd been living in Changsha when they met. People said they looked alike, almost like brother and sister, so it was natural that they'd fall in love. He talked about his past and the future, said: I can't paint what I want here. *I want to paint foreign skies.* Those sentences struck her, stayed with her for a long time afterwards. I want to paint foreign skies. She decided then that she liked him. Liked him enough to lean in and kiss him. She'd kissed other boys before, but that May Hunan night of 1998, sticky with early summer heat, she felt as if she was weightless, as if the world around them ceased to exist, and when they walked back home that night, leaning against his arm, she felt that she was in love. "Can I see you again?" he'd asked and she nodded and smiled and then stopped herself and hoped that she wasn't appearing too keen. She'd never been in love before, she realised then. It was like being an ox, led by the nose. In the days that followed she clung to him like a shadow. They lived together for two years. She never told her parents. They didn't understand the new world; its rules and slang and opinions. Their minds were as narrow as old village alleyways: when the world she knew had busy five-lane highways.

When she spoke to them she felt a gulf between them, and she thought it would be easy to leave them behind. She helped Wen Jun fill out Green Card applications; scholarships; dreams of leaving Changsha and Hunan and China behind.

A letter arrived one dull Spring Festival morning. Meili was granted residency to Hong Kong. They danced round their room that morning, taking it in turns to re-read the letter. "Foreign skies!" she toasted that lunch and they drank beer till their cheeks shone red and their world seemed to be full to the brim.

If Wen Jun and she were married then he could come too. They agreed to it without talking about it really. The next day she picked up her phone. "I'm getting married," she told her mother. "His family name is Wen. His name is Jun. He is an artist and he is brilliant and we are going to live in Hong Kong." It all came out in a rush, which wasn't how she had meant to say it all, but she could see her mother there, despite the miles between them, crumpling like a tissue. Meili listened to the sobbing and rolled her eyes and said, "Is father there?"

Her father took the phone. "What is it?"

"I'm getting married."

"Who to?"

"My boyfriend," she said. "Boyfriend" was one of those new and modern words that he didn't understand.

"Is he a good man?"

"He is, father. He is a very good man. He was born in the Year of the Ox so he will be hard working. He is an artist. He is 165 centimetres tall, and he is not so handsome, but very kind." It sounded silly trying to reduce Wen Jun to sentences, but her father seemed impressed.

"Does he make you happy?" her father asked, and the shift of emphasis threw her for a moment.

"Yes. Of course!" she said and his questions ended there.

Meili and Wen Jun went to her hometown for the wedding banquet: a lunch-hour affair in a huge eating hall called Zhao Yang Wedding Palace. Shaoyang was grey and concrete and hectic, but it was Meili's home: the place she had to escape, the people whose opinions she resented, the only place that made her feel small again. The place where people's opinions were set in stone, like the writing on tombstones.

She felt small all that day as she went through the rekindled customs of papercuts and firecrackers and bundles of bedding. She wore a white dress and deep red blusher; and Wen Jun looked stiff and uncomfortable in a black dinner jacket and clip-on bow tie. They were both glad when it was all over, and they went to their hotel room and smoked.

They'd had their wedding photos done two months earlier, and somewhere between the photos and the wedding they actually went through the legal marriage ceremony at the wedding office. It was just a piece of paper. Just a ten minute ceremony, and a lot of paperwork. It wasn't the wedding day she had imagined, but then the next day, leaving Shaoyang wasn't quite how she had imagined either. She felt odd as her parents slipped from view, as if she would never see them again, and as the town was swallowed up by the jostling hills there was a brief but sharp pain, like a cord snapping. Good riddance, she told herself, but the sight of her parents haunted her.

Meili was too busy to think in the following weeks. Friends in

FIFTY-FIFTY

Changsha were happy and tearful all at the same time, as if they thought Wen Jun and Meili were going to ascend into Heaven: happy and tearful all at the same time.

"We'll be back," Meili promised her friends. "We'll bring you all kinds of presents! And you must come and visit!"

It was an overnight train from Changsha to Guangzhou; an hour's train ride from Guangzhou to Hung Hom. Hong Kong was wonderful and daunting at the same time. The size and the colours and the water left Meili dumbfounded. She cried the first time she saw the harbour because it was like a dream come true. When she looked back the people didn't seem very friendly and Meili had been surprised at that. She'd always thought that Hong Kongers longed to be returned to the Motherland. Well, not *thought*, she realised—*told*. When she looked back to that morning of arrival she disliked the way the border guards looked at her and checked her paperwork. And after the border guard a policeman looked at her the same way. But then they found their hotel and the manager was a Mainlander from Hunan as well, and they were happy to find someone here who spoke with the same accent, ate the same food, knew the same places where they had grown up.

The lady helped them, and they gave her the bottle of Open-Your-Mouth-And-Smile Wine that they had brought from home. She gave it back to them, but they pressed it on her and the third time, she took it. The lady helped them find somewhere to live and they ended up bunking down in a flat with six other Mainlanders, who all worked the same temporary jobs.

Wen Jun started painting at Tsim Sha Tsui, painting the harbour and the neon reflections. He sang silly country songs as he walked up to his spot, and she joined in as well, and sometimes they danced the old-fashioned peasant dances and laughed like drunks. Their cup kept overflowing; Wen Jun could barely sleep at night he was so excited. This was his dream, everyday to paint a place like this. "The locals don't know what they have!" he laughed. "They have no idea!"

Most of all Wen Jun loved the evening, adored the fading after-sunset yellow light, filtered through a glaze of drifting Shenzhen smog, when the straight blocks and bobbing waves seemed to meld together, and the office lights gave way to neon adverts and the small squares of apartments lives. He frowned as he painted the scene, so eager was he to get the image down. Meili sat nearby on the harbour front, her knees drawn up to her chin, and listened to the Cantonese tongue: soft and pretty, like cooing birds. Sometimes she watched him paint; sometimes she looked at the view.

That evening hour was magical, and when the last light had faded Wen Jun would put his brush down and let out a long sigh and she would light a cigarette for him. "Here," she would say, and pass it from her lips to his and he would look up at her, almost in surprise, as if he had left the real world of his art, and found himself back here on the harbourfront. "Smoke," she'd say gently, like she was telling a newborn child to breathe, and he'd take it, warm from her mouth, and put it in his. Each evening there was something new to excite him: an underlit cloud hanging above the Bank of China building, a junk, a tug boat, a new neon sign. They were so happy and in love that people turned to look at them on the return journey, and in bed he lay and dragged on his fag as she rested her head on his chest and he said, "Are you happy?"

Yes, she ummed contentedly. "Are you?"

"Heavens!" he said. "So many paintings. Such horizons!"

People liked Wen Jun's paintings and sometimes they wanted to buy them. "They think you're good!" Meili encouraged. Wen Jun was shy of selling but she pushed him out of the door and smiled at passers-by, and took their money. Hong Kong was kind to them. They made more money than they could dream of and when two of their friends were caught in an ID check and sent back to China they were sad but not too concerned: after all they were in love, and happy. And legal.

Meili still went down with Wen Jun to the harbourfront at five o'clock to watch the day fade, and she looked at the lines of home lights and fire escapes and felt surrounded by people that she liked and who liked her. All of them—that constant stream of randomly produced passers-by of all shapes and sizes and ages—like computer generated characters flowing past her in a constant stream. She loved them all, and she thought for a long time that they felt the same way about her. But it was a year after she had arrived that she read a newspaper headline that dented this belief. *Mainlanders Threaten Hong Kong Stability*, one headline ran one day. *Hong Kong Swamped with Mainlander Babies*. A month later she was stopped by a policeman a hundred yards from her home and checked for her ID. She had it of course, but the way that he looked at her disturbed her. "Who cares as long as we make money," she said that night. "And as long as you can paint!" she said aloud.

The next morning, Wen Jun came back from the shop with a handful of large blue chrysanthemums. She set them in a cup of water on the table next to the TV, and she cherished them like a pet. She felt strangely sad one morning when she woke to find that they had shed their leaves in the night, silently and surely, as women shed their youth. Wen Jun loves me, she told herself, even if no one else does and that is enough.

Wen Jun's brush strokes became bolder and they made more money than they had ever dreamt of. "This city brings up money like old men brought up phlem!" Wen Jun laughed.

Six months later they had enough money to pay the rental deposit on a 20th-floor shoebox, with a small barred window looking into a gloomy fire escape. Meili tutted at the cost of this place, the small dingy window, but it was *theirs*. She bought window cleaner and cloths and scrubbed the glass clean, but the dullness of the view made her shiver and she thought of the newspaper headline about Mainland babies and an odd thought came to her, like a long-forgotten friend who comes suddenly to mind. "We should never have a baby here," she said. "We should go home and have a baby."

Wen Jun was brushing his hair. "I don't want a baby," he said.

"What do you mean?"

"I don't want a baby."

"But now we're married."

"We're married," he said, "so we could move into Hong Kong. It's just a piece of paper! Don't look at me like that."

Meili didn't care about children before, but there was something about her life here that made her want to build a family around her, like a blanket. She told him that but he looked at her as if she was mad and she felt cold and hollow, like a porcelain figure. "I don't know what you're talking about," he said, and his voice was half defensive, half desperate. "You don't care about me. All you care about is painting that stupid skyline!" She cried then, and he let her cry, which made her cry more – but at last, after a long and unhappy silence, he put a hand to her cheek. "Don't pout. Maybe we will have a child. Sure, when we are rich we can have a child." And the next morning when she woke, she found a painting of a chrysanthemum propped up on the table next to the TV and she kissed him to say thank you and thought that it was all decided.

Meili worked harder then, and they made more money, but the more their savings grew the more separate from her friends they became, as if wealth was measured in distance. People came and peered over Ma Jun's shoulder, and she talked to them and told them how famous Wen Jun was in Hunan, how all the teahouses had pieces of his calligraphy, and sometimes they bought a picture or two. Bird flu made life tough for a while, and Meili felt the panic fluttering inside her. But then the crisis passed and people returned and business was even better than before. Wen Jun enjoyed the way the growing IFC towers tilted the pictures off balance, enjoyed the changing scape in front of him.

At the end of each day, Wen Jun would clean his brushes and light a cigarette and look up from his easel. "How many?" he'd say.

"Thirteen," she'd say. Or sometimes fifteen, and sometimes twenty-three and he'd nod and close the lid on his tin of oil paints and ask how much. She checked her sums, just for show of course,

FIFTY-FIFTY

but each day her pouch grew pregnant with Hong Kong dollar bills and she'd keep the total in her head, humming it like a nursery rhyme. Sometimes it was three thousand. Sometimes four, and each day he'd nod and smile faintly and pack all the pictures back up, and stuff them into the bag, then they would octopus their way back onto the tram and slip back down into the depths of Central.

It wasn't hard work, and it was good to be up high looking down on the world, like one of the spirits in heaven, floating on clouds. And Meili was happiest up there, as if all her cares and worries blew away on the wind. But as the tram slipped quickly below the high-water mark of high-rises, she felt she lost something on that descent, as if her angel wings dissolved. This must be what rabbits feel when they flee back underground to their stale tunnel air, she thought, or termites into their tunnels.

"Do you feel it?" she asked Wen Jun.

"What?"

"This!" she said and the pitch of her voice alarmed him. "Pressing down on you?"

"My ears pop," he said and she punched him.

On a Sunday morning, after three years, Meili took out the bank book and held up the money they had earnt the previous day and totalled it all up and burst into tears. "We've done it!" she said. "We've made a hundred thousand!"

"We can go home now!" she thought to herself, and touched her stomach, but Wen Jun brought up all kinds of reasons why they should stay. We can make money here. We're both still young. Let's get another hundred thousand and then we'll go home and be really rich. Meili cried, but he talked to her and she understood.

"Well, I'm sick of living in this hole. Let's find a flat with a window."

Wen Jun was sitting on the window ledge, as he always did for breakfast, eating pot noodles. "If we move somewhere with a view then it will take longer to save the money," he said. His tone was as neutral as a set of scales: he let her decide.

She frowned at him and felt a wave of anger as if he was trapping her, and she thought of termites dying in sunlight. "Okay, we stay here," she said at last. "But let's brighten it up."

"I'll paint you a picture," Wen Jun said. He was a little disturbed by the suddenness of her exuberance. "Chrysanthemums?" he asked.

"No! Paint a waterfall," she said quickly, "in a forest in Xishuanbanna, with minority women washing their clothes!"

He painted a picture and hung it in place of the window. That picture had hung there for nearly six months, as the summer warmed to a boil and simmered all the way through October, when she asked for a picture of the moon rising over the West Lake. "We haven't been to the West Lake," Wen Jun said. Meili scrambled about their tiny room, knocked over paintings and piles of clothes and books, lifted the camp bed in the corner, and finally sat up with a triumphant look and read him the ancient poem in the fine Mandarin they'd learnt at school. She read and he painted quickly, in traditional Chinese style: the moon and lake and pavilions hanging on a sea of white paper. It was pleasant to look at as the summer began to boil. When the heat dripped from every building, and, she thought, "I'm so glad I'm not going to stay here to turn old and dry and sterile as a concrete road. We won't bury ourselves under dollar bills." He painted the Shaoyang skyline, the Mongolian steppes, the limpid Guilin rivers, and Tai Shan. Each one he painted filled the dirty grey windowpane. The change of scenery made Meili smile, but her smiles seemed increasingly distant, like someone who was walking away from him. He painted a photo of them standing outside their Changsha apartment block, standing close to each other, but not quite touching. Meili put her arms around his neck and the two of them stared at themselves in the past.

"It makes me nostalgic," she said.

"For Changsha?"

"No," she said, "for the past."

FIFTY-FIFTY

That night they made love, and afterwards she held him tight, and felt he might leave her and he stroked the hair from her cheek and kissed her in a way that reminded her of their first night together, when they walked into the park and life gaped open ahead of them.

Two months later she missed her period. She was busy and it was a week later when she took the test. She told him one evening on the return trip from the peak. It all came out in a rush, just as it had when she told her mother she was getting married, five years earlier.

"How can you be pregnant?"

"I don't know!" she said.

"Are you taking the pill?"

"Yes!" she said, but then it struck her that once they'd passed HK$300,000, she'd forgotten to take it. They'd agreed, hadn't they, when they had enough money they'd go home and have children. It wasn't deliberate.

"We can't go home," Wen Jun spoke with an air of authority.

"Why not?"

"Meili," he said. "Look what we have here! I have a career. We have no bosses. Remember Changsha? Do you remember what you used to call your boss? Why would we go back to that?"

She turned her head away from him then, and took her hand out of his.

"I'm your wife and the mother of your child! You should do what I say if you love me!" But Wen Jun grew angry and they shouted at each other, said terrible and hurtful things, and when they had finished he would not look at her or touch her or even sleep in the same bed as her. In the days and weeks that followed she understood what a powerless word "wife" was. She wore it out till it had less meaning than a ten-cent coin. In the flaming middle of a row he shouted, "Well then, let's get divorced! I never wanted a wife anyway!"

Meili paled. The look on her face made him turn away, but he was too angry to feel guilty and he stormed out and slammed the door. She took a moment to react, but when she looked for him the corridor was empty, the lifts languishing on other floors.

When she came back to the room she found that the picture had fallen off the window. The window was thick with grey soot. The soot was so thick it had started to form icicles of dirt. She thought of the stories her grandfather had told her about his time in Inner Mongolia. How the sky was bigger there, the stars brighter, the moon more luminous. And she wondered how life had brought her here to a place where no grass grew.

"I can't stay," she said to herself. "I must leave."

Wen Jun came back with a bunch of white lilies, and they were both sorry and hurt and they held each other and did not go to the peak to paint that day. "I don't know who I am any more. So much has changed. Last year feels like a lifetime ago. I think of my childhood and how small and quiet life was and I want to go back there. But there's no way back. It's all changed so quickly."

It worried Wen Jun to hear her talk so strangely, and he held her hand. When she was empty of speech he put his head to her stomach to listen for his child.

"Let's go have dim sum." There was a little place nearby where old men sat and smoked and read newspapers and they ordered a selection of dishes, but Meili saw the waitress looking at her stomach and put her hand there protectively. "She's staring at us!" she whispered to Wen Jun. "And you know what she's thinking!"

"What?" he said not understanding at all.

"You know what!" she said.

"What?"

"She's staring at me. All that stuff about Mainlander babies."

"I'm sure she's not."

"She is. Look at her! Ugly turtlehead!"

Wen Jun held Meili's hands and pressed them together, and his forehead furrowed with concern. "Even if she is," he said, "who cares."

"I care."

She sat there, staring at the bamboo trays of dumplings and cried. "When it is time to give birth we will leave here and go home, won't we? Promise me we will not stay here. Promise me so that I can believe it. I do not want to grow old here. I want to go home."

He looked down for a moment and she knew he was about to lie to her. "Of course," he said.

"No, you have to promise me. We're no-one here," she said. "Let's go home and be ourselves again."

"But Meili, I like it here," he said. His face looked pained. It was as if she was going to take all that loved he away from him.

"You only care about this city." The realisation was as cold as December water.

Meili phoned her mother that night, and they talked for over an hour. It was the first time in a year that they'd spoken, and she found she had so much to say to her mother, so much in common with her, that she had never thought before. The next morning they caught the ferry over the harbour and walked up to the Peak tram, and he set out his paints and easel and she looked across to the mountains opposite her and thought of home.

"Why don't you paint the mountains?" she asked him that afternoon. "Why do you always paint the silly buildings?"

He seemed hurt by the question, as if she had failed to understand everything that inspired and excited him – and Meili read his hurt and wondered how they had grown so apart, and then wondered if they had ever been close at all. He'd fallen for a mirage, she told herself, a reflection of the moon on the surface of the sea. A cold light that did nothing but dazzle.

She left a note in the flat one day, caught the KCR and set off through the mountains towards her home. There were many mountains between her and home, but they seemed like bumps now that she knew she was returning home, and a line from one of Mao Zedong's poems came to her, strangely and unbidden, like the words of an oracle, mysterious but relevant:

Do not say the water of Kunming Lake is too shallow
To watch fish it's better than Fuchun River.

She thought of Shaoyang, and it made her cry: joyful tears to think that she would be in the slow lane again, and as the north train set off, she felt Hong Kong and its opportunities and highways and wide open water move south behind her, like the drifting clouds of Shenzhen smog.

Personal histories

Two Parallel Motions:
Mapping Hong Kong
Jennifer S. Cheng

The water was always there, rising and falling.

It rose and fell from different distances.

She waited in the concrete place for the boat to arrive, water sloshing against wooden beams.

She liked crossing the plank, like a drawbridge, ridges under her shoes.

The green and white painted colors, the rows of slippery seats.

(From the downstairs window of the apartment, the waves were small and silent.

There was a cove from the upstairs window which she could not now place.)

Her family waited every Sunday to reach the mainland, then back again by nightfall.

Minutes spent waiting, then crowding.

There were three different concrete places she could count in her head.

But always one boat rocking from side to side.

The air was mostly cool, but usually it was warm, saturated, and thick with moisture.

The slight foul smell of the ocean.

In summer months the smell mixed with her body, sweating.

(Like the dampness of certain streets were secret and hovering.)

Up close the waves were larger, noisier, and you could make out all of the movements.

As if you could see every detail yet still be unable to discern—

Changes in color, or the layer just beneath the surface, or where creases began to fold.

The ocean which was never clear but always slightly opaque.

Waters were worse in certain parts, dark and clouded with pollution.

(Her dress soaking up dirt, soil, chemicals, dust.)

They were like parallel motions.

Waiting for their edges to overlap translucence.

Personal histories

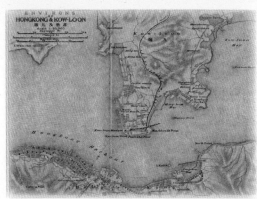

*to find the thing shaking
underneath, in that
nebulous place outside*

*where the murky can exist
as in twilight*

where intersecting stories

THE FIRST FRAGMENT: A DISCONNECT

It begins immersed in water.

She has discovered in the Midwest that in some environments an American-born woman can lose the language she most easily speaks, and turning to a language that is comforting but ultimately broken, she becomes silent. Sounds are fractured, vocabulary in any one set of words is insufficient. She has trouble communicating with her mother over the phone.

When she was young, the child had a prayer song before dinner at the large white table her father had built in their Texas home. The tabletop slid occasionally because it was not nailed down. Outside the window of the kitchen the disappearing light was a feeling deep inside her stomach. The prayer song, which was full of sounds, was full of only sounds. The sounds had no beginning, they were just there, like all the other sounds.

(In wintertime, she would come in from the snow and begin to unzip her snowsuit by the kitchen door, and seeing that it was stuck at the top, begin peeling apart the zipper at the bottom near her ankles, and when this could go no further, she would stand at the door unsure of what to do next.) It was the southwest, which was the ranch-style house that held her family, the yellow-haired doll in her closet, and the neighbors outside playing on the street.

It would be years before she realized the sounds in the song had no explicit meaning for her, were incomplete, were missing this other part. At that point, *sounds* became *languages*.

The figure of their grandparents, the names they called them which were also in Shanghainese, neither the Mandarin they spoke at home nor the English they spoke at school, but a language often heard in bedroom corners or family gatherings of summer. Her mother standing at the counter and spooning *lu dou tang* 綠荳湯 into plastic rose-colored bowls. Weekday mornings as they waited by the door and chanted: *man man kai che* 慢慢開車, *zao dian hui jia* 早點回家, adding *stop sign, ni jiu* 你就 *stop* when their father was almost ticketed by a policeman. These lay inside her body like an overexposed photograph, saturated colors. Pure, protective, as if her flesh would evaporate without them. Now, sounds have acquired rules, leaking into words that no longer belong to a person, as if you have no claim. Now, she tries to decipher the sounds until they are empty and cold on her tongue.

(Her Mandarin is her childhood Mandarin, as if in that way she is still a child, never able to move on or move away. So that when she dreams in her mother tongue, she is dreaming a child's dream.)

But it is not only language, as language is merely a starting point: where sounds become languages is where a child becomes self-aware, and in doing so, in the course of twenty or so years, finds that she is made of tepid, lukewarm water.

IT BEGINS IMMERSED IN WATER

It rains every day the first week of my return after
ten years. Rain streams down all over Hong Kong:
the mountains and hillsides and alleys, water
gushing down stairwells and forming pools on tiled
platforms. At the college where I am meeting other
writers, I wade through drenched paths after riding
on a bus that slowly makes its way up the mountain.
   Standing outside and leaning over the railing, I
suddenly remember the sensation of always looking
downward, below me, wondering what it would be like
to fall.

DISTANCE BETWEEN TWO POINTS

Here, everything is smaller than in my memories.
Here, it has been more than ten years, and when
I tell people that my family decided to leave before
the Handover, I forget how many countries exist,
how many masses of land count as one. There was
an island floating on the sea here. A shadow danced
in the bathroom window here. The air blew drops of
water and floods, here. I was not born here.
Upon returning, I realize how much more complex
the place is, the traffic motions, the array of
advertisements, pedestrian bridges, and I am
picturing my motions when I walk.
   I lived here for a few years, and then we left.
My mother and father spoke Cantonese, but their
children were unable to do so. There were chestnuts
from the street vendor at night and crabs in our
kitchen sink which we poked with chopsticks. On the
crowded street side I jumped over dog dung while
hanging on to my mother. We threw rocks down the
steep tapering stairs just to see them finally land.
Here, where grandparents and great-uncles and
aunties and other less familiar relatives shouted
over the noises of *ma jiang* 麻將 at regular late-night
banquets as my cousins and I played *choi dai di* 鋤

FIFTY-FIFTY

大地 underneath tables. Where a secret pathway hid in the fenced bushes on Platform 2. Where we ate purple ice-cream while waiting for the bus and the fumes rose and wafted around our bodies. Where there has always been a language barrier. Where crossing the ocean to the other side of the world left a ghostly imprint: the terrain of my apartment building like an uneven maze, the womb of dark-green hillsides and leafy trees cocooning the school, the dark narrow streets after it had rained. These specters appear in my sleep, on the doorstep of my house, as I meander the grocery store.

A body of water beginning with the tilt of her reflection.
A body of water now cloudy with pollution.
A body of water rises and falls with imprecision.
A body of water shakes.
A body of water claims no legitimacy: it is made of too many parts.

When does an image, a sound, a ritual, belong to a person?

In Hong Kong, the rain pours heavily on the pavement and the next moment stops as blue skies suddenly appear.

My Grandmother orders our dishes in multiple languages as the waiter continues to nod multiple times and then is gone.

In America, I tell people that I spent most of my life here as if apologizing because I am afraid of being found an imposter, a hybrid that cancels itself.

A body of water is being evaluated.

Personal histories

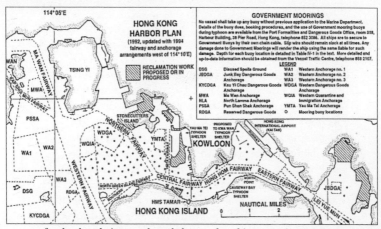

firmly placed signs and symbols reveal nothing, exterior measurements, unaware of something edging, creeping, rustling

THE MIDWEST (i)

During their first year of marriage, they prepare dinner together. Still just children, they decide to stop calling their parents to ask for directions. She chops the vegetables and dried bean curd, careful to make even slices. They take turns adding and mixing ingredients, and he flavors the dishes using various dark bottles and some sugar. The noodles they have fried, which her parents insisted on sending to them, are slightly burned. As they sit down at the small square table to the red glow of the lamp, he turns to her and asks, *So is this fake Chinese food, Chinese-American, since we didn't really know what we were doing?*

Is it? she says, trying not to feel irritated.

It doesn't look exactly like anything I'm used to, he replies.

TRACINGS

Beginning with.

Beginning with some dates, some numbers, some 235, some two sets of laws, twice. Beginning with "ending 156 years of British rule", 1841-1997. In the year topography amorphous. (In the year of processing information and spatial arrangements, your body will be yearning.) In the year of mass emigrations. In the name of fear, of love, of every person for herself, for wealth, for survival, for undisclosed ambitions. In the name of nationalism, of ethnic pride, of Canto-pop and memory-encoding. Of the imperial mother. The motherlands. The Manchu dynasty. (For your crisscross movements, and in the same space, filtering in and out—your mother's birthplace, your father's adolescence, or your earliest childhood.) Beginning with indigenous in way back when, or 1984, or 2047.

And the word 'globalization', meaning multiple memory sets, inconclusive structuring, resin with plastic. Every immigrant, a multitude of immigrants murmuring their echoes their air their clouds of smoke and residue. 1661. The 1960s. To burrow through or stay afloat. (Beginning with reverberations, like lines leading out. Your first word, your first word overseas, such questions beginning "why you are here" or "how light is refracted through water".) For loyalty to the crown, to the emperor, to the party, the lesser of two evils otherwise called the devil that is known, to your father, your art, your Victoria Harbor and Avenue of Stars, to your waking moment, your birth. Intervals of time suggest here is a sliver, a gap, some space to move around, fill in, wander sideways, exhale.

WHERE TO FIND TRANSLUCENCE

I had a memory, see, or maybe something from a dream while I slept. Little squares of Spanish rooftops on the edges of hills, seen at an angle a few feet above. Along winding paths filled with black trees and leaves which shadowed the structures.

I would float up the rainbow staircase at 6:15. I would feel the largeness of things, like the moon. I would believe that if I climbed up the massive set of steps, it would turn a corner and keep going. The seventh floor playground like a deserted land. So I thought that this was why my primary school should remain here in this place, expanding and contracting like jellyfish.

In her dream she was walking in the sand.
I don't understand your dialect, the old woman frowned.
Which she thought were plants, but were in fact shifting
  figures.
Her own skin, mottled and impure, making her evaporate.
Disembodied own.
She buried her feet and then went home.
Like faraway layers in the atmosphere.
Thin and sparse.
In her dream it got into the water, and colors spread
  against the tide.

And there, sitting on the top of a double-decker bus looking from an angle a few feet above, I suddenly realize it is less of a dream, which is to say dreams and memory have an elusive connection.

Expanding and contracting

An elusive connection: an electric current

An elusive connection: an electric current
A person's identity: her sense-making: two parallel
  motions: the world through which

A patchwork, asymmetrical: altogether tangled and imprecise at the edge of my throat.

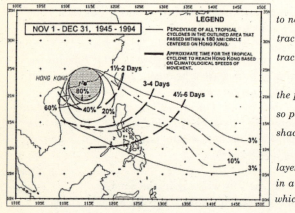

to navigate a map:
tracing and falling off,
tracing and waiting.

the pointing of a light,
so perhaps their
shadows may converge

layers upon layers
in a filter through
which to breathe

WAITING

Later that morning while the rain continues to flow downward between paths, the bus stops at the top of the hill. The driver turns off the lights and I am sitting in the back, gathering my things. There are no other passengers left on the bus. I call out to the driver asking if it is the last stop and he grunts something indecipherable. At the door there is some hesitation, and I turn to ask, *ma fan ni* 麻煩你, not the right language but often familiar, and he doesn't look at me but points in the direction of the rain.

In Hong Kong I memorize maps, learn the routes of buses and the layout of districts: the footprints I leave behind on the land are too careful, too unfamiliar, and sometimes circular.

I slip from one language to the other, Mandarin to English and back again, not like others who may do so unconsciously, but because I have run out of the words in one.

In this physical space I am always running out: of breath, of water, of tissues, of time. My bones are too weak and my mouth too misshapen for these acres of inclines and steep uphill slopes.

THE MIDWEST (ii): A WATERY RUIN

She cannot say what it is. It is too embedded, a word that means both 'hidden' and 'essential'. She can only try to follow it closer to the surface—her intimacy with relics and rituals is equal to her insecurity with belonging to them. That is to say, her feeling of water is the same as her feeling of intensity. When she is in a room full of white faces she becomes self-conscious. When she is in a room full of overseas speakers. When she is alone in her kitchen trying to remember the character for 'ghost'. In this case 'ghost' is neither a foreigner nor a native because it is not a person but a shadow version, an unshapely figure eluding set boundaries and rules. She will arrange her food in perfect symmetry, align her pictures at exact right angles, wipe her table until the surface is solid. She will desire a precise outline of her appearance, as if a mark of presence, as if 'illegitimate' causes one to fade into air. What does it mean to feel what is called your 'culture', to feel it inside of you, and yet at the same time to feel that something further, deeper, truer, lies inexorably outside your bodily limits? What does it mean that your body has no substance, is full of holes? Sometimes the relationship between what you cannot say, your wayward attempt, and the thing that is haunting you feels more imminent than anything rational or coherent. Other times it only feels. Either the sounds are sounds of her childhood, from underneath the table, or all words become accusations, all things part of a definition—one that is untainted, concrete, singular.

Ba ba 爸爸, *nong de ge hao che ve* 你這個好吃嗎?
Gei ba ba 給爸爸 ... *Ni mei you chi xie* 你沒有吃蟹.
*Just a little bit ... No, no, that's enough, give
   it to her ...*
Wo zi ji hui na 我自己會拿.
Ni zi ji na 你自己拿? *Wo cong lai mei you kan dao
   ni na* 我從來沒有看到你拿.
Be ni zi che 給兒子吃. *Ni zi hui xi che* 兒子喜歡吃.
Ni zi du lei xi 兒子多得很, *nong che va* 你吃吧.
Be ni zi 給兒子, *be ni zi* 給兒子.
Ni zi si ga wei de che 兒子自己會吃.
Ngo sik jo lo 我吃過了.
Hao le 好了, *hao le* 好了, *xia ya* 謝謝, *xia ya* 謝謝.
Bin go 誰 ... *yao che de ge* 要吃這個?
Mei you ren yao chi zhe ge 沒有人要吃這個 ...
   You want the head?
Viao be ngu 不要給我. *De ge ying gei nong che ge*
   這個應該你吃得 ... *Nong viao be ngu* 你不要
   給我, *ngu ve che le* 我不吃了.
Oh, just a little, gou le 夠了, *gou le* 夠了. *Xie
   xie* 謝謝.
Che le ma 吃了嗎, *che gu la* 吃過啦? *Che gu ye
   die die* 吃過一點點?
Wo chi le yi dian dian 我吃了一點點.
Nong ting de dong 你聽得懂?

EXPANDING AND CONTRACTING

On the steps of my old middle school, I remember
everything and at the same time it is nothing like my
memories. The green fence overlooking the field is too firm,
too unyielding. The concrete ground beneath my feet, the
dimensions of the outdoor eating area, they are steady and
angled without any shifting lines or contradictions of space.

   It has followed me, dotted lines across a map. But it
is not my home and has not been my home for centuries
of heavy rainfall, during which countless girls and women
were here, walking to school, buying green fruit, holding
their umbrellas as they slipped underground.

The first glance always physical in nature.

Precise, simple. Present.

Where the air is so thick, caught between descending and hovering, I can barely breathe. Where elusive particles of water, of dirt, of smoke-filled fog, seem to infiltrate my body and settle into corners. Where the earth is fickle and cannot be categorized into rain or sunshine, land or sea, rocky green hillsides or concrete forest. Where the sky rises and falls behind the hills as whitish clouds begin to drift lower. Where even the physical shape of the island is fleeting. And the rows of food alongside the street, creating smells in masses that seem always to be in-between: fish and meats and *gui yuan* 桂圓 fruit and bitter green melons, alongside computer arcades, alongside cafés, alongside clothing that is one-size-fits-all.

The land shook, burst forth
People fleeing from northern regimes.
Decades later an old woman said,
We are Chinese, we are one nation.
Or, perhaps: God save the queen.

My husband joins me ten days into the trip, and I meet him at the airport with a bag of candy in my hand. We are awkward, unsure of how to navigate such a different space together. I lead him around the next day, stopping in the bakery and feeling self-conscious about sharing places of my childhood with him. I bring him to the market, to my school, the pier, the bus stop, pointing to where the bookstore used to stand and the snack vendor used to sell popsicles. On the MTR he says to me, *You sound like a child when you speak Mandarin here.*

Not out of loyalty but out of lingering fears
Seeping across the waters.
Or, jaded voices scattered
Along a shoreline in flux:
Anticipate change, and change accordingly.

At the Museum of Art I read about an exhibit, *Bu Zhong Bu Ying* 不中不英. 'Not Chinese Not English' or 'Non-Chinese Non-English'. The exhibit consists of visual and multimedia pieces relating to language. Characters dance and break apart on a screen according to the body's motions. Beautiful wallpaper patterns are really comprised of foul language. What appears to be calligraphy is actually a series of unintelligible, invented "characters".

Outside, the mist has somewhat cleared and the sun glistens through. We walk to a restaurant and sit at a table drinking milk tea, which as a girl I believed was something Chinese, since we didn't drink it in America, and only later learned was first something English and then something else.

Or, like residents who spanned the globe
Feeling everywhere, nowhere.
(Beginning with
Blood is different than
Papers is different than
Government is different than
Language is different than
Upbringing.)

The streets are full of people. We walk, almost aimlessly, with sections of the crowd, against the crowd, buried amidst the crowd. There is movement in every direction, movement engulfing the pavement. People waiting at cross sections, then washing over the ground as the ticking sound speeds overhead. The day is intermittently rainy: the streets are dark, and even when the sun appears it is still shadowy on the gritty streets that lie obscured between massive buildings. At a music store we decide to enter and find ourselves drifting from one listening booth to another in random skittish paths; sliding on the headphones, being filled with Japanese rock, experimental Chinese opera, familiar Singaporean voices. The music against my ears swallows up the room in which I stand.

*Or, the land shook and poured forth
A history of multiplicity and adaptation indicating
Its own quiet self:
Neither midpoint nor mixture;
A subtle undercurrent beneath a chaos of surface waters.*

My room in my grandparent's tiny eighth-floor flat has light red curtains and a dusty pink blanket that lies folded at the bed's edge. I shuffle around in dark pink slippers small enough to fit my feet. Whenever they give me too much milk, I pour the last sip outside my window, never afraid of where it will land: the ground always covered with isolated puddles, the air always filled with a thousand different sounds.

And down below me, the turtles are falling off rocks into the pond.

They are falling upside-down, shell-first, turned over, eyes squinting.

and the ghostly can become radiantly bright, though blurry, under the light of the moon

OUTSIDE IT RAINS

The professor we meet at Lingnan University sits on the edge of a table with his arms crossed. He has a familiar accent, an air of assurance, and wire-rimmed spectacles. He reminds me of someone's father or an uncle. He is saying: *Cantonese speakers should not feel that their Mandarin is inferior to the mainlanders'. A language belongs to someone not when they follow the 'correct rules' but when they have made it their own, with all of their idiosyncrasies.* He is saying there is a difference between owning a sound and following the rules of a language. He is saying if a sound is something pure and a language something precise then perhaps precision and purity aren't the same, perhaps purity is forgetting to be self-aware.

THE MIDWEST (iii): WHERE SOUNDS BECOME LANGUAGES

Colors are breakable or beginning to fade: take a jar into your hands and breathe reds as far as Mars, darks as cold as raven.
This is how it ends: with my figure stretched thin as I am reaching, reaching.

So that she is remembering the past, and in remembering, feels it something so deeply inside and wound against her bones. It swells, belly forward, as if too great for her grasp.

So that she is holding it with a light, trying to find the holes—
The cracks. The half-hidden corners, the moonless stains.
The heavyweight cloth, obscuring her face, bruising her body into light grayish tones.

What constitutes a foreigner, a person seeing a foreigner.
How many words you have to know, how many memories you have to own. How foreigner means something

different to her in each country: first *family* and then
white.

And she measures the curvature of the eyes and the
movement of her hands for the inscription of the eyes
(mine or yours).

Because that which lacks color becomes nonexistent,
tinged with the silent rhythm of her body. There is a
history of things surrounding her since birth, like home
and family. She stands there, measuring, and instead
of a number there is the sensation of her fingers
partially dipped in something.

It is like earth-streaked leaves and soaked tissue
mellowing in a secret see-through container. A girl who
likes to be covered, vaporous glass windows and her
dark half-hearted reflection.

At a gathering of unfamiliar white faces, she does not
talk to anyone and wears the long woolen socks she'd
won in the game on her hands to keep them hidden.

As if the word *foreigner* was at once too much and not enough.

In the same way she hides behind the stories of her
parents because she does not know how else to make
them her own.

It is not two opposing halves but something else entirely—
a milky mixture, cloudy particles that cannot be
identified.

A voice becomes silent because it is diluted, weak; it is
the same with the body.

Or I am merely a shadow, a fallacy, a watery figment
billowing in dark closets.

POINTING A LIGHT

It is not, ultimately, to prove the purity of her blood or
her ability to stake claims. It is the need to make sense
of the girl in her snowsuit and the images that swirl in
her sleep. The need to look for the places that lie between
cracks or in corners of bubbles.

FIFTY-FIFTY

THEY FALL INTO PONDS

There is not a singular moment, a defining scene with intricate details. There is your grandfather shouting down to you from the apartment window. There is the early morning silence on the MTR as you are pressed flesh against flesh, passengers reading their newspapers. There is winter melon soup, your grandmother's *jiu niang* 酒釀, and her voice on the phone dictating recipes to your father. There are pieces of a day that continues.
At some point I grow tired of being spoken to in a language I do not know, weary with having to say, *Putonghua* 普通話? By the last week, I am simply nodding when store workers speak to me, nodding and waving them off.

In Hong Kong, the day begins like this: half-muffled sounds of construction behind a closed window, the steady beeping of a truck backing up, older women and men basking in the slow fluid motions of *tai ji quan* 太極拳 on the terrace eight floors below your window.

Supatra's Buddha
David McKirdy

5.30 a.m. Hoi Ha Village, Sai Kung Country Park.

I'm woken abruptly by the first high-pitched staccato volley of the dawn-chorus; today should be a $2,000-day. I gaze through the window, bleary-eyed, at a dark monochrome world of brooding, burgeoning tropical-vegetation, shadowy below a canopy of dark grey storm-clouds. I drag myself to the kitchen, put the kettle on and mentally order my schedule; 7 hours at $300 per hour equals $2,100. I almost forget, I also have to meet Supatra's Buddha.

I brush my teeth to the accompaniment of the mournful avian two-tone call-and-response from across each side of the bay, expanding and soaring, sung with gusto and passion, a coloratura enhanced by the natural amphitheatre of hills, river-beds and sea-shore. Returning to the kitchen, I pour the water into a mug and hear the barely audible fizz of the expanding porcelain as it sips its share. I sup mine and stroll out onto the open-air balcony. By now the day is sepia-tinged and the sound and the smell of the sea omnipresent. The steady put-put of diesel-engined fishing-boats, returning through the mist, vies with the percussive clop-clop of hoof on path, as the village cows, stoic and unattended, go about their morning processional. Suddenly there's a flash of orange as the warming sun pours through a gap in the clouds over the surrounding hills. Throughout the village stark maroon-tiled roofs, glazed and shiny with dew, reflect the newly arrived solar glare. Trees flaunt their lilac flowers and orange berries. Low, fast, dark clouds swoop over the mirror-calm tranquil bay. Alternately obscuring and revealing the sun, a shining corona behind them, they crowd and push their way across the stage, grumbling as they go. Details of near and distant mountains are gradually muted to a soft impression, receding range by range, shade by shade, until all are finally obscured by grey drapes of ocean-rain. Time to hit the shower, I think.

I need to buy some necessities and be in the city by 11.00, if I'm to achieve my monetary goals. On the way, I'll pop in to see Paul and Supatra who live in a neighbouring village. They are due to be married in two weeks and have asked me to be their best man. They are hosting Supatra's Buddha, who is an abbot from a Temple in Chiang Mai, together with one of his acolytes. He has advised them of the most propitious date for the proceedings, and I've been invited round for lunch to meet the 'Venerable Bede'. I won't be able to stay for lunch as I have a busy day ahead; I need to make some money. I have, however, agreed to call in for a cup of tea and a biscuit and to pay my respects.

I arrive at 9.15 as the clergymen are eating their one and only meal of the day. The abbot is younger than I expected: he looks about my age with a round, cheerful face. He is a compact man, muscular, with well-developed calfs and a toned body more apt in an athlete than an aesthete. He could probably beat me in arm-wrestling. I wonder where this physical prowess comes from—the legacy of a past life, this life? Mahogany-brown, indelibly and literally covered in dark-blue tattooed hexagrams and religious scripts encompassing his head, neck, arms and legs, his adorned chest and shoulders are revealed from time to time from within the draped pleats of a maroon habit. With his freshly shaved head and lack of eyebrows, the roundness of his head frames his typical Indo-Chinese features; the full, dark, clearly-delineated sensuous mouth, wide nose and hooded almond-eyes set above high angular cheekbones and below an expanse of forehead.

The abbot talks over his shoulder in rudimentary English, asking how old I am, am I married yet and do I have children? His voice is soft in tenor but loud in authority as he interrogates in his halting English. Paul is serving, while a worried-looking Supatra scurries back and forth from kitchen to table, bringing food and making sure that neither Paul nor myself commit any serious social faux pas. Paul is indulgently deferential, but I sense the deference tends more towards Supatra than towards this holy guest. He has to retrace his steps several times as he constantly forgets and leaves a plate or a glass of juice on the table rather than placing it two-handed into the palms of the junior priest as an offering; this is alms-giving, bestowing spiritual merit on the donor; the monks should be passive recipients rather than aggressive trenchermen. Supatra keeps up a barrage of one-sided conversation with salvo after salvo in her native Thai, lobbed from the kitchen into the dining room; her nervousness is palpable, this is the equivalent of an Italian receiving a house call from the Pope. She tells me, between snatches of Thai, that since I always seem to happen along to alleviate her problems when she is in trouble, the abbot has weightily proclaimed that we must have been related in a previous life. I suspect she is permanently in some kind of trouble and I could become her personal good samaritan unless I'm very careful.

The monks finish their meal and retire upstairs, ostensibly for the performance of their post-prandial priestcraft, which turns out to consist of smoking miniature cigars and watching highlights of World Cup soccer matches from the previous evening. We remain downstairs and partake of our own modest repast, which in my case consists of a large mug of tea and a fist-full of Hob-Nob biscuits. We join them after ten minutes to sit at the feet of His Holiness and enjoy the vicarious pleasure and privilege of pungent piety. His smoking is clearly not a hidden, sordid, guilt-ridden vice, but a flamboyant acknowledgment of corporeality and good cigars.

Doy, one of Supatra's friends, arrives. She is a 27-year-old Thai woman who has lived in Hong Kong for two years and speaks excellent Cantonese but no English. We break the ice, beginning a four-way conversation between us and the two priests. Supatra is once again rushing round in mother-hen mode as Paul sits bemused in a corner. The abbot is very impressed with my grasp of the language; although most Asians speak several languages, they are always view it as a bit of a rarity and in some strange way as a compliment when a Westerner deigns to learn an Asian tongue. This strikes me as a sad testimony to our colonial past and the lost opportunity of a cultural heritage richer than a grudging acceptance of the Chinese takeaway on the corner, or a turbaned bus conductor. Both monks are extremely sociable, with much idle banter, belly-laughs and slapping of thighs. They alternate between a serious and somewhat aloof demeanor, adopted for the more formal aspects of their duties, and a degree of levity normally found only in lottery winners and the clinically insane. The abbot calls each of us over individually for an audience, during which he chants and dispenses nuggets of good luck, consisting of strings of wooden beads, spiritually-charged red-twine bracelets and tiny gilded-metal buddhas. He then advises each supplicant of their luck for the foreseeable future. He is considered a link between the physical and the spiritual world and is not expected to instruct the members of his congregation on points of religious philosophy. I wish we could discuss aspects of buddhist thought: I'm sure that I would be considerably enlightened by the experience. Instead, I find myself unintelligibly but thrice blessed and make a mental note to buy a lottery ticket today. Armed with my trio of fetishes, surely I must win something and if I don't get out of here soon my day, which is already down to about $1,500, will be shot to pieces.

The abbot and his assistant approach the dark rosewood altar. Offerings of fruit and flowers surround the golden-Buddha statue. They chant and their resonant, nasal tones reverberate through the house and into the village, a litany of Eastern liturgy. After this brief ceremony we are assembled for a walk, and traipse downstairs into the hot midday sun. Paul and I start to perspire while our Asian friends stroll in front, unaffected. The villagers are Hakka; they have their own language and culture and although they are Taoists and animists by religious inclination, they are very superstitious and deeply respectful of any visiting God or spirit. Taking no chances, they are deferential to this auspicious guest, in stark contrast to some foreign residents; dismissively horrified by these heathen rites, they visibly tighten their buttocks and their grip on curious young hands and minds as they pass: These people probably have Buddhist statues and art in their own homes, but recoil when they encounter someone who sees a statue of the Buddha as a focus of reverence rather than a stylish interior design feature. At the conclusion of our walk, we return upstairs to sit in air-conditioned comfort.

Unexpectedly, the abbot decides that Paul and Supatra are to be married immediately. Paul looks a bit shell-shocked. He thought he had another two weeks of freedom, but is now led to the front of the altar, looking sheepishly like some death-row inmate whose execution has been unexpectedly and ineluctably brought forward. The abbot removes a package from his bag and unwraps it to reveal a collection of herbs and a delicate white string. He breaks off a length and attaches it to the Buddha in the altar, then wraps it round the altar and finally through his own palms and round Paul and Supatra's heads. As the chanting begins anew the happy couple become inseparably linked by this spiritual umbilicus. In my capacity as best man and Supatra's spiritual brother, I am instructed to hold one end of the string, as the newlyweds are raised to their feet by the abbot, who then leads us all into the conjugal bed chamber. Here, various herbs are carefully placed around the room, to the accompaniment of the deep sonorous tones of the incantations designed to ensure a harmonious and fruitful marriage. The string is wound up and attached to the window directly under the headboard and the abbot, who is by now cracking a huge grin, pronounces "for much children". I think to myself that this could be a bit difficult! Although Supatra already has three children from a previous marriage, she has recently undergone a hysterectomy. The laughter sweeps away the tension and solemnity which is replaced by a light-hearted air. I ask Paul what it's like being a married man and he says he'll let me know when the shock wears off.

After toasting the happy couple. Supatra tells me about the abbot's temple in Chiang Mai where they have programs for AIDS sufferers and drug addicts. His main reason for coming on this trip is to raise funds for this work. I ask Supatra if I can contribute; she says that it is not expected but would be gratefully received. I excuse myself and pop downstairs to the car where I have some red lucky-money envelopes, I put $1,000 in one, go back upstairs and offer it to the abbot. He accepts it with both hands and passes it to the monk without opening it. He then blesses me yet again and Supatra solemnly informs me that I will be very lucky in the future. I finally feel I can make a graceful exit and note that the time is now 4.18. Perhaps I can get to Mong Kok before the shops close in preparation for an early start tomorrow.

Supatra asks if I can drop Doy off at the bus stop in Sai Kung. It takes another fifteen minutes for her to collect her things and for us to say our goodbyes. We finally reach the car and make good our escape. As we reach the Ma On Shan intersection I drive past the Sai Kung turn-off and up the road towards Tai Po. This is a long straight road and I get up to about 80 kph. As I draw alongside a large rubbish-hopper on the verge to the left, I spot a tripod and slam on the brakes. I go through the speed-trap with all four wheels squealing in protest. I've definitely been nabbed, but I just hope I slowed down enough to avoid penalty points. Just over a rise, 200 metres up the road, I am flagged down and politely informed that I have been clocked at 67-kph in a 50-kph zone. "Shit!" That's a $450-fine and 3 points. Still, it is a good 15-kph slower than I was actually doing and it could have easily been a 5-pointer. On the other hand, if I had dropped Doy at the bus stop and gone into Sai Kung, as originally planned, it would have been a no-fine, no-pointer. Doy is completely silent and looks as if she fears I might kill her, or at the very least throw her out of the car at-speed. Resuming our journey, we stop briefly for $382-worth of petrol and a couple of soft drinks, after which she visibly relaxes and we chat pleasantly all the way to Tai Po. Here she alights, apparently delighted to be alive. It is now 5.20 and I've absolutely no hope of getting anywhere before 6.00. I might as well go home, read a book and try again tomorrow.

I make myself a cup of tea and reflect on the day. The figures are: income zero, expenditure $1,832. Not quite a $2,000-day.

Emotions
Karen Shui-wan Leung

Sugarcoated world
Makes you cry, scream, laugh and sigh
Life is marmalade

Composed on 23 April 2005, at 00:10

Random Fragments From These Years
Tammy Ho Lai-ming

One day I wrote her name upon the strand
But came the waves and washed it away
—Edmund Spenser

1.
Union of the upper and lower lips:
you like *bamboo, member, Ming,*
and many more: random words
you whisper in my ears from multiple
rudimentary and spontaneous scripts.
The unveiled night seems perpetual
and perpetually ours. Meanings are
arbitrary, unnecessary. Perhaps—perhaps,
in both time yet to come and time afore,
this sensual game of earlobe-warming
with words—words that precede
and succeed us—was played, is played,
will be played in eternal present.

2.
Summer smeared my face with melting butter. Thirteen
dinners after the first Indian meal, tonight was a
delightful compound of white wine, over-cooked chicken
breasts and cheesecakes. I told myself I must remember
this: being held by you, finally, on your bed—kissed,
touched, licked, squeezed and fucked. All verbs sublimely

FIFTY-FIFTY

passive and telling of passionate physical gifts. When you fly away—for you are a frequent flyer and majestic liar—what I remember is useful: fingers, index and middle, tiptoe swiftly on somewhere wrinkled until an impatiently self-inflicted orgasm. How I want you to know this; how I want you to echo this brilliance of sorrow.

3.
This morning were you warming your feet? How? Who else was involved? For how long? Do you play with the snow which is never seen in Hong Kong? A snowman with a pointy nose in a fairytale in a glass ball. Absence of years. I mean ears. Why aren't you writing? Because I say silly things? Because I say things I mean? Do you light cinnamon-scented candles on your dinner table? Do you hold someone when watching Wong Kar Wai's *2046*? Do you still wear a white T-shirt whenever you feel sinister? Is that a protest against terrorism, war, and sending a Chinese into Space? Do you look out of the window and pray that someone would delightfully appear, a flash of an image, and plant a kiss on your lips? Which is more in this world? Love, or raindrops? Which is longer? Our distance, or this particular evening when you are absent? Two time zones—clocks' arms understand and pickpocket us—yet my now is your present.

4.
The stairs to your apartment are perfect to walk on. I enjoy the clear sound my high-heels create on them—knock-knock-knock—before I am at last standing in front of your wooden door. Most of the time, I walk alone, and there is distant music drifting over the doorjamb, or you are playing the piano and I hear that too. Other times, there is silence, and I get worried. Then, when I open the door, I see you sitting back on the sofa, reading a limited-edition book, or sketching something with crayons on your notepad, and you smile to me, your hair a bit messy, and I am relieved. Sometimes I reckon, walking on the stairs, alone, is the very first part of our foreplay. That sexiness,

that boasting noise, somewhere between my thighs begins
to shudder. That untamed excitement.

5.
You have noticed, in this poem "you" always refers to
you. You have no name. Names are burdensome, names
identify. You'll remain anonymous, mysterious. I pray
that some day in the future, your shadow, slender and
speechless, will collide with mine again. Long live
logophilia; sexphilia; youphilia. It is not forgiveness I ask
for, but un-forgetfulness. One afternoon before Death stops
his chariot for me, I will make a bonfire and burn all
those heyday e-mail correspondences I have printed and
stored in a locked closet. Dickens did not want to preserve
words from Collins, Tennyson and Thackeray—why should
I keep you and me for posterity? Burning; let us choose
fire over ice. Not stupidities that are destroyed, nor fears;
but unpleasant surprises for our separate offspring of
different hues of darkness. Who's deciding how much of us
should survive?

6.
One sleepless night
I dreamt of you. And hey there
was also your bob-haired wife,
a silhouetted shape from my
imagination: the two of you sleep
on the same bed, dream two different
little dreams. That's acting,
and thus that's art. How peculiar –
I didn't cry or feel uneasy. Not at all
absorbed by this repetitively
dislocated imagery.

7.
Tell me things, such as: if you ever get a tattoo, would
it say "I love Ming"? The words stained under a picture
of a non-demolished Star Ferry Pier or a woman with

breasts like ice-cream cones. Tell me things, including why in anger you switch off the phone and why you want a girlfriend who can write but not dance, or sing. Is performing with words better and less intimidating? Tell me things, for example: how you know I love strawberry milkshakes and burnt chicken wings instead of Claret and T-bone steaks. Tell me things. Tell me things. Tell me. Tell me. Tell. Tell. Tell.

8.
The same day I sat facing you in the kitchen with greasy Indian food displayed in front of us, Prince Charles and Chris Patten sailed out of Victoria Harbour in the Royal Yacht Britannia. It was the first time I dined with you after numerous false starts and coy e-mails written with decorum. Half past eight in the evening, eyes were still adjusting the wondrous closeness of the other's dilated pupils. I listened attentively to your words and in a moment of drowsiness, the consonants and heavy vowels seemed to sit on the four corners of the table, lingering, mocking my ineloquence. Towards the end of our glistening meal, you said to me, 'You are the only one' and I was afraid. I was afraid that you were drunk.

9.
You do not like to have hair, ice cream and semen on the floor or on the sofa or on the mattress. You are angry when you discover them and poor black strong hair poor sweet ice cream poor milky semen are picked up or wiped away in haste. Then you look at me, you are still slightly angry, and I can't help laughing. You fall in love with a younger girl and you know you have to tolerate some things. Not just hair and ice cream and semen carelessly found on the floor, but also slammed doors, giggles, Cantonese colloquial ('your head') and unreasonable complaints: I cannot guarantee I will be a better person when I grow older, but love me anyway, love me.

10.
A novelist can spend a whole chapter on whether the main character—a male—wants to buy nail-polish and after fifty pages he decides not to buy it, so why can't I use the last section of this poem telling you why I like having your tongue dance with mine? Now look, your tongue is rather ordinary, but I like it anyway because it makes me realize in more than fifty years' time, when I am in a crowded elevator and everyone's face is younger and more innocent than mine, I can still stand straight and smile to myself thinking of the taste and roughness of your tongue. Nothing is going to steal this memory from me. Not time. Not *1984*-ish government policies. Not age. Not even your death which will come sooner or later. No.

White
Alan Jefferies

I am being ground to whiteness
at the moment,
the whiteness of a white bone.

That is the purpose of my whole existence

and was it not yesterday
a man came to me and said
as he touched a big beard hair
growing out from my cheek,
"pure white".

Mirror
Viona Au Yeung

The mistress of lightness and delicacy was not I, but she. When I danced, I felt a tension between reserve and passion. But she danced to the voice of her heart, where lightness and delicacy had begun to ripen.

Luna shuffled onstage in her pointe shoes. Occasionally, she paused and looked through a transparent curtain separating her from Stella. On the other side, Stella played her role as the mirror image of Luna. She moved swiftly at exactly the same time as Luna, so at ease that even she would doubt any effort had been put into achieving such perfect imitation.

"Stella." The music stopped and the dimmed lights were turned up as the director spoke with his assertive tone. "Stella. Remember in this scene we're showing the slightly distorted image of Luna. So I want you to vary your style a bit. Don't imitate Luna completely." Stella nodded, fixing her eyes on the floor. "Yea. We're the same, yet different," Luna added with her hands folded. Stella looked up and stared at her proud smile. Arrogance puffed out from her lips with each word she uttered.

9th August

Today when we were doing the 'mirror' scene I was told not to imitate Luna completely. I have to say, I've made a mistake. Two months ago when the script was in my hands I was so excited that they picked me as Luna's supporting dancer. I had long been impressed by her light, delicate steps. I didn't even care to read into the other details, including the 'distorted image' part, because I was focusing on the same steps that I'd have with Luna. But her words today really made my heart ache. She's keeping her distance, and doesn't seem to like my close imitation. Perhaps she's afraid next year I may replace her as the leading dancer. Well, by the time she said those words I really did want to shake off her style. But how am I supposed to do this? I tried not to look at her when I danced. I tried to forget I was her mirror image. I changed my pointe shoes from Freed to Capezio. But still, when I stood en pointe and turned, Luna's spirit crept into my toe and swirled my body around.

Stella

"Look! Her hairstyle goes well with her dress, don't you think?" Stella's friends busied themselves with her hair, her make-up, the ribbon on her dress. "Thanks, Sheenie," Stella said flatly, her vague smile reflected in her eyes. "So this is Stella, a creature of fantasy," mocked a voice in her mind, and Stella was engulfed with disdain. The expression in her eyes, her smile, the way she tied her shoe ribbons, the lightness of her steps, all were shadowed by Luna.

Luna and Stella were, as usual, well matched in their dance. The two drew closer to each other. Luna stood on her toes, facing the curtain. She clung to it with her right hand reaching out, touching her own mirror image. Stella did the same at the other side of the curtain. But as her hand was about to touch Luna's, she heard, again, "We're the same, yet different" and and kept her hand from reaching further. She remembered the proud smile. She remembered the air of arrogance. Would Luna be grateful to know somebody was copying her? No. She would look down on this false copy, despising its every step and gesture.

Stella fixed her eyes on the floor instead of looking straight into Luna's eyes. The girls skipped away from each other and stood still on either side of the stage, heads lowered and upper backs curved. The lights dimmed and the grey curtain dropped. The audience clapped anyway, as if to cover up Stella's mistake. They would rather the show draws to a perfect end.

11th August

When I went back stage after the performance, Sheenie tapped on my shoulder and said, "It doesn't matter." I said thanks but actually, I didn't care if my ballet coach was going to come and scold me. I was calm. Triumphant joy stole through my heart, and I secretly praised myself for finally distorting Luna's image—not just by varying her style, but by dancing a real step. Luna was right. "We are the same, yet different." And I proved it.

Stella

Guitar music played. In the practice hall, Luna stood at the centre, arms raised to her shoulders, her fingers curled. Eyes closed, she lifted her head, as if to let the notes sprinkle over her face. Every muscle in her arms moved with the drumbeat. Luna stepped out, and to Stella's surprise, clapped coarsely on her thighs. She swung her right arm out and lowered her head to the left, vitality and pride seeming to burst out from her. Stella could barely stand these extraordinary movements. What was this dance? Was this not Luna, queen of lightness and delicacy?

"What are you doing here?" Stella's deep breath caught Luna's attention. She felt like she had stolen a secret. She was speechless, and simply stared at Luna.

"Don't you dare tell anyone about the Flamenco." Luna's voice was stern.

"Why?"

"Lightness. Delicacy. That's what they expect from me. I'm not going to disappoint them."

"But why not show this passion and abandon in ballet? Maybe they'll add something new to your performance. Who knows."

"They've spent years shaping me. Everybody loves Luna. Everybody looks up to Luna. She's a queen, a butterfly, a sylph. You name it. You think they'll accept me if I'm actually passionate and wild?"

"I wouldn't fake others out if I were you. You can't fake yourself out, can you?"

"Do you think you're being true to yourself and to others with all your imitations of me?"

"It won't happen again, not after that performance. I'm fed up with it, and now I know the truth." Stella avoided Luna's gaze. She walked away without looking back. She couldn't believe her determination, nor the lie that was Luna.

There in a garden Stella was sitting alone. Fragrance in the evening breeze. She stood up and looked around, but she could not find its source. Perhaps it was from the small white flowers, which Luna said were osmanthuses. The fragrance did help a little to calm her down, but she couldn't shake her image of Luna, a delicate sylph, juxtaposed against the real, the passionately burning Luna. Stella's heart started to lose its weight and float, light as the petals of a dandelion in the air, blown away from their roots.

15th August

I'm lost. I tried to escape my thoughts through practice, but failed. I doubted the reflection in the mirror; it no longer was the copy of Luna that I had been so proud of. It was a statue without flesh, hollow. I turned away from the mirror in horror and got back to my dance. But as soon as 'The Maiden's Prayer' played, I discovered that I'd lost the ability to create. Three months of practice had ground away my originality, which had been an obstruction to the performance. And now the casual directness I used to have in my dance steps is nowhere to be found. I tried hard to lose lightness and delicacy. At one point, I almost succeeded, but as I opened my arms and brought my right arm in front of my chest, I saw my middle finger, slightly curved downward, and knew I'd lost. Luna was back again.

Stella

Stella and Sheenie were sitting in a café. As usual, old-fashioned love songs were playing. "I decided long ago ... never to walk in anyone's shadow ... if I fail ..."

"Hey, didn't you used to take brown sugar in your lemon water?" said the ever-perceptive Sheenie.

"Oh, yes." Stella put down the pack of white sugar and picked out a brown one. "Do you think I lack character?" she asked.

"It'll be over soon. This is normal for actors and actresses, too. It takes time to get away from the roles they've played."

"Well, maybe ... but you know, it's scary. Sometimes I try desperately to find my old style, but then when I fail and become Luna again, I'm at peace."

"You like Luna very much, don't you?"

"I have to say I do. She knows that, but apparently she doesn't care."

Stella's heart raced when she heard the news.

Sheenie asked. "Are you going to Luna's farewell party? I'm sure you will, huh?"

"Why? Where's she going?"

"Europe."

"What for?"

"Not sure. Why don't you ask her? You two were partners."

Luna looked different in her jeans and red T-shirt. Two ballet coaches were beside her, talking about Luna's journey. One coach suddenly burst into laughter. Luna giggled, the proud smile still evident. Stella was watching Luna, and never even sipped her orange juice. She badly wished to join them, to find out why Luna had to go. But she held back—those disgusting words of praise for being like Luna rang in her head. She hated those! Stella turned. She was about to walk away without looking back, but this time she couldn't. She turned and gazed at Luna. The proud smile had disappeared and her eyes were filled with sorrow.

20th August

Finally, Luna's farewell party. I didn't plan to say anything to her. I thought if I was forced, I'd say something like "Have a safe journey." She wouldn't care anyway. The best thing was for me to slip away without being noticed. I had planned to leave without looking back, and failed, as expected. But this time it was different: our eyes met as I gazed at her. Perhaps I shouldn't accord too much importance to it. We had practiced this dance a thousand times, looking back at each other at the same moment. It had become instinct. But I don't understand the sadness in Luna's eyes.

Stella

"Which book are you looking for?" Sheenie asked.

Stella flipped through a travel book with colourful pictures of Europe.

"Just looking around. Where do you think Luna is at the moment?" Stella paused at a page upon which a gondola drifted along a canal under greasy sunshine. The boatman's pole did little to sweep away the haze.

'In Italy. Sitting in a gondola perhaps?'

"You know me, Sheenie," Stella smiled. Of course she took Sheenie's words as a joke, but she hoped they were true too, so she'd be able to trace Luna's footprints.

"Hey! Look at this photo. Is this not her practising in Spain?"

In the hall Stella and her friends are practising as usual. Stella stands en pointe and turns. Now she can do four-and-a-half turns.

"Well done, Stella! It's been almost a year and you still turn like Luna," yells June, who is tying her hair into a messy bun.

"Do I?" Stella sounds casual as she looks at herself in the mirror. Her ribbons had come loose. She kneels down on her right knee, places the platform of her left pointe shoe flat on the floor and lowers her head. She crosses the ribbons and circles them above her ankle. She ties a knot.

14th February

Haven't written in my diary for a long time. Life's changed a lot without Luna. It's not easy to develop my own style without a model. I'm still not sure where I'm going with my dance, but I know Luna's style has become part of mine. (It took me quite a while to free myself from the constraint of her.) June said I was still dancing like Luna, and I admitted it, without feeling offended nor extremely happy. When I knelt down and finished tying my shoes, I did not tuck the extra ribbon in. I never do. Neither did Luna.

Stella

Stella dances, remembering the Flamenco, the true voice of Luna's heart.

kinesthesia
Viki Holmes

i will present to you
delicate fictions
as the rain falls
as the rain falls again
our words meet
across the electric city
purple to grey
looking almost
like a real sky
your hands sift the real sky
ferry me across the water
and your tongue
searching me out
a tiny fish
at the coral
of my teeth

the night we subside
in each other
such fictions!

today the fountains are alive
today people sit on the walls
and look up at the rain
today it is all so super-magnified
even the streets sleek their way
up the hills

the way we kiss is like
raising a hand to the sky
like a real sky

how your head rests
on my stomach
is all the history
i will ever care
to read

i have forgotten
nothing

this is all
touch

i open my palm
and the words
pour like sweat

away, away
i am looking over
your shoulder
the words spill
across your back
where the light
gathers
i gather you in
we are all over

white-like noise—hush!
the sound of a breath
released
and my tongue
searching
you out, a tiny fish
at the coral
of your teeth

Conversations
Monica Chan

One cloudy night without stars
I asked,
"If I can fly,
What do you want from the sky?"

You adjusted your glasses and looked
Diligently as if examining the scaffolding of another
construction project.
You asked,
"How high can you fly?"

One rainy day without umbrella
I ran in the downpour
And shouted,
"I'm soaked!"

You put your cap on and strolled
Calmly as if tackling another long mathematical problem.
You said,
"Just walk, between the drops."

Live It, Love It
Keane Shum

From every angle, at any time of day, Hong Kong can blow you away. You can be crossing the street in Causeway Bay with what I think are literally thousands by your side, and the sheer chaos of it all—not to mention the highest pollution ratings in Southeast Asia—suffocates you. But it's almost a good suffocation, because when you end up on the other side of the road you're smitten with the intimacy. So you take a minute (and a breath) and then you say, damn, where else in the world can I do that?

Or you can be out clubbing, on a Tuesday night, the day *before* New Year's Eve. It means you're dishing out the bills every other night for drinks and cabs, but it's almost a good waste of money, because although you're putting the hurt on your immune system you're also making new friends, seeing old ones, and just chilling with everyone in-between. On a Tuesday night. The day *before* New Year's Eve. Despite your empty wallet (save the cab money, of course), when all's said and done you walk down Lan Kwai Fong and say to yourself, damn, where else in the world can I do that?

On the way home, the cab driver asks you ever so innocently whether you'd like to take the tunnel or drive unnecessarily over the Peak. You actually choose the Peak, so that this cab ride won't be like all the others. And damn straight it isn't like all the others, because as you ride up and down the hills of the island you catch the stunning glimpses of a megalopolis asleep. Its lights reflect in the utter stillness of the harbor, by day a shipping industry mainstay but at night a somber, rippling mirror for the canvas on which the city's painters have dreamt up true miracles of architecture. By the time you get home—especially if you live out on some island off of Aberdeen—the meter has hit $120. But it's $120 well spent, because as you step out of the cab you say to yourself, damn, where else in the world can I do that?

And then you get home, write self-consciously about it all in your diary, and try to squeeze as much literary worth out of you before you call it a night. You feel like it's all a bit much, a little over the top and far too dramatic for your subtle tastes, but you click "submit" anyway, because god knows that you're just going to do it all over again tomorrow.

Damn.

Where else in the world can I do that?

And a little real history

Remembering 1967
Jesse Wong

When I asked Chak Wai-wah what she remembered about August 9, 1967, she started by telling me about the heat. It was the height of the south China summer. The windless air dripped with humidity. Her room had felt like the inside of a steam boiler when she went to bed the night before. She was 13, the younger of two sisters. Her father was a publisher of school textbooks and her mother an heiress to a jeweler's fortune. Despite their affluence, air-conditioning was too novel to find its way into their home, a hillside apartment overlooking the Hong Kong harbor. Unable to sleep, she and her sister stretched out on a rattan mat on the living-room floor with an amah fussing over them. She tossed and turned through much of the night. Daylight was a couple of hours away when the doorbell rang. Within seconds the lights were on and the apartment was overrun by strangers. They were six men, all wearing normal street clothes, she recalled, and "one of them carried a very big rifle."

For Hong Kong, where 3.7 million Chinese lived under British colonial rule, 1967 was a year of high anxiety. Some 33 kilometers north of the city center, a skimpy wire fence separated them from China. There, the year-old Great Proletarian Cultural Revolution, part political theater, part farce, but above all a huge man-made tragedy, was continuing to unfold. Mao Zedong initially used the campaign to lash out at rivals, the "capitalist roaders", within the Communist Party. He then stood by as the young Red Guards he unleashed went on to hijack government institutions and subject millions of victims to abuse and violence. Soon anyone with a grudge or an opportunistic eye was in on it, too. Although the country was largely closed to the outside world, what little news trickled across the border depicted scenes of worsening chaos. By May, a local version had erupted on the colony's streets.

What began as a minor labor dispute quickly turned into a wider struggle against British imperialism. The local communists choreographing it employed quintessentially Red Guard methods. There were the waving of Mao's little red book of quotations, the chanting of venom-filled slogans and the public pasting of "big character" posters. Protest marches escalated into clashes with police and into the random planting of home-made bombs. As the authorities struck back, crackdowns made heroes and martyrs of pro-communist figures, among them Chak Nuen-fai, who had passed up an earlier invitation to join the party, yet remained a stalwart supporter. They also energized young believers such as his younger daughter, a witness to his arrest in a predawn police raid.

I first got to know them three years ago. It was in the summer of 2004. I had been digging into old subversion cases to explore an idea for a book (which eventually came to nothing). The father was by then a retired widower and the daughter a housewife, and she and her hospital-pathologist husband had two teenage boys. She and I had been born in the same year, I learned, and we had grown up on the same street, Seymour Road, which in my memory was lined with ghostly mansions skulking behind wall-clinging banyan trees. From there, I had gone away after secondary school for university in the U.S. and so had she. She didn't seem to mind my questions and neither did her father. Over time, I asked more questions as I got to know them better. Their answers opened a window on a murky aspect of our past.

The Chinese government has never addressed the subject of the anti-colonial violence head-on. Glimpses of the decision-making on its side are available from only a few non-official sources: Party apparatchiks in Hong Kong took it upon themselves to launch the struggle and were cheered on by central-government radicals who had sidelined Premier Zhou Enlai. According to *The Cultural Revolution in the Foreign Ministry* by Ma Jisen, a former ministry worker and *China Daily* editor, a resurgent Zhou sequestered the apparatchiks in the Beijing Hotel in late 1967, explaining, "You are being kept here for two months so you can cool your heads." In the end, no one is known to have been held accountable, a muddle that compares poorly with China's treatment of the Cultural Revolution. Not that the latter is much to crow about. A full account is lacking, and discussion continues to be restricted. But at least, the episode was officially condemned after Mao's death in 1976, a few culprits, notably the "Gang of Four", were punished, and amends were made to some victims.

Since colonial rule over Hong Kong gave way to the resumption of Chinese sovereignty ten years ago, some things have changed and many things have stayed the same. Gone, for the most part, are the British faces but otherwise, the establishment is still dominated as it used to be by the same business tycoons and civil-service bureaucrats. The left has remade itself, as its big brother in China has done, into the party of prosperity and stability. It dutifully plays a supporting political role, helping to shore up the social order it once worked hard to subvert. Its scope to revisit the anti-colonial struggle is limited by the lack of interest on big brother's part but when it occasionally does, the old party line tumbles out: the protesters' cause was just, the police were sadistic brutes, and the bombs appeared mysteriously, origin unclear.

Mr. Chak is an unlikely one to parrot such a party line. With his fondness for books and conversation and the benefit of his wife's inheritance, he could be quite at home, had he been born an Englishman, in a London gentlemen's club. Not the stuffy sort for snobs, for certain, but a convivial one, perhaps in Mayfair. He might own a small publishing house specializing in works as clever as they are hopeless of bringing a profit and he'd give happily to other causes, too. And on the weekend he might retire to his Surrey country house to drink tea on the lawn, weather permitting, or stroll across the wind-swept downland photographing the fauna. A place on the Queen's honors list at some point wouldn't be a big surprise.

In fact, he was born among the rice paddies of south China. The last imperial dynasty had collapsed eight years earlier and he grew up, as his landowning family's modest fortunes declined, in a nation much abused by coarse military men and avaricious foreign imperialists. He went into debt to finish university in Guangzhou and taught school there for a while. In Hong Kong, where he applied for a teaching post two years before Mao's communists unified China, he met his future wife. He also found a worthy cause. With her blessing, he used her money to support patriotic printing and publishing ventures—a good man who gave, asking nothing in return, another leftist said of him. Because of his loyalty to the cause, he was sucked into moral dilemmas a good man shouldn't have to face. His loyalty became his daughter's and, in time, his dilemmas hers, too, as she grew older and re-examined choices made long ago.

Ahead of my first meeting with Mr. Chak, I mentioned the upcoming appointment over dinner with my father. He and I exchanged a few comments about events in 1967. Back then, he was 44 and running a toy business but, as we spoke, his 81st birthday was behind him. Although his health was sound, his recollection of the rage and fear that ruled our streets was hazy. At some point I asked: "Do you remember the bomb under your car?"

Instead of a verbal response, I received a quizzical look from across the table. I repeated my question on the chance that he hadn't heard clearly. Still wearing the same look, he replied: "No, I don't remember it."

If you had been at the table and seen his expression, you wouldn't have believed that he really did discover a suspicious-looking package one morning when he left home to go to the office, and it was sitting under his car which was parked in our apartment building's open-air garage. Not only that, but he also got down on his hands and knees to study it, then he got the watchman to call the police and warn all the residents to keep away, and then he got behind the steering wheel and drove off. I described each detail carefully, hoping to hit a button that would stir his memory. I reminded him that while many suspected bombs proved to be duds, the one he came upon turned out to be the real thing. Concluding my account with the blast set off by the police bomb squad, I threw my hands into the air, and I went "BANG!"

He continued to look at me after I was done, and I looked at him, and eventually he asked: "How come I don't remember any of this?"

To my relief, I found as soon as I started talking to Mr. Chak that he had an excellent memory. I also found abundant contradictions in his feelings about the party. To him, Mao was a tyrant, and post-Mao China, despite achieving great economic progress, continued to be ruled by a ruthless dictatorship. I wondered when he began to feel this way. He replied, "After June 4", the day in 1989 when gunfire and tanks crushed peaceful pro-democracy demonstrations in Beijing's Tiananmen Square; but then he said "No, it was earlier, maybe as early as the late 1970s." If so, why did he accept a place in the Chinese People's Political Consultative Conference, a do-nothing body filled with people who had been of service to the party? (First appointed in 1983, he resigned in the 1990s.) He glared at me with his one good eye. "There is such a thing as vanity. Haven't you heard?"

We were in his Seymour Road apartment, a dark interior weighed down by heavy Chinese wood furniture. A portrait of his wife sat on a piano. Two bigger-than-life portraits of her parents hung from the wall above. He sat with those unsmiling faces behind him and I to his left, and we drank tea brought by a Filipino maid. I was at the same dining table where the policemen sat interrogating him back in 1967.

There had been a crackdown on three newspapers. Three people who ran them were charged with sedition, publishing false news and attempting to cause disaffection among the police. Applying another law that held printers responsible for what they printed, the authorities also arrested two partners of Nam Cheong Printing Press

Ltd on similar charges. One of them was Mr. Chak.

I had scrolled through library microfilm containing press coverage of his arrest. It showed a lanky figure stepping toward the camera with eyes downcast, shoulders stooped and wrists manacled to other prisoners. He was 48 years old, and he was about to tumble from a genteel existence into that of a convicted criminal, for which he would spend two years in prison. Seen close-up 37 years after the event, he appeared alert and vigorous despite the usual ailments that came with age. His hands looked as soft as a baby's. His shiny cheeks exploded into pink whenever our conversation dredged up less agreeable memories.

For China, the 1950s had been a cruel decade. Fresh from his civil-war triumph over a corrupt Kuomintang regime, Mao plunged his people into a bloody conflict with the U.S. in Korea. They were further subjected to a succession of political campaigns. Branded counter-revolutionaries, reactionaries, rightists or spies, many lost their careers, their liberty and even their lives. The decade closed with the Great Leap Forward, an exercise in forced collectivization that severely disrupted agricultural production. Scholars in the West estimate that around 30 million Chinese starved to death, victims of the worst man-made famine in history.

Life in the colony went on as normal in the meantime, more or less. At the Hong Kong Club, majestic with stone arches and columns, you'd see British gentlemen sipping cocktails and taking in the harbor view on the verandah as they mused about the red menace. A short walk away, you'd find Mr. Chak and his fellow patriots debating ways to further the cause. Meeting in traditional teahouses under Chinese-tile roofs, they shouted to be heard over a symphony of humming ceiling fans, pet birds shrieking in cages, waiters pitching dim sum and patrons clearing throats into spittoons.

He hadn't been active in politics in China but said things that had got him into trouble with the Kuomintang. Fearing retribution, he slipped away to Hong Kong, where he taught school and enrolled in correspondence courses in his spare time. A fellow student introduced him to communism. He joined the Chinese New Democracy Youth League, forerunner of China's Communist Youth League. Little was asked of him except to report on the words and deeds of those around him. Feeling uncomfortable about the task, he asked for time to consider when invited to join the party. Not that he doubted the cause. All the true believers he knew were decent people who wanted what was best for China. "In my heart I was as much one of them as if I were a party member."

In the mid-1950s, he was asked to help with the printing of a newspaper newly started by communist friends. He consulted his wife and she gladly went along. I would hear this pivotal detail again over weeks and months and almost every time, he would insert the same comment: "Well, you know what they say. Behind every foolish man there's usually a foolish woman." He was asked to put up half the capital and also to have his name appear on a government register of printing-firm bosses. In fact, he didn't run the business; they did. The subterfuge reflected Hong Kong's status as a "white", or enemy-held, territory. Having no overt presence in the colony, the party carried on sometimes discreetly and sometimes less so via organizations and individuals serving as fronts. The authorities kept a close watch and, depending on the political mood, turned a blind eye sometimes and took a tough line at other times.

More newspapers were added to the stable of customers after the printing firm got off the ground, bringing him a share of profits though not necessarily satisfaction. He had some say in the management at first but gradually got elbowed aside. When business got turned away for political reasons, he objected but to no avail.

Listening to him, I was reminded of Louis Cha, one of his contemporaries. Originally a journalist in the leftist camp, Mr. Cha branched off to found a largely apolitical newspaper, *Ming Pao*. Still on amicable terms with his former colleagues, he followed their example in avoiding reporting on the famine. After all, the official press in China was declaring the Great Leap a huge success. A moment of truth arrived when the trickle of refugees from China turned into a deluge. His reporters brought back daily eyewitness accounts of desperate Chinese throwing themselves at the border fence in broad daylight. After suppressing their accounts for a while, his newspaper broke its silence, a decision that caused him to become a target of vehement attacks in the leftist press.

I asked Mr. Chak if he had been reading the newspapers coming off his presses. Did they mention the exodus? What did they have to say about Mr. Cha, who had become, in the words of former colleagues, a turncoat and an agent of the Kuomintang government-in-exile in Taiwan?

He said he glanced at one or another of those papers, but only rarely. "I hadn't time. I was busy with other things."

What about the famine? Did he believe the party line trumpeting bountiful harvests and well-fed peasants?

The question, which I raised more than once, seemed to irritate him. At times he admitted to having doubts about the official propaganda. Mostly, he looked away, impatient to move on to another subject, and he would say: "I didn't think about it. It didn't concern me."

He was thinking in those days mostly about how to put together a decent natural-science textbook. For local schools teaching in the Chinese language, teaching materials were often clones of originals written in Beijing or Shanghai. As a result, schoolchildren learned little in natural-science classes about indigenous animal and plant species. Aiming to fill the void, he commissioned writers to compose the text. His wife, serving as his assistant, edited and copied manuscripts in long hand as Chinese-language typewriters weren't available. Meanwhile, he took off every day with tripod and camera to look for samples for use as illustrations. Trekking across woodlands and streams, he was reminded of his childhood in the Chinese countryside, and he felt truly happy.

He had no part in the violence of 1967. He was present at one meeting of a "struggle committee" and learned after the fact that his name had been included in a published list of committee members.

He came as close as he ever did to a demonstration when he drove by one on his way to an exhibition showcasing one of his textbooks. He didn't follow the news and didn't pause to think about what went on until the police turned up at his door, he said.

The public library hasn't kept copies of the newspapers printed by Nam Cheong's presses. Still, you can get a sense of what they were about by looking at others because the leftist press spoke with one voice. Here's how *Wen Wei Po* reported the death of a policeman, the result of a godown-district confrontation in which a coolie was also shot dead by the police: "A courageous coolie filled with the hatred felt by his entire race rushed forward and, grabbing a yellow-skinned dog that had committed much evil, plunged a sharp hook into its neck, chest and back. This yellow-skinned dog didn't even have time to make a sound. It lay down and was still."

Following the crackdown on the three newspapers, the colony was hit by a stepped-up bombing campaign. The leftist press celebrated it with terms such as "magnificent" and "wonderful." Although many of the suspected bombs were duds, some, such as the one under my father's car, packed enough punch to kill. One went off one Sunday afternoon on a quiet side street. Hearing the explosion, a mother of four rushed from her home into the street. She found her two-year-old son lying on the sidewalk. His face was blackened and part of his brains had spilled onto the ground, and his tiny body was covered with fragments of shattered windscreens. Nearby lay his eight-year-old sister. Her insides were splattered on walls across the street. A policeman combing the scene later scraped one of her fingers off the side of a parked car.

As the family tended to the children's funeral, in the Chinese capital some 1,200 kilometers to the north, tens of thousands of Red Guards assembled to condemn oppression of Hong Kong compatriots by British fascists and imperialists. Britain received a diplomatic ultimatum demanding release of the defendants in the newspaper case plus 14 detained leftist journalists. After the 48-hour deadline had been ignored, a mob set fire to the British embassy in Beijing.

Soon afterward, Mr. Chak was given a chance to speak in court. He praised Mao's thoughts, denounced British fascism and predicted that "brightness will come very soon". He and his codefendants were convicted on all charges. The bombings and protests fizzled out toward the end of 1967. The official toll came to 51 dead, 832 injured and 1,936 prosecutions.

As one who works with the printed word, I dislike laws that make criminals of printers. I think of the case against Mr. Chak as an injustice. Even so, in the time that I got to know him, I became intrigued by how he saw himself.

The violence of 1967 had taken place against a backdrop of simmering discontent. Workers' pay was not keeping pace with prices. The police were corrupt. The colonial government was aloof and insensitive. The British often were superior in how they treated the Chinese. Those in the leftist camp were disadvantaged in additional ways, the most glaring being rough justice such as deportation to China without trial. But after all has been said, the hateful propaganda and the killing and maiming of innocents still couldn't be justified. He wasn't directly responsible and yet, as a loyal supporter of the party, was he entirely blameless?

Over time, I received a range of responses. "Of course we were right to resist because they were beating up Chinese," he said of the police response to the protests.

Sometimes he was critical of the party leadership. "As soon as the bombs went off I knew all was lost because they had made themselves enemies of the people."

And sometimes it wasn't clear at all if anyone was to blame for the bombing campaign. "Oh, it was probably just some kids taking matters into their own hands."

But he never spoke about himself or reflected on his possible choices. Could he have withdrawn from the printing business? Could he have walked away from the cause? How did he feel about the innocent victims of the struggle? On one occasion I pressed him perhaps too hard, and he seemed to feel terribly aggrieved.

"You young people have no idea what it was like to live under the Kuomintang," he said, slapping the table top with both hands.

But then again, he could have been trying to make amends in less direct ways. He spoke up in 2003 when the post-colonial government proposed a harsher version of the laws under which he was convicted. His old comrades were parroting the party line of the time, asserting that while those laws were bad under the British oppressor, the same laws under Chinese sovereignty would be no problem. He opposed the proposal—which was eventually dropped—in press interviews, which he supplemented with a stinging aside. His faith in the legal system was much greater when Hong Kong was under British rule, he said.

Also, he frequently made self-deprecating comments to me about his relationship with the party, usually by quoting his daughters. "They tell me I lack an independent mind," he confessed. He also said of the younger one: "She used to be much more of a leftist than I ever have been." I decided as soon as I heard that remark that I wanted to meet her.

As a child she had looked up to her father for his ready defiance of convention. He stood up for a niece who was being ostracized for wanting to wed a divorced man. When she felt overwhelmed by her science studies, he took her to the beach to hunt for seashells, saying that observing was as important as homework. No preaching by him was necessary for her to convert to causes he considered worthwhile.

Too young to play a role in 1967, she became politically active two years later. The violence having ceased by then, the struggle was being continued by other means. She joined the Hok Yau Club, a cultural organization where teenagers were offered help with their studies, then incrementally exposed to capitalism's seamy side. There were visits to squatters' slums, curbside chats with street-sleepers and journeys to China for study sessions with party cadres. She continued to be active in Maoist circles while studying microbiology in Cornell University. The end came, for her as for many believers of her generation, with the downfall of the "Gang of Four" in 1976, the event that heralded the end of the Cultural Revolution. Still in

Cornell then, she withdrew totally from politics but she wasn't able to completely leave the past behind.

My first meeting with her was in the Conrad Hotel coffee shop in mid-2004. Petite, with straight, short hair and no visible makeup, she had a schoolboy look about her. It sent a message that her swift responses to questions reinforced: Here's someone with nothing to hide.

I learned that upon returning from the U.S., she was deeply ashamed of having been a leftist. She avoided former schoolmates and comrades. On her first date with her future husband, she spent the whole time coming clean, not wanting him to think later that she had been covering up. She was upset, too, with former Hok Yau leaders whom she felt had led her and other youngsters down the wrong path. One of those bygone leaders happened to publish a memoir a few months after my Conrad meeting with her. She sent him angry Internet messages charging that he had whitewashed the past.

She also introduced me to two former Hok Yau comrades. The pair, being slightly older, had participated in protests in 1967 but never went beyond chanting slogans and raising clenched fists. Looking back, they felt, as she did, that they had been victims of foul propaganda. They looked startled when I mentioned other victims of the struggle. What did they think about the children blown to pieces? Or the strike-defying tram driver stabbed to death? Or the anti-communist radio broadcaster incinerated in his car by a gasoline bomb? "We've nothing to do with that," one of them said.

It echoed her response when I put a similar question to her earlier. "We were told that in war casualties are avoidable," she had said very matter-of-factly. Questions about shared, or moral responsibility, were not for her.

But that was back in 2004.

We met one day this past summer to catch up and, over coffee, she disclosed that she had converted to Catholicism. She had been inspired at least partly by the nuns she had come to know from doing volunteer work, she explained. I congratulated her, and we chitchatted about local politics and other inconsequential things. At some point, without prompting, she began talking about victimhood—not hers, but that of people unwittingly injured by her leftist endeavors. They included schoolmates she had tried to manipulate, a victim of on-the-job injuries she had treated as a class-struggle specimen, and a teacher despondent over her rebelliousness. Her turn toward religion has made her see the past—and herself—in a new light. "I committed sins, not knowingly, but I have to bear responsibility for what I did," she said.

Finger, Flower
Madeleine Marie Slavick

I

She sees, cannot see

surrounds her face
with a band of black

stands in the center
of a peopled street

Her finger writes
6 and 4 in city air

6 4 6 4
6 4 6 4

The sigh needs
to sigh

And the air
remembers

II

He collects
white flowers

puts the petals
by the harbor

says nothing
does not bow

Whiteness is all
Whiteness is all

All that has been
lost, buried, retold

White evening
White morning

We believe, do not believe

(for Ko Siu Lan and Tsang Tak-ping)

Hong Kong, 3 June 2007

Victoria Park
Woo See-Kow

Thousands upon thousands
of candlelights
dotted Victoria Park

She handed me a leaflet
in neat short phrases
heralded
the injustices
the cruelties
the things
I must not forget

Her fiery eyes
firm matter-of-fact voice
sheltered
the blazing compassion
shielded
a tender heart

Fighting her battle
preaching her cause
by the park's swimming pool
where I once almost drowned
as a boy

Red eyes and white-prune fingertips
staying in the water for too long
drenched with too much chlorine

I was there
candle burning in my hand
for a reason

We were on the same side

But
watching her quietly
from a crowd
all I could think of
was to tell her
how beautiful she looked
in the soft candlelight
and
she was gorgeous
even
when
she was
mad

202 | Painting Statues Red and Blue
Peter Gregoire

You can't avoid or prepare for a phone call like this. All you can do is sit there and let the words tear your tranquil world apart, like a spade ripping through turf on a bowling green.

"Your father's been taken into hospital," Mum said. "He's critical."

After hanging up, I must have asked my secretary to book a flight, gone home, thrown some clothes into a suitcase and headed to the airport. I can't remember doing it, but it must have happened because I'm now two hours into the flight to Heathrow, the dinner trays are cleared away, the cabin lights dimmed and the numbness is starting to wear off.

He'd had this cough for weeks, Mum said. She'd been nagging him to go and see a doctor but "you know your father". The stupid old curmudgeon hated doctors. "It's just a cold, woman! Stop fussing!"

He was diagnosed with pneumonia minutes after arriving in casualty. The next few hours would be crucial, the doctor said, so now I'm in a race against time to get to his bedside before ... no. I can't think about that. Not yet.

The night looms ahead of me like a cavern of nothingness. I shut my eyes and let my thoughts take their own course.

In the darkness, Dad is in full-blown technicolour. The morning sun highlights his craggy features. White hair sticks out from his head like a candy-floss salesman's first efforts. His podgy tummy nestles snuggly under that mauve toweled dressing gown Mum bought him from the outfitters in the village. It always was too big and the collar bunches up round his neck, squashing his cheeks so he looks like a disgruntled bulldog.

I remember exactly when this was.

He's sitting at the kitchen table, a grim captive of events thirteen thousand miles away, unfolding on television. On screen, the Union Jack is lowered above Government House in Hong Kong as a bugler sounds "Taps", signaling the end to another chapter of the British Empire.

"Never thought I'd live to see this." Dad's voice is always gruff in the mornings, like sandpaper on splinters. "I'm glad your mother's at work. She'd be in tears watching this. That's a piece of your heritage disappearing."

"Don't be so dramatic," I snap back, like the precocious youth I am, irritated by his dated opinions. "It's not like I've ever really been there."

"You spent the first eighteen months of your life there!"

"... and the next twenty-three years here. Face it, Dad. I'm English."

Dad stays silent for a minute, regroups, tries again. "That place," he points his teaspoon at Chris Patten receiving the folded up flag, "is part of you whether you like it or not. It's where I met your mother, where we got married and where you were born. You're part Chinese, remember?"

I should have known better than to argue, but then again mornings aren't my thing either. After two weeks living in each other's pockets we're getting on each other's nerves. I'm about to leave before this degenerates any further, but then I catch sight of his watery blue eyes, still fixated on the television, and I see something other than the usual proud defiance that runs to the core of my father's being. There's disappointment, even defeat, and it's so ... so un-Dad-like.

Then it hits me. The realization why what's happening to that tiny pimple on China's backside needles him so badly.

My father is a textbook product of the British Empire. Born in 1947 in Singapore, where his parents were posted, he was then dispatched to a Scottish boarding school and an education designed to equip its pupils with the tools they needed to staff Britain's imperial domains. On leaving school, he was sent out to Hong Kong by the only company he ever worked for. It was supposed to have been the first step in a long career overseas, but it never panned out that way. As Britain's imperial territories diminished, so did Dad's usefulness in the far-flung places where he served. He was eventually retrenched home and spent twenty years commuting to London. He hated it. He never said so, but I knew he did. So when three weeks ago, he finally received notification of the redundancy that he knew had been a long time coming, I thought it a blessing in disguise.

But to a proud man, there's no pride to be taken in being told you're no longer needed; in being condemned to history's scrapheap, just like Hong Kong was being condemned today.

"It must have changed a bit from when you were there," I say, hoping a show of interest will overcome my insensitive dismissals.

It seems to work, because in the next forty minutes Dad loses himself in reminiscences. It's like he's traveled back to when he first landed in Hong Kong as a twenty-one year old, ready to take on the world. I nod, ask questions and chuckle in all the right places pretending that I haven't heard these tales before.

Eventually Dad pauses and nods, as if to thank me for humoring him. He gives a rueful sigh. "People are worried the Chinese are going to crack down there, now. Wouldn't be the first time they've tried."

"You mean Tiananmen Square?" I ask.

He shakes his head. "I mean in Hong Kong itself. When I went out there in '67 the place was in turmoil. The Cultural Revolution in China sparked off rioting against the British in Hong Kong. Whole thing got quite serious. Places were bombed, people were killed. We were all petrified the Chinese were going to waltz across the border at any moment. I was in the auxiliary police at the time.

Got called up to do my bit."

I see the defiance reflate. It doesn't last, though, as on-screen the scene cuts to Hong Kong's border where a platoon from the People's Liberation Army is goose-stepping through its drills. Dad's chest rises and subsides in a deep sinister sigh.

"The rioters used to carry around Chairman Mao's little Red Book," he says. "I managed to get hold of one. Kept it as a souvenir until you scribbled on it with your crayons when you were a toddler! Your mother must have chucked it away." He chuckles, then sips his coffee. "It was a crazy time back then."

"Sounds quite scary," I say

"It was, I suppose. But it was also good fun."

"Really? How come?"

"Well," he drawls. "I was twenty-one and didn't have any family, so I guess I found it a bit of a lark. In fact, one night..." He interrupts himself and changes tack. "I don't know if I should tell you this, not even your mother knows about it. It happened well before I met her."

If he didn't before, Dad now has my full attention. I pull my chair towards the table. "Oh, come on! You can't say that and then just stop."

He glances left, right and over his shoulder. I'm not sure why, it's not as if there's anyone else here. Then leaning forward he continues in a hushed, conspiratorial tone:

"One night, me and a group of lads were down at the Hong Kong Club. It was after curfew, we couldn't go out anywhere, so we ended up having a skin-full. Anyway, one of the guys starts reading this story from the newspaper, about how the communists had gone and graffitied Queen Victoria's statue in Victoria park with red paint. Well, that was it, as far as we were concerned! Making us stay indoors after dark was one thing, but defacing the Queen's image?! Let's just say, we weren't too happy about it." He leans back and grins mischievously. "So I had this idea."

I feel my eyebrows furrow.

"The club was having its dining room refurbished," he continues, "and the decorators had left some paint lying around. So we found ourselves a couple of tins of royal blue, snuck around the corner, and dumped them over the two stone lions outside the Bank of China. Monstrous things, they were. Trouble was, when we legged it, we ran straight into a couple of policemen on a fag break. We all had to spend the night in the lock-up!"

By now Dad is laughing at the memory.

I, on the other hand, sit there with my jaw half-way to the floor, wondering if I have really heard my father—the boring old sod who embodies middle-class dutifulness—just admitting to vandalising public property.

"You've got a criminal record?" I stammer, "and mum doesn't know about it?!"

He shakes his head. "They didn't charge us. Too scared of what would happen if it got out that a load of *gweilos* had made such an inflammatory political statement. I mean, all hell could have broken loose. So the lions were cleaned that night and we were released the next day after a bollocking from a Colonel Blimp superintendent who told us never to mention it again."

"Wow!" is all I can say, stunned at thought of Dad instigating a cover-up amongst the higher echelons of the colonial police.

We sit there in silence for a moment, listening to Chris Pattern's farewell speech.

"The story of this great city is about the years before this night and the years of success that will surely follow it."

There's something in those parting words that resonates with Dad.

"Wait here," he says to me excitedly. "I want to show you something."

He disappears. Footsteps clump up the stairs. A cupboard door clicks open. He groans at my mother's fastidiousness as he can't immediately find what he's looking for, but it's soon followed by a grunt of satisfaction. Footsteps clomp on the stairs again and he settles back into the chair opposite me, glancing towards the TV to see where proceedings have got. A torrential rainstorm engulfs Hong Kong.

"Have a look at this," Dad pulls something from his pocket and hands it to me.

It's a tie, rolled into a thick coil, reeking of mothballs. The cloth feels fragile against my skin. I carefully unravel the thick end. It's black, although the passage of time has greyed its edges. Dotted around the material in triangular formation are miniature embroidered figures, each one red, yellow or white.

"Five of us were arrested that night," he explains. "Like I said, we couldn't tell anybody what we'd done, but we wanted to commemorate it somehow. So we each had a tie like that made."

"What are these figures?" I ask, fingering the delicate embroidery.

"Those depict the insults that were traded during the riots. You've got your white skinned pig—that's what the communists called the British. And the red fat cat is what we called them."

"What about this yellow whippet?"

"Actually it's a greyhound—a yellow running dog. That's what the communists called the vast majority of Hong Kong's population—people like your mother—for not joining them in trying to throw out the British."

"White-skinned pig. Red fat cat. Yellow running dog," I repeat.

He nods. "From when your old Dad was a political prisoner."

"Pah!" I choke down my laughter. "More like an alcohol-fueled prank."

Dad smiles philosophically. "You're right. But there was more to it than that, at least for me there was. I mean, when you read about the British Empire nowadays you'd think it was the most monstrous creation in the world, but that's simply not true. Hong Kong's probably the best example of the good it did. It was a rock before we came along. British government and British justice, that's what's turned it into what you see there today," he gestures towards the television. "I'm not going to pretend it was a major hardship for me going out there, but I left behind a lot of friends and family! And, yes, I had fun. But I also felt a sense of responsibility towards the people who lived there. We all did. So to have a load of Marxists screaming they wanted us out, for no other reason than we were white-skinned pigs was … was …"

"Not cricket?" I venture.

"Exactly!"

The television has now moved on to another set of programmes, as if the interruption posed by the Handover was just an inconvenient aberration.

"Well, time to start the day, I suppose," Dad gets up to leave. As he passes, he pats my shoulder and points to the tie. "You can keep that. It's a piece of your history. God knows what's going to happen to the place now."

Another voice enters my consciousness.

"Excuse me sir!"

A stewardess is standing over me, her hand shaking my shoulder. "The seatbelt sign is on."

Suddenly I'm transported back to the cold, dark cabin of the 747.

"Yes, of course."

I spend a few moments blinking myself awake and do up my seatbelt.

Then, as the plane judders through turbulence, I remember the reason I'm on this flight.

"Hold on, Dad," I mutter under my breath.

"Hold on until I get there."

Life can be so cruel.

Being forced to make funeral arrangements in the days after a loved one's demise proves it. With the loss still raw, you have to force yourself through the trauma of choosing a coffin, applying for a death certificate, changing names on utility bills and performing all the administrative steps necessary to bring someone's existence to a formal end.

When it's all over, when the hymns are sung, when Dad's in the ground and Mum's upstairs trying to catch up on the sleep that has eluded her, I find myself for the first time this week on my own in the living room.

I stare at Dad's empty chair. I'm never going to see him sitting there again, I realise.

That's when the juggernaut of grief rams me at full speed. I cry guttural sobs from deep within my core. They clog my throat in staccato bursts. My whole body aches. It's physical and emotional, as if some part of me has been cut away.

I wasn't even close. He died while I was somewhere over Russia. So there were no last words between us. All I'm left with is the guilt that comes with having made my life on the other side of the world.

Don't be so stupid!

My breath stops at the sound of his gravelly voice.

Silence hits the room like ice-water. It's a loud silence, a dominating silence, the kind of silence that replaces an air-conditioner's constant drawl when you flick the off-switch. It stretches out in all its awkwardness, until I let the breath I'm holding spill from my lungs.

My mind is playing tricks, that's all.

And I know why.

There's a discussion Dad and I should have had but never did, and him chastising me for feeling guilty about living so far away is exactly how I imagined it would start.

It's his fault, you see. That story, the one I re-lived on the flight over, about him dumping paint over those Chinese statues back in '67, that's what started it, that's what ignited the craving I'd spent my whole life trying to suppress.

For Mum and Dad, Hong Kong was truly where East met West and I was the product of that union. But before Dad told me that story from his past, I had no interest in the place. England was my home, where I'd grown up, where I was going to stay. And back in

FIFTY-FIFTY

June 1997, it all seemed so easy. I'd just finished law school and was starting work in London after the summer. My life-path seemed set.

Then Dad told me of his brush with the law thirty years before and, somehow, it unbalanced my contented equilibrium.

It was jealousy, I guess. As a law student, I'd grown to love the common law system, the way it found dispassionate black-and-white answers out of grey, emotion-filled questions, and how it served the demands of justice in a changing world. But I knew that whatever else I went on to accomplish in my legal career, it would be nothing compared to the dramatic blow Dad had struck for British justice when he'd blue-painted those Bank of China lions that night.

The common law was English society's mighty oak, with roots stretching back 800 years to the Magna Carta. In Hong Kong, by contrast, the law was a mere sapling which, under the new constitution of the Special Administrative Region, had 50 years to take root. As auditions went, that wasn't long. The place was in need of good lawyers. The challenge piqued my interest.

But it was more than just an intellectual yearning that Dad had sparked. Whether I liked it or not, I was part Chinese. I'd spent my youth ignoring it, but Dad had made me question that decision. Could I ever be complete as a person, if there was this part of me which I continued deliberately to neglect? Soon, the issue plagued me like an embarrassing itch. Every time I went to a Chinese restaurant with my mother, and had to admit to being from Hong Kong, the looks of disappointment when I said I hadn't been back since I was 18 months old were shaming. I wondered if my own children would one day look at me that way, when I proved incapable of telling them anything about their heritage.

In 2003, just after my 30th birthday, fate finally intervened. My firm's Hong Kong branch was desperate for new staff. I hardly needed my arm twisted to sign up for two years.

Two years. It's a long time when you first step off the plane into that wall of unforgiving humidity. But two years has now become five and the English lifestyle I once dreamed of is a long-distant memory.

I dry my eyes and stare at Dad's empty chair again.

He understood why I went back. He never said, but I know he did. And I longed to tell him how I felt after five years getting to know the place. We never talked about that sort of thing in our telephone calls, so Dad never got to find out how my experience compared to his. He never got to ask whether I've managed to satisfy the yearning he ignited in me.

As I sit there in that hard silence, I want to have that conversation. But I can't just pretend he's sitting in his chair. If this is going to happen, it's going to happen in the confines of my own mind.

I shut my eyes, take deep breaths and begin slowly.

I imagine myself saying: "Hello Dad."

There's no answer. I begin to think this is futile, that it's stupid to think I can just conjure him up and ...

So you made it then!

His sandpaper voice is clear, as though it were smoothing down my inner ear.

"Dad? Is that you?"

Who do you think it is!

I should have known. Even in my imagination he's a grumpy old sod.

So how have you been?

"Fine," I say. "Apart from you dying."

Yeah. Sorry about that.

I'm still not convinced that my mental state can stretch this far. Then again, maybe this is what grief does to you? I decide just to see where it leads.

"Sorry I didn't make it back in time."

Don't worry about it.

I can picture him now. He's in that same toweled dressing gown, but it's only a head-and-shoulders shot. There's something peaceful about him. His cheeks still bunch up like a bulldog's, but his skin is shiny and fresh. His hair is white, but a vibrant, bountiful white. And I swear, even though I know this is only happening within the limits of my mind, I can smell Brut aftershave. A brand so cheap never had such a loyal member. It made Christmas and birthday gifts easy enough.

A sudden sadness moves through me, but Dad's voice is quick to stem it.

How's Hongkers then? You enjoying yourself?

"It's good," I say. "Work's going well and ..."

You think I want to hear about work? Tell me how you feel about the place?

There's a punchiness to his tone that's so unlike him and it sends me spiralling to the very heart of what I want to tell him.

I dish it up raw and devoid of sugar-coating.

"I'm never going to be as Chinese as you want me to be, okay?"

Silence. Disapproving, headmasterly silence.

"I've tried, believe me. But it's just never going to happen," I plead. "My Cantonese is so bad, people just laugh when I try to speak."

The corners of his mouth twitch upwards.

It's always good to have a party piece.

I look at him with incredulity. Here I am, expecting another lecture on how important history is, and all he can do is poke fun!

Oh come on, it was a joke.

Obviously death hasn't affected his sense of humour. He called it 'dry', I called it 'non-existent'.

Okay, so you don't feel Chinese. Well the truth is, you're not. Not fully, anyway. But at least you've tried to find out a bit more, that's something.

He then changes tack by asking: *How do you find living in Hong Kong?*

"Exactly the same." I blurt out. "I try to feel part of it and to an extent, I am. But I'm just a part that's been bolted onto the side. Like I'm half observer, half participant, and no good at either."

He nods his understanding. It encourages me to continue.

"The most terrifying thing is that's exactly how I feel about my English life now. I'm not part of it anymore, but I don't want to leave it behind. It's like being constantly suspended between two different worlds. Totally unsettling, I tell you."

Great, now he's chuckling at me.

"What?"

You know what you are? You're Eurasian.

I bristle at the thought, but that's as far as it goes. In the past, I would have been more vehement in my reaction, probably reeled off the names of the schools I'd attended and the football team I support, just to prove the depth of my Englishness. But all I find myself saying now is:

"I guess I am."

Dad moves the conversation on before I can retract.

Everybody felt displaced there in my day. They were always in transit, you see. Hong Kong was never a place to settle down in. People were there to work their socks off and make enough money to start a new life somewhere else. The place always had a temporary feel about it.

"Not anymore," I say. "Many of the Hong Kong Chinese from your generation have moved abroad, but the funny thing is their children have all come back. Most of the friends I've made were brought up in Australia or Canada, but they've all chosen to settle down in Hong Kong. They work hard, sure, but they don't want to leave. In fact, most weekends they spend on family shopping expeditions, just like we used to."

Dad's eyebrows furrow in disappointment.

Sounds more like Milton Keynes than part of China.

I feel myself smiling. "I wouldn't go that far, but in a way you're right. When I first arrived I was more impressed with how similar everything was to the UK rather than different."

So there's no more rioting in the streets then?

"... or people pouring blue paint over statues."

His face creases into a mischievous grin at the memory, but his brow soon crinkles again.

I bet no one's standing up to the Chinese, though.

"Hong Kong is Chinese," I say.

You know what I mean.

"Hardly ever." This time it's my turn to joke and his not to laugh. "Look," I say, "Hong Kong people do stand up to the Mainland government when they need to. But it's different from your day. They can't just riot and expect to be taken seriously, or they'll risk a crackdown. So when a protest is needed, it's a lot more ... what's the right word ..."

Boring?

"Subtle," I correct him.

Hmm.

I try to explain further. "Take the July 1st march, for example. That was in 2003, just after I arrived. People were fed up with the government's handling of SARS and annoyed at the way the Chief Executive was trying to introduce these new anti-sedition laws. Half a million people stood in the sun for over four hours and then walked from Victoria Park to Government House. And do you know what the amazing thing was? There wasn't a single arrest. Not one. Can you imagine that happening in London? Things would have kicked off big-time."

Did it work?

"The sedition laws were dropped pretty quickly and within a few months a new Chief Executive was installed, so what do you think?"

I see his mouth twist into a pout as he ponders that.

This march. Did you go on it?

"I did."

I can tell that pleases him.

"The sedition laws they tried to introduce could have undermined the whole justice system," I tell him. "I don't know if I was hallucinating because of the heat, but I thought of you that day. It felt like we were all defending the same thing that you'd stood up for thirty years ago. It was like, I don't know ..."—I try to reach for the right words— "like the past was reverberating and sending a ripple of shockwaves through to the present."

I see him nodding.

Nicely put.

We stay in silence for a moment.

You think the place will survive?

"Can't say for certain, but I like its chances," I say. "Hong Kong people seem to have an instinct about deciding what's negotiable and where to draw the line. I think that's what makes them unique. They're not brash like New Yorkers, or terribly polite like the Japanese, or world-weary like Londoners. But they do have this innate realism in everything they do, whether it's work, relationships or knowing when to stand up to the Mainland government and when to keep quiet. They don't follow the local politicians, who are constantly moaning about everything. They dictate the agenda and let the politicians catch up."

Funny. All people wanted to do in my day was make money.

"Well that hasn't changed," I say. "And I guess that's part of it. Hong Kong wants to be part of China because that's where the financial future lies. One-point-three billion consumers' worth. But people also realize that to make the best of it, Hong Kong has to preserve its own systems. That's what one country, two systems means and it's sort of become part of Hong Kong's national psyche. I mean, when Hong Kong people go abroad, they identify themselves as Chinese, but in the same breath say that they're from Hong Kong, as if to emphasize they're the same, but different. If you ask me, the more that distinctive identity takes root, the more chance there is of Hong Kong being there in fifty years."

What about you? Will you still be there?

The question catches me off-guard and even though I'm unprepared for it, an unequivocal answer seems to force its way to the surface.

"Unless I'm where you are," I say.

Dad looks at me then with an intensity that seems to envelope me in love. Our relationship was never touchy-feely, but still we had the strongest bond that any father and son could wish for. My mother was always my driving force. But Dad was my rock. Strong and dependable, always there for the big things.

I realize how much I'm going to miss him.

My chest tightens with the sense that we are nearing the end. Sadness and elation washes through me as Dad holds me in that one-in-a-million stare of his. His face transforms into a smile that seems to power out from the depth of his soul.

Give Mum a big hug from me.

"I will," I say.

I love you.

"I love you too, Dad."

Then, he gradually evaporates into the watery fingers that shimmer across my vision.

When I open my eyes, tears cascade down my cheeks. Mum is moving about upstairs. I don't want her to see my like this, so I wipe my face with the first piece of cloth that comes to hand, and when my vision clears, I find myself clasping the end of the tie I was wearing at the funeral.

The yellow-running-dog, red-fat-cat and white-skinned-pig are now damp with my tears.

And in that moment, I feel immensely proud of the man who was my father.

Chine
Alan Jefferies

The following objets trouvés (found poems) were collected from the "Around the Nation" column in the South China Morning Post *between 1998 and 2006.*

A taxi driver in Nanjing fell asleep at traffic lights for two hours before someone finally called the police. The driver failed to wake up until he was moved into an ambulance.

∞ ∞ ∞

A two-year-old child who superglued his eyes closed was turned away from four Nanjing hospitals. At the fifth, a woman doctor spent over two hours peeling back his eyes.

∞ ∞ ∞

A Chengdu resident plans to turn his house into a public toilet—to improve his standard of living. He Ming says there are only a few toilets in the area where he lives so providing one would increase his family's income. Mr. He is now awaiting Municipal Planning Bureau approval.

∞ ∞ ∞

A Chengdu temple is forcing a 72-year-old Taoist priest to reimburse it for the fake bank-notes he unwittingly collected during the Lunar New Year. A check of the forty-two 100 yuan notes found 28 were fakes.

∞ ∞ ∞

After snacking on soil for 11 years a 19-year-old woman from Inner Mongolia is seeking an explanation for her unusual eating habit, the *Dong Fang Jin Post* reports. The woman reportedly couldn't get to sleep without eating 100 to 500 grams of dirt a day.

∞ ∞ ∞

Liu Shu, a 19-year-old girl from Shenyang is hoping to get into the Guinness World Records by keeping her eyes open for more than two hours without blinking. *The China News Service* reports that people normally blink 15 times in a minute.

∞ ∞ ∞

The 13 winners of a secondary-school student beauty show were left red faced after they were given condoms as prizes. The organisers of the "Youth Image" contest defended the decision saying it promoted safe sex and a condom manufacturer had sponsored the event.

∞ ∞ ∞

A dentist has built three tooth towers using more than 50,000 decaying teeth, Xinhau reports. Yu Quin says he built the towers to remind people, especially rural residents, to take care of their teeth.

∞ ∞ ∞

The owner of a BMW returned to a Panjin car park on Sunday to find a letter on his vehicle. Tucked under the car's door handle, the letter said "I love you because you have a BMW." It also included a telephone number and a brief personal introduction.

∞ ∞ ∞

A professionally trained classical singer has offered to lament for a fee at funerals to make the services sound more touching. In advertisements, the singer says she can provide various kinds of laments. *The Liaoshen Evening News* reports she usually charges between 100 and 500 yuan an hour.

∞ ∞ ∞

A Daqing man has committed suicide after consuming the remains of his wife who died last year. A note detailed how he exhumed his wife's ashes on August 27, crushed them into a fine white powder and consumed a little each day for the next six months. After eating what was left of her, he took poison and died last week.

The Spoken Word
Susan Blumberg-Kason

Maybe I was ahead of my time or maybe I was yet again doing something unconventional, but somewhere between the signing of the Joint Declaration and the Handover, I landed in Hong Kong at the age of 19 to study Mandarin. I'm from a medium-sized town in the middle of America and ended up having the same conversations there before landing at Kai Tak in the summer of 1990. These were often awkward and confusing.

"Hi, Susan! Where are you in school these days?"

That was the easy part. "Well, college in Baltimore, but I'm actually going abroad this year."

"Wow! Where to?"

I knew they were expecting me to say England, France, or Spain, or maybe even a more exotic locale like Germany. "Hong Kong!"

"Do you speak Japanese?" they would ask awkwardly.

"No, I mean, yes, a little, but they speak Chinese in Hong Kong," I'd say, trying not to make them lose too much face. "And I've had a year of Mandarin here."

"Oh." They would be slightly embarrassed. "That's great!"

"Well, yes, but people speak Cantonese, another dialect. And a lot speak English since it's a British colony."

Now, confusion set in. "Are Cantonese and Mandarin that different?" they continued, feigning interest.

"Yeah, like English and German."

"Then why didn't you just start with Cantonese?"

"There are no Cantonese classes in the US, so I decided to take Mandarin to be able to read. Chinese writing is all the same, no matter the dialect."

I knew the next question, or rather, statement.

"Oh, so at least you can read the signs there."

"*Well* ..." and here, complete exasperation was obvious. "People in China use a simplified script, which is what I've studied. In Hong Kong, they use the traditional characters."

"Then *why* would you study Mandarin there?"

Tiananmen meant many people just assumed going to China wasn't an option, and they were correct in a way. My interest was Hong Kong.

I wanted to live in Hong Kong and decided to study Mandarin before going, not realizing the difference between simplified and traditional characters. But it didn't matter because I would be able to continue Mandarin back in the US. No one, though, seemed to have the patience to hear all that.

Back in the early 1990s, I had to go searching for Mandarin speakers in Hong Kong. Apart from my teachers, all of whom were either from Taiwan or not-so-recent arrivals from the mainland, I was hard pressed to find other native Mandarin speakers. Sure, there were the Taiwanese professors who taught my elective classes, but they spoke English to foreign students like me, Cantonese to the local students, administrative staff and the tea ladies, and Mandarin only amongst themselves.

Rumor had it that some antique dealers on Hollywood Road in Western district spoke Mandarin as their mother tongue. I found it odd that this very specific, small stretch of road on the Island was the only place to find native Mandarin speakers. After I had been in Hong Kong for about a month, one of my teachers told my class that it might be time to start practicing the language in a real-world context and mentioned the Hollywood Road proprietors. My five classmates and I all had had a rudimentary year of Mandarin in our home countries of the US, Canada, or Japan before coming to Hong Kong, but had little experience speaking it outside the classroom.

There was also a Mandarin-speaking enclave in a remote area of the New Territories, far from the university, at Rennie's Mill, where more than 6,000 former soldiers and Kuomintang sympathizers had settled. The coastline of Rennie's Mill was lined with Nationalist flags.

It seemed less invasive, though, to explore the shops on Hollywood Road than to trespass on residential spaces in Rennie's Mill in search of Mandarin speakers. So I made my way—an hour by train and subway—to the lively and crowded Western district with the aim of finding a Mandarin speaker. But alas, my shyness got the best of me. I did not have the guts to mill around until I heard someone speak Mandarin.

I had to fly out of Hong Kong to speak Mandarin outside the classroom. For Chinese New Year, I traveled to Nanjing and spent a week there in the countryside with the guide from my first trip to China three years earlier. Then, at Easter, I had a week for spring vacation, so I flew to Taiwan. That summer, I was on a domestic flight in Vietnam and sat next to a Vietnamese helicopter pilot. His English was minimal, my French was poor, but we found our common language in Mandarin. He had studied aviation in Beijing. It seemed like I could speak Mandarin anywhere but in Hong Kong.

Fast-forward three years. I'm back in Hong Kong after finishing college in the US, and working. With one suitcase, one carry-on, no job and a three-day reservation at the YMCA on Waterloo Road, I've returned to either find a job or start graduate school. On that flight back to Hong Kong, I sat next to a young, American missionary who had also lived in Hong Kong a few years back and learned about localization from him—the policy of hiring a local over an expat unless the position required "expertise" that only a foreigner could provide.

As luck would have it, I got accepted to graduate school and at the same time found a job in publishing. A local resident could have also done that job, but I guess the magazine was desperate to hire someone. I chose graduate school and was once again living on the same campus as I did three years earlier. This time, however, I found many more Mandarin speakers. About 200 mainland graduate students were enrolled that year at the university. Back in 1990, there were only a handful of mainland students on campus, but in 1994 there were enough to form a mainland student and scholar association. By then, I already had about five years of Mandarin, and became a member to practice the language and meet new friends. We went on day trips to the lovely beaches of Shek O and had karaoke and ballroom dance parties in the recreation room of one of the post-graduate hostels.

I also found opportunities in Hong Kong to speak Mandarin outside the university. Each time before I traveled to China, I visited a dark, sleepy China Travel Service (CTS) branch in Mongkok, rather than the busy office in Wanchai where all the foreigners went. Mr. Zhang, a northern Chinese who staffed the visa desk, got to know me because I was one of the few foreigners who regularly went to that branch for a China visa. I enjoyed my small chats with Mr. Zhang. I also answered an ad in the *South China Morning Post* for a Mandarin-English conversation exchange with a former editor from Beijing who now worked in Hong Kong for a small import-export company. I waited a few days before answering the ad, but was the first to call Mr. Wang. So, the exchange was arranged for each Friday in his Sheung Wan flat and was something I enjoyed that first summer back in Hong Kong. I stuffed *jiaozi* with Mr. Wang, his wife, and their seven-year-old son, Pinker, before my school work became too demanding.

In the few years before the Handover, some of my political-science professors from Taiwan began to plan their retirement, returning to Taiwan in 1996, 1997, or at the latest in 1998. Mainland professors who had studied in the US or the UK were hired as their replacements—the first wave of such mainland returnees. I was also able to speak Mandarin with my Hong Kong classmates, since most of them now spoke it. Even something as basic as eating became easier. In the past, I had a hard time ordering food at the canteens on campus because my Cantonese was so poor. During my first four months in Hong Kong, I ordered toast and jam every morning at the campus coffee shop because I could say jim do, but was too scared to attempt to say anything else on the menu. The canteen staff dispelled the notion that "everyone in Hong Kong speaks English", as I had been told by some Americans before I ever set foot in Hong Kong. I found that to be true only in touristy areas like Tsim Sha Tsui and Central.

Just before I started graduate school, a family from Beijing moved onto campus and ran the canteen in the post-graduate hostel. Then, I could converse away! Since the canteen proprietors spoke Mandarin, most of the mainland students ate there. It also helped that 75% of the post-graduate hostel was filled with mainland students. I married one of those students—a marriage that lasted 10% of the time period for which the "one country, two systems" was guaranteed. After graduation, my mainland husband and I searched for a flat near campus. The real-estate agents in the New Territories mainly spoke Cantonese. Some spoke a little Mandarin, and few spoke good English. My then-husband often had to speak Cantonese, with a strong mainland accent, to the leasing agents. But as it turned out, our landlord spoke fluent English, but no Mandarin, so he mainly spoke to me about our lease.

As the Handover came and went, mainland tour groups began traveling to Hong Kong for pleasure. Not since before 1949 had so many mainland citizens been able to travel for leisure outside of China. The service industry in Hong Kong is one of the best in the world, and without a doubt lived up to its reputation by adopting Mandarin and catering to this new demographic of travelers from north of the border. Mainland couples are also coming to Hong Kong as a wedding destination these days. When I got married in Hong

Kong in 1995, the marriage official did not speak Mandarin, so she spoke in Cantonese and English, I spoke in English and my then-husband spoke in Mandarin. In academia, there are now so many mainland students at all the universities in Hong Kong, not only at the graduate level, but at the undergraduate one as well. The universities are recruiting the top mainland students and offering them scholarships they can't refuse.

Some Hong Kong friends recently told me that Cantonese was rarely spoken in U.S. Chinatowns 30 years ago. It used to be only Taishanese. Then Cantonese became the predominant language, and now Mandarin is quickly becoming more popular. I wonder how long Cantonese will stay the predominant language in Hong Kong? In less than 20 years, native Mandarin speakers have gone beyond the antique stores of Hollywood Road and the KMT settlement at Rennie's Mill. One can now hear Mandarin almost everywhere in Hong Kong—in stores and restaurants, on the KCR and MTR, and on the streets. It seems that the post-Handover mainland immigrants are bringing their language outside the walls of their homes and into Hong Kong society—for good. What will the next few decades bring in terms of language to Hong Kong?

Ten Days of Cholera Epidemic
Kwai-Cheung Lo

Let us walk on tiptoe, you say, the salty toothpaste in the morning
Or the lingering odor in the mouth which rises when you hiccup after
A hastily consumed Chinese, sometimes Western, meal at noon and the slight tremble of the body
The already upright toes

Slowly become soles falling solidly on the road surface, you go on talking about ballet dancers and
Tightrope walkers whose movements suggest the way
Foreign tourists maneuver chopsticks, nervously breaking up some hard-boiled seafood
Use an unstable medium

Working on something and enjoying something, you think the use of
Language is just as bizarre and strange, like you can hold on
And then you cannot. The reality of photographs, television screen and radio finally catches up with us
Yet that which is around cannot be seen

There should be a kind of power that touches, that impresses us, you say
All images disappear all of a sudden, reality is something with part of the real omitted
During the time of epidemic, put aside conventional life

Seek a kind of disorderly ease

Teeth no longer feverishly kept clean hum a sweet song,
   you sing out
The colorful explanations printed on the labels of canned
   food, to the previous
Angry generation the world is still so new, amid ideas
   unable
To be sorted out, shoelaces wrongly done up, and buttons
   fitted into wrong holes

You gesture with your hands, say you would have your
   hair cut short and then let the short hair grow long
   again
You refuse to stay in a certain image, every time you try
   to find dainty patterns
Round the clothes you take off, you perform a ritual dance
   and sprinkle some white powder
As homage to the new tradition

You always like to look down as you repair the lamp
   hanging from the ceiling
To estimate wind speed, gradient and obscure distances,
   just like the mode of expression
You want to speak and as a rule you cannot speak out
   what you want to speak, so you talk nonsense
To keep the equilibrium of the roof

Maintaining balance in mid-air, your feet toy with your
   pair of high-heels to feel
The delicious taste of fish, the entangled but depthless
   content of its opened belly
Send a line far off, among the sun-dried laundry you
   search for hints of the wearers
Journey between crevices and darns

Well how can you keep a door open at the same time you
   close it
As easily as you switch off the television, press the
Polaroid, and let reality emerge and disappear
Face strange people and events, try hard to make words

FIFTY-FIFTY

        sound more tactful
Defend while implying offence

In order to see your name in the telephone directory a hundred pages thick
To persist in retaining from the publicly acknowledged instrument of communication
A tenuous thread of personal romance, to believe in spite of everything that between cut-up frames and the fragmented reality
All that is not pure has the possibility of beauty

Mapping moments

Reinterpretations of Three Poems by Leung Ping Kwan
Arthur Leung

I. Tea

The teacup refuses
to show a face within,
only the tealeaf heralds
a visiting friend
bobbing its stalk.

I raise the solitary
teacup showing shadows
flickering within,
sending fragrance
intruded by bitterness

while hidden jasmine petals
gather and disperse
sewing patterns.
Light spots on the tea,
hot and brown, counted

like eyes
drifting in silence,
or stars of summer
that appear from sky's
entrance and vanish
through cloud's exit;

trivialities

FIFTY-FIFTY

    make distance,
    there is no moment
    to drink to each—
    meetings by chance
    were felt like fragrance
    of tea, far away.

    II. Old City

    So neat is a row of bicycles
    that pass but not the ringing bell,
    pass the gray buildings and separate.

    Some pedal far and vanish
    at a turn, others stop by the queue
    of a foodstore dimly lit, customers
    eating under banners, heads lowered.

    So neat row by row as they pass
    the door, so neat their fading behind
    gray buildings, but not the ringing bell.

    In Cultural Park we sit by roots
    of an old tree, sipping tea for a cent.
    My friend wonders where to buy soap
    to wash away the dust on his face.

    I keep silent, watch the woman
    sweep away fallen leaves
    but not the dust of this city.

    III. Opening Sea Urchins

    By the hut
    women in blue open sea urchins
    in heaps black sea urchins
    in heaps furious spikes
    in heaps clamps break and pry open the tough hearts
    in heaps women scoop out

tenderness
from that golden yellow.

Walking a day's journey, overcoming black rocks
in heaps worn-out faces
in heaps finally we see
in heaps through a mountain crack
gentleness
of an ocean.
By the store you sit
amidst women in blue.
Out of seawaves
out of broken urchin shells
out of the coffee you sip and say

face of spring—reflection in coffee
as the milk dissolves slowly
out of the soft heart.

Leung Ping Kwan is one of Hong Kong's leading men of letters, a literary, film and culture critic. Mr. Leung is a professor of Chinese Literature and a contemporary Chinese-language poet, with ten published volumes of his works.

Penny's Bay
Woo See-Kow

Will you dance with me
under the moonlight
at Penny's Bay?

We'll get our ourselves lost
in the sound of the waves
by the smell of the sea

Let the warm fingers
of the damp sultry air
caress your face

Put your hair down

Slip off your shoes

You and I will tango
across the wet dancing floor
swing to the music
from a singing sea

Nothing will be left behind
in the morning
not even our footprints
but our tender memories
of what this place once was

Before old Penny's Bay
is no more

Before the music stops

Will you dance with me?

volar
Akin Jeje

stares
blank hidden by glazed polaroid aviator glasses in the crush
of the blaring club, glitter and indigo fluorescent shadows
over finely-set grimaces, fierce animation with the white crystals,
the crystal hi-balls
chopped ice, Grey Goose and golden Red Bulls jet-set fuels
for pride and prejudice
complete with waves of aural narcotic syncopated bass
swaying and crashing tumultuous currents
over black marble walls
over the chattering and gnashing of pills
where I am alone,
as everyone else is, in the forced intimacy
of this ninth circle, where everyone is a name
on or off a membership list
but nothing but electronically churned black ink
on a financial sheet matters,
no hot boy or it girl
or any other writhing body
shimmering on the dance floor
tonight or any other

void of compassion beneath the well-sculpted smiles
unspeakable pain under practiced arrogant
stares

pity or envy wasted emotions, in an enclosed space
where there is little left
to care

Ode to the Mass Transit Railway
Arthur Leung

One day you take a train
that travels west for east,
don't feel regret,
quit and shift your feet
to the opposite platform,
the few extra minutes
aren't too much for you to lose.

Or simply get out
at the farther Tin Hau,
have a sunny stroll backwards,
or take a breezy break
at Victoria Park—
what's wrong will easily
become alright.

Worse still, you nap
until the train stops
at Sai Wan Ho,
forget the clock striking
12 hours 53,
be relaxed & leave,

take the bus 14
to Stanley & change the plan
with your whatever friend,
perhaps indulge yourself
in an exotic restaurant
for a romantic afternoon,

your hours so wisely spent.
Oh, some day you'll be on a train that passes
the terminus (Chai Wan) & keeps going,
You'll break the ground & shoot up for the sky,
experience a few turnabouts
in the air, fly with planes & galaxies,

scream highly above
where you'll come to land.

I for Illness
Nicholas Y. B. Wong

"From the beginning the construction of the illness had depended on notions that separated one group of people from another—the sick from the well ..."

—Susan Sontag

Ian habitually opened his wallet to see if he had enough money for the night. Tuesday, and the Venice Club should be featuring Swimwear Night, the Double E: Entertainment and Excitement. It was the only night in a week when he could fully indulge his fantasies. Satisfied or not, he at least had the chance to fantasize. *Being Ian is wonderful but unbearable*, he always thought.

In his wallet, there was a photo of himself as a toddler. Little Ian was smiling at the people out of the frame. He does not know who was there when the photo was taken, but the hands of those unremembered strangers were touching his reddish, untarnished skin. His face, his chin, his hair, his shoulders were all touched. A significant and reassuring human touch. Ian sighed and prepared to leave his office.

He glanced over the compartment that separated his seat from Harvard's and was disappointed to see that he had already gone. His new colleague was in his early twenties, six foot tall, with broad shoulders and a physique Ian would die for. His single eyelids seemed to send out seductive signals to Ian from the moment he arrived. *There's always something about his eyelids.* Those eyelids had the power to create a cult among all the gay men living on this lost planet! Even so, Ian did not cross the border of work ethics. Occasionally, his head climbed over the compartment and they would chit chat, usually for less than a minute. The desk compartment was the Berlin Wall, dividing two species. Its solidity, however, invited trespass.

At the elevator lobby, Ian couldn't help comparing his reflection on the door to Harvard. Total loser—chubby, fair skin, a few wrinkles on his 32-year-old face, receding hairline, average height and mediocre fashion sense. He looked okay, but unable to amuse anyone by existing. At this moment, Harvard appeared.

"What're you looking at?" Harvard asked. His voice was manly.

"Oh! You're here. I didn't see you leaving."

"I went over to HR to fill in some forms. Shirley said the first paycheck didn't make it through to my account."

"Don't worry, you'll get the money sooner or later. I hope you're not too tight financially."

Harvard looked embarrassed and his flushed face simply made him more adorable. "Well, to be honest, I'm quite tight this month," he admitted.

"I'm sorry. But, you know, it's a miracle to know someone in Hong Kong who has savings," Ian comforted the Adonis, his mind sorting out the implications of *tight*.

The elevator door opened. There was hardly any space for two people to squeeze in. Harvard stepped in first, attracting the hideous gazes of all the overworked office ladies. "Come on in, Ian."

Ian put his right foot forward, worried that the elevator would be overloaded once he got in. Safe. His arm was against Harvard's chest. His fingers brushed the inviting fabric of Adonis's suit.

Harvard was speaking. "Yeah, you're so right. I need to do some savings and investment as well. Since '97, the stock market has kept rising. Can you believe the index passed 20,000? Anyway, where are you going now?"

"Me? Well, I need to buy something in Mongkok and then I'm seeing some friends for dinner." The silence in the elevator was an amplified truth detector.

"Really? What're you trying to get?"

"Just a gift, for my friend. It's her birthday next week. So how about you?"

"I'm seeing my girlfriend."

"Good! Dating is good. I wish I had a date. A girlfriend can make you feel more existential."

Harvard grinned. Meanwhile, Ian was cursing his mythical girlfriend: *That lucky little cunt must have done something great in her previous life. She must be St Joan of Arc or Mother Teresa.*

The elevator reached ground, ending the intimacy. "I'll see you tomorrow," Harvard said.

The MTR train was crowded, as usual. Thank god, it was his sacred chance to be closer to people in his daily life. Around him, the singletons were texting their friends or families to make dinner plans, while some were reading magazines or newspapers. Of course, the couples were cuddling and submerged in a world of their own. Ian fondled his mobile phone and pressed the buttons meaninglessly, entertaining the hard metallic cold, until the train reached Causeway Bay.

At the entrance of Venice Club, Ian closed his eyes and rang the bell. Harvard, wearing only a cowboy hat and muddy boots, was waiting for him at the reception counter. *You're probably tired of herding sheep. Riding too much on a horse does your butt no good, buddy.* Harvard wasn't sweating at all. His naked and hairless body smelled better than lavender. The cowboy tilted his hat with one hand and stroked his semi-hard penis with the other. "Welcome, Ian. The admission fee is $120 tonight."

Ian's eyes opened. The door was unlocked and he went in. At the reception counter, he saw the same old arrogant sissy. "How much?" Ian inquired. The receptionist looked away and pointed his bitchy finger at the price stand on the desk. Ian opened his wallet and saw his own childhood photo again. Visualization of human contact overwhelmed him. He placed the money on the desk and was given a locker key to unlock the heavenly door of the Double E.

Inside the total darkness of Venice Club, everybody was wandering around in their swimwear. No pool in the world could contain water enough to quench the cruising desire. Ian was wearing an over-priced white Speedo that he just got from ebay, hoping someone would recognize it as the latest summer collection. The tight fabric provoked undressing, but no one stopped thanks to his belly and flaccid arms.

In the distance, Ian saw slim young fitness fingering the nipples of a medium-build in the dark corner. The man's head was back against the wall, revealing a curved and solid Adam's apple. Ian walked towards them and gradually, the man's moaning reached his ears. Ian stopped next to the boy, wanting to entertain him while he pleasured another. Ian extended his arm and closed his eyes. Harvard had abandoned his nomadic cowboy image and transformed into Satosi Tsumabuki in *Waterboys*, Ian's all-time favourite movie. Ian looked down and found that Harvard was also wearing the same white Speedo, but it was too small to hide the erect penis, which was escaping from the tight trunks, reddened and a bit wet. Desire defeated the powerless foreskin. Ian slid his hand along Harvard's muscular arm and let the skin guide him through ecstasy.

"Get your hand off me!"

Ian opened his eyes.

"Just get off, would you?" the young boy repeated. He pushed Ian's arm away and walked into a dark room with the medium-built man, abandoning Ian to melancholy.

Ian was humiliated but he was already used to it. He just couldn't feel *more* humiliated. Here at Venice Club almost every Tuesday, he deserted his dignity if he wanted to touch and to be touched. Laying a hand on someone's body made him feel connected. It enhanced his existence, this landscape of numerous nameless chests. He felt at ease as a functional being in the bustling city, where individuals were segregated. Just a hand and a touch was all that Ian had longed for.

Wandering in the lightless aisles, Ian passed several locked doors, behind which gorgeous men must be fucking like hell. He cruised a while, stopping at spots where men gathered to flirt. Whenever he joined in, the crowd would scatter, either moving to another Ian-less spot, or going into a dark room without inviting him. The countless rejections of the night made his penis shrink like a snail into its shell. Just before Ian made up his mind to call it a night, he saw a short hairy guy jerking himself off in the reading area, with his eyes closed. His penis was not magnificent, but the gutsy masturbating in the most lighted area in the club aroused Ian. He walked and sat quietly next to him. The hairy guy neither moved away nor shot him an inviting glance. *Am I too invisible to be noticed?* Ian wondered. *Or is he actually welcoming me by not kicking me away? I shouldn't think too much. It makes my dick go soft.*

Ian made his move. "Do you want to go in there?" He whispered into the hairy guy's ear.

The guy opened his eyes. "Go in where?"

"The dark room."

"Only if you're good."

Ian closed the sliding door of the dark room. In the shadowy space, Harvard appeared again, lying naked on the stinking mattress, waiting for a good fuck. Ian was completely turned on. He climbed over Harvard's god-like body and licked every inch of his delicate skin. Harvard took a submissive and quiet role. Whatever Ian was doing to him, he simply lay there without doing anything in return. This satisfied Ian's desire to be on top. Maybe Ian was being too rough. During the course of foreplay, he had hurt Harvard a bit, by either biting too hard or fingering too deep. Harvard made uneasy noises. But Ian the barbarian did not notice his partner's discomfort and continued to exert his erotic hostility. His tongue moved from

Harvard's pelvis to his slender but firm legs, wetting the hairs with his saliva. And finally he reached his toes, where Ian's magical tongue exhibited its speed and rhythm. At that point, his partner pushed him away and flicked the light switch. In a blink, the room was not dark anymore.

"What the fuck are you doing?" the short guy complained.

"Don't you like it?" Ian replied innocently.

"Oh! You still need to ask? What's your problem?"

"Problem? What problem? I thought you would like it."

"Toe-sucker? No fucking way."

"That's what I saw in the porns. The guy being sucked gets very high and keeps yelling for more."

"You're *insane*, pervert."

"If you don't like me sucking your toes, I can still make you cum without it."

"No, thanks. I'm just not kinky enough for you."

"But we can still fuck! I brought the swimming goggles with me. They're in the locker. I can go and get them if you want. Goggles and my white Speedos are erotic, aren't they?"

"Are you out of your fucking mind?" the short guy sighed. "You're the craziest freak I've ever seen." He stood up and headed towards the sliding door.

Ian blocked his way. "Where're you going? We're not finished here."

"We're so finished. Now, you step aside."

"How so? You still haven't touched me."

"How dare you still have guts to ask me to touch you. I told you I am not into this kind of sex."

"Oh? Why not? You could call me names, any names you want when I'm inside you. It'll be a lot of fun!"

The short guy shook his head. "You're pathetic. I mean it. Move away from the door."

Ian didn't move. "I could fuck you without a condom. We can do bare back. I know a lot of guys like doing that here. I tried that and they couldn't resist."

"Fuck! Without condoms? Now, don't you ever touch me. I don't want to be infected."

"I wouldn't be that lucky, would I?"

"You never know." The short guy pushed past Ian and made his way out.

"You're really going? Can you at least touch my dick for a while before you go? It's so hard. I'm sure you'll like it."

The short guy turned around. "You're really sick. Go get yourself a shrink." Then he walked away from the dark room.

"Hey, you! Come back!"

The short guy kept walking and raised a middle finger. "Go fuck yourself."

Ian had no choice but to leave the room. He headed to the shower and let the hot water wash away his failure. On his way out, he found a secret portal that he had not noticed before. There was a light shining at him. All the people were gone. He advanced slowly towards the light, hoping some sexy guys would be miraculously hungry for his body. The light swelled larger and he discovered that the end of the portal was an opening to another room, one he had never visited before.

The room was all white. There was a sofa on one side and a chair on the other. A man was seated on the sofa reading the papers. Ian could not see his face clearly because he was wearing a pair of swimming goggles, the same pair Ian had. He was also wearing the same white Speedos. The man's physique was similar to his. For a moment, he thought he was looking into a mirror.

"You're finally here," the man sounded like an oracle.

"What do you mean? I've been here for two hours." Ian said.

"No. I don't mean there. I mean here."

"What here and there? What are you talking about."

"Never mind. You wouldn't understand even if I told you. Anyway, please take a seat. We have to talk."

"Why should I? Who are you?" Ian asked, feeling confused.

"When I ask you to sit down, you sit down. As simple as that. So now, take a seat in that chair."

"No. You're strange and I'm leaving." Ian looked around to leave, but the opening to the space had disappeared.

"As you can see, there's no exit. We're locked, in a way. Don't worry, I'll let you go after we're done talking."

"Why should I trust you?"

"First, you have no other choice but to listen to me. Second, I rule this dimension and my words are golden. So now, sit down."

Ian reluctantly succumbed. "Tell me who you are."

"That's a tough question." The man put down the papers. "I can be Mark Anthony, Keanu Reeves, Jake Gyllenhaal, Josh Harnett or even Daniel Wu, if you don't know the names I just mentioned. Simply put, I can be anyone you fantasize about."

"You're insane. Stop your bullshit and let me go," Ian said impatiently.

"You want to go? But your body hasn't been touched yet. Is that what you want? To drag a rejected sad body into your own bed and jerk yourself off ?"

"That's not your business."

"Why?"

"Because I don't know you. Got it, lunatic?"

"You think you don't know me? Every time you're here, I'm here, reading papers in this funny room. I've been waiting for you to come talk to me."

"That's impossible. I know this place very well. That portal didn't exist!"

"Then, tell me why you're here," the man retorted.

"I don't know. I really don't. I wish I did."

"You only see what you want to see. I don't blame you on this. Every gay man is like this. You and I are the same. We're all cruisers in the ghetto. Wonderful and unbearable at the same time."

The man removed his goggles. Ian stood up and scrutinized the man's face. It was like looking at the elevator door once again. "Now, come over and sit next to me." The man patted the sofa to signal Ian to move. Ian sat down slowly, still staring at the face. Suddenly, he was calmed by his proximity to a person who had no intention of leaving him. The two men were now on the same side and gazed at the empty chair opposite.

"Would you touch me?" Ian asked.

The man hesitated for a while and said, "I've always touched you. You just didn't notice."

"When?" Ian asked.

"So many times that I can't even remember."

"You sound very vague. I'm not sure I follow what you're saying, actually. You popped out from nowhere all of a sudden and gave me the most enigmatic talk I've heard. But I *do* feel secure around you. I don't know why."

"It's nice of you to say this, but the fact is ... I will hurt you if I touch you."

Ian smirked. "No. You'll like the feeling after putting your hand on my body."

"See? You still don't understand," the man disagreed. "You're not going to be satisfied, are you? It's like pouring water into a leaking glass. But you refuse to see a tiny hole at the bottom of it. You're deceiving yourself. All the people in Venice Club are dreamers. They fantasize about being kissed and touched. They want someone to remember them, to know of their existence. No one will! Men can't remember a thing after getting laid."

"It's just a touch. Don't make a fuss about it."

"Gay men ask for too much but they never give anything back. Even if I touch you, I only touch your skin. I can't reach your heart. The only people who can touch your heart are the doctors. They cut you open. You lose a huge amount of blood to get your heart touched. Everything has a price."

Ian did not respond. He gazed at the empty chair, imagining Harvard sitting in it and opening his legs to welcome him.

"Not that I want to sound like a saint here. I'm saying this to you because I'm sick," the man said.

Ian turned to look at the man who was still facing the empty chair. "Go and see a doctor. You'll be fine soon."

"No, I won't. That's why I come here just to talk. I dare not touch anyone. I'm afraid of hurting them."

"Don't be such a drama queen!"

"I'm serious and so is my illness. My body will finally turn into its own rival and defeat me. My only killer will be myself. Isn't that horrible?"

"Oh, you mean you are one of those ..."

The man interrupted. "Yes, you're right. I'm one of those 487. Before you came, I was reading a headline about myself. The stock market has ups and downs, but *this* figure hasn't dropped since '97. It keeps rocketing to stunning levels. If this figure can be invested, many people in Hong Kong wouldn't have to live below the poverty line." The man pointed at the papers he was reading.

"How does it feel to read news about yourself?"

"It's like eating something you've cooked for yourself. It's not very good but you still have to eat it. When you take the first bite, an inner voice says, *Only you can take care of yourself*. Maybe you should read the papers as well, then you'll know how I feel." The man passed Ian the papers. "I'm about to go."

"How about me? How can I leave here?"

"Just read the papers and take a rest. When you wake up, you'll be back in the dark room where you came from," the man murmured and strolled towards the wall. His body slowly twisted, deformed like an amoeba. In a few seconds, it was devoured by the whiteness of the walls.

Ian opened his eyes and gazed at the black ceiling. He was still in the dark room where he drove the short guy away by sucking his toes too hard. He woke up on the semen-stained mattress and headed towards the shower. He was the only one left in the club. Ian had not cum, but the exploding urge was gone. After a hot shower, he looked at himself in the mirror. He touched his own face softly with one hand and looked into his own eyes. *Do I look familiar to myself? Do I only see what I want to see?* He did not know the answer, but he had no problem identifying himself now. *This is probably what I am.*

Before he left Venice Club, he returned the locker key to the sissy receptionist, who was impatient for him to leave so that he could close down the place. Ian shook his head slightly to express his dissatisfaction at the frigid hospitality. As he turned around and headed to the door, a six-foot-tall man crashed into his shoulder and hurried to the reception. He asked, "Are you closed yet?" Ian was attracted by the manliness of the voice. He looked back. He could barely see the face of the man through the closing door, but he was glad his shoulder was touched.

The Beautiful Game
Martin Alexander

Beautiful game? Don't give me that—football
Diminishes us all, coarsens the soul
Makes the mild man vicious: watch him put ball
And foot together—whack—the only goal
Is "Put the boot in!" on or off the field.
Zidane was football's gent but there he went,
A head-butt, just because he wouldn't yield.
But wait—you know a sonnet has to turn
And here it comes: there's no amount of stick
Or whingeing at the cash those comets earn
Will counteract the magic of the kick—
That moment when, three-nil, your team is spent—
They're fucked, with fifteen desperate minutes left to go—
Yet make their miracle: a draw. And *then* you know.

10 October 2006

Chung Yeung:
Lamma Island 2006
Kate Rogers

I

Along the path to old Mo Tat, a sweet flag
of scent flutters in the Feng Shui woods.

Pale ginger flowers crowd the lotus ponds.
Untamed banyans, disorderly stands of bamboo
colonize the temple's grey skeleton.
Every empty house promises bird song at dawn,
kitchen geckos chirping through purple night.

II

But it is Chung Yeung, so we seek the highest point
to save ourselves and the family
friends have become, from historic danger.
We strain up this steep slope, bending our backs,
filling the flabby sacks of our lungs with gritty
oxygen. Shoulders scoop air, yet chests cannot
inflate enough to float us to the top of this scrubby
mountain. I dizzy with trying, joints grate
their sockets. My gaze treads water
in the South China Sea, where thirty cool minutes ago, I swam
among rented junks, discarded bagels and the deflated red sails
of cocktail napkins. Where the jab of a sea urchin spine
   was cause

for celebration—something still bristling with life on the ocean
   floor.

Here at the top, the coal-fired air of Lamma Power Station sears
my nose. From this dragon's back I stare at Sham Wan beach
and wonder where green turtles will nest when the sea
swallows it whole. We each inhale a puff of Ventolin,
wait for our ragged breaths to slow and smooth.

III

In twenty years, after the poles have melted,
the white bears of my northern
home become myth,
the sea reclaimed Hong Kong,
who will tell

the story of Chung Yeung? Who will offer
the children rainbows
as the flood waters rise?

Once Upon the Lamma Hills
Agnes S. L. Lam

Once upon the Lamma hills,
there was a man
in flowing white,
one of the ancients,
so it seems,
painting into the air,
with his hands, his feet, every
muscle of himself, every cell
in his body, all emotions
he had ever felt
blended into one,
bare contours
of a crane,
another,
and another ...

There was no one around him.
There had never been anyone—
only the hills from of old
and the sky hanging low.

He needed no palette
of ink in different tints ...

... for at the cleft of time when
a particular sun shines through the fog,
a few times in each century,
the cranes he drew will flutter alive
into the wind

in shades of all
imagination, always
a little before
the colours of a season.

If you take the ferry
from the IFC in Central
after you pass the Pokfulam shoreline
on your left, walk for about fifteen minutes from the pier
through the bustle of restaurants from every clime and land,
rattan baskets from Taiwan, Thai desserts spilling from shops,
estate agents selling apartments, a million each, goldfish
circling each other in glass bowls, silk scarves from
China caressing your arms
as you pass,

you will find
a narrow footpath
winding its way
up to the Lamma hills ...

If you leave
family, lovers, strangers
behind and go

alone

to the crest of the Lamma hills,
at the crack of time when
the mist lifts, the dawn breaks,
you may see these birds of heaven still
rising above the hills,
one flock but
all alone—

a pale rainbow floating
across the forest sky ...

On Mark Malby's photograph, "Misted Hills", December 2006

254 **Petal Beauty**
Yuen Siu Fung Phoenix

A petal can't resist the wind,
Falls, remote soil where it withers.
A frosted remnant, under cruel foot quivers,
Floats to make hoarse gloomy flutes.
Armed leaves drop to pacify brutes of winter
As they decay in fertile ground.
A petal's kept fresh by its foreign collector.

Line of Division
Shirley Lee

standing in a bikini
water up to my neck
I plunge in
to the halfway point of my eyeballs
waves divide the two worlds

there must be a line of division
between
the air
that does not sink
into water
and
the water
that does not spill
into everywhere

but even when I'm half submerged
my head exposed to the midday sun
there is no line of division

Apocalypse now & then

The Mangrove Island
Michael Gibb

"If survival is an art, then mangroves are artists of the beautiful."
—*Annie Dillard,* Sojourner

Ternia and her father Arnal reached the island under cover of night and hauled the kayak out of the waves, their bare feet sinking in the mud. The man pulled with one hand, the other reaching for balance. He squinted to keep the rain out of his eyes, raincoat buffeting in the wind. Ternia struggled to keep her footing in the waves and dropped to her knees, breathing heavy, limbs numb.

—*Over there.* Her father at her side, lifting her up, his voice stolen by the wind.

—*Over there.* Pointing into the gloom.

They pushed inland across the soft flats, the boat leaving a scar in its wake. The soil hardened as they drew further from the sea and the rain became a thick drizzle. Moonlight illuminated the terrain during breaks in the cloud cover and they stopped where the vegetation grew thickest.

Ternia slumped, eyes dulled with hunger, her face pale as the stars. Arnal looked for dry ground where the tallest shrubs grew.

—*This'll do.* Working fast, he retrieved his backpack and a bolt of canvas from the hull and shoved the kayak under the bushes and crawled in after. Using the bamboo stick around which the canvas was wrapped, he erected a lean-to. Ternia followed, stooping to avoid catching her jacket on the over-hanging branches and sat and dried herself. Arnal squatted next to her and dried himself, too.

—Are we there yet? Ternia's fringe falling in thick strands over her forehead, head on her knees. She still felt shaken from the crossing and gripped handfuls of earth as if for balance. Ternia had been petrified the boat would capsize and they would risk contamination. No-one could be sure if this stretch of coastline was clean. No-one knew the extent of the damage.

—I reckon we've got to head west, over that ridge. Leaning out of the shelter, Arnal felt the prick of rain on his face. To the west a hill arched like a hissing cat. *Yep, that'll be it.*

—Will there be food? The dull ache of hunger had drained Ternia of energy.

—I don't know.

—People?

—I'm not sure. We'll see. He passed Ternia a fresh mask.

—Dad? The cord tight round the back of her head.

—Do you want to stay and rest?

Ternia shook her head, eyes widening at the thought of being alone.

—Let's get going then.

They strapped on their boots, their feet smeared black with mud, and crawled out from under the shelter. Arnal shouldered his backpack and the pair trudged off, chins tucked into their chests. They found a track and ascended the hill in stages, Arnal pausing for his daughter to catch up. When she did, blowing hard into her cheeks, Arnal had to suck back the emotion. Her frail body, sunken cheeks. Weeks without adequate nutrition and Ternia was running on empty. Not finding food was not an option. A fever or whatever bacteria now drifted in the atmosphere could end his daughter's life. He'd already lost his wife, Ternia's mother, to a disease no-one had understood, and his sole reason for continuing was Ternia.

As they journeyed up from the south, past the rows of apartment blocks that stood like giant tombstones in the suburbs of the emptied cities, past dried-up rivers and fields of rotting crops, he repeated the promise he'd made his wife. That no matter what, Ternia would survive.

Within a half hour they were at the top of the hill. Arnal waited while Ternia excused herself and stepped off the path, brushing sodden branches out the way. She crouched next to a grave that overlooked the black sea, the cold breeze on her face. She felt like lying down and sleeping. When finished, she pulled up her jeans and leaned over to read the inscription next to her. The lettering was barely visible and the marble slab on which the headstone stood had fractured, as though stamped upon by an enraged spirit. She ran a finger over the faded characters.

Ternia rejoined her father and they continued along the ridge in silence, negotiating a path wet with decaying leaves.

Eventually, a set of steps appeared.

–This it? Ternia leant against a tree trunk, cushioned by her backpack. She was taking deep breaths.

Arnal didn't reply. He stood at the top step and peered into the darkness. What he saw didn't look promising. Not a single light. No evidence of camp fires. Nothing. The only sound branches scratching in the wind, like old men fencing with canes.

–We'll go down and look. Arnal took his daughter's hand. The air felt heavy with soot, reminding Arnal of the mining towns they'd skirted on their journey up from the south where ash blew in the breeze and the horizon glowed yellow. They pressed their masks close to their mouths, listening for signs of human activity, heard none.

At the bottom of the steps, a pathway led them through the main village. They advanced in silence. Most buildings had fallen into disrepair. Walls caved in as if punched out during a neighbourhood dispute. Doors hanging off hinges like consumptive men hacking in the dirt. Bundles of rags down side-streets covering the bones of the unburied.

Ternia read the faded storefront signs as they passed underneath. Poon's Seafood Restaurant. Dai Dai Thai Food. Betty's

Ice-cream Parlour.

　—*Are you sure this is Lamma?* Ternia stopped outside a derelict restaurant. *Was I born here?*

　—*No, I was. You were born just over the border.*

　—*Mum?*

　—*Kowloon.*

　—*So don't you recognize it here?*

　—*No.* Arnal took a look around. *Not at all.*

Rumours of survivors living on an island off Hong Kong had filtered down to Arnal and Ternia weeks before. Arnal guessed that island was Lamma, where he'd been born forty years ago.

　Now, looking round the Lamma village, Arnal reckoned any survivors had slaughtered each other over what scant resources remained, or had left, probably for the northern cities.

　Arnal gripped his daughter's hand and they traipsed on, mulching the grey cinders into the wet mud underfoot, until they reached the end of the main track where one building stood taller than the rest, its walls mostly intact. The sign above the doorway read in faded lettering Sunshine Property and Real Estate.

　The irony almost made Arnal smile.

　—*Shall we look inside?*

　Arnal nodded, patted the walls and then pushed the door open, the metal panels scratching against the cement. Boots crunching on bits of glass, he ducked into a damp office, his flashlight casting troubled shadows over the ceiling. A computer monitor lay on a low desk splayed open as if awaiting surgery and rusted metal supports in the walls were revealed like bloodied bone.

　Arnal checked the overhead shelves, stooped to look inside cupboards for anything they could eat. Nothing but an old screwdriver, a mug with no handle and a jar of nails. As he looked, his flashlight caught something shiny under the desk and Ternia reached down and picked up a thin plastic phone. The numbers on the buttons had faded and the screen had smoked over. She held it to her ear, then placed it on the desk.

In an adjoining room was a heavily stained gas range. Arnal flicked the ignition and tapped the gas bottle with his boot. Not even the scent of gas. On the floor was a charcoal ring, remnants of a camp fire. Scorch marks ran up the wall like the prints of someone trying to escape. The charcoal didn't smudge when Arnal scrapped it with his heel. The fire went out long ago.

The back of the office led into a small open yard where two empty oil drums stood next to a bricked-up annex. What caught Arnal's attention was the single window above the drums. The glass was intact. He looked around but couldn't find a way in.

–*I'll give you a bunk up?*
–*There might be someone inside.* Ternia's eyes widened.
–*There's no-one inside.* Though he could not be sure.
–*Then why look.*
–*You hungry?*

Arnal shifted the drums and hoisted up his daughter. The flash tucked in the back of her jeans, she cupped her hands to the glass, then elbowed out one of the panes, her face turned. She squirmed in, groping for something to take her weight and felt the back of a chair leaning against the inner wall. She slipped to the floor and listened. Nothing. Just her breathing and the steady patter of rain outside.

Hands trembling, stomach a knot of uncertainty, she flicked on the flash. The beam lit up a camp bed, computer screen, bucket, two wooden barrels, several cardboard boxes. No door.

The boxes looked untouched, sagging. The tape broke easily on the box nearest and when Ternia pulled back the cardboard flaps, she took a moment to realize what she was looking at.

She looked back to the open window and called out.

–*We're going to need a bigger backpack.*

The haul was impressive. Tins of ham, fruit, nuts, tuna. Plastic bags of dried beef and squid. Packets of juice and coffee sachets. And a small bar of soap which she slipped inside her pocket. The food was lowered in red and blue patterned plastic bags that Ternia had found under the bed. Once his backpack was full, Arnal told Ternia to put back what they couldn't carry. She clambered down into her father's arms.

—*There's no way out or in from inside.*

Back in the damp office, dinner was served at the desk. Tins of fruit and beans. After, Arnal pulled Ternia to his side, ruffled her hair. She looked up at him, the eyes of her mother.

—*Is there no-one else here on the island?*
—*I doubt it. They'd have taken the food.*
—*Maybe it was too well hidden?*
—*No, there's no-one here.* Arnal wanted his daughter to feel safe. But something was not right. There was no way in or out of the annex except through the window, which had been locked from inside, or so it seemed. He went back into the yard, leaving Ternia to finish up eating, and checked again. The annex felt solid to touch, no secret entrances, but about five metres away was a manhole cover dug into the concrete compound. Arnal crouched down and picked at the displaced soil and grit around the lip of the plate. Clearly, the cover had been lifted recently. Arnal guessed there was underground access to the annex, possibly leading to a hatchway of some kind that was hidden under the camp bed. Ternia couldn't have spotted it.

Arnal went back inside and said nothing of this to Ternia.

—*Let's take this lot back. Get the rest tomorrow.*

The rain had stopped and water dripped from the stooped trees as they headed back over the hill. Dawn was beginning to break when they reached the mudflats and they found their kayak undisturbed and no signs of visitors. The ground under the lean-to was hard but dry. Arnal stored the provisions in the boat and they removed their damp clothes and wrapped themselves in sheets. Ternia fell asleep where she sat and had to be lowered by Arnal. He stayed awake, worrying, until it was light and then shielded his eyes and slept.

Ternia woke, groggy, and scratched at the bites on her ankles. She could hear her father muttering.

—*Hey, sleepy-head. We have to move.*
—*Why?*

–Tide's coming in.

A thick mist had rolled over the bay and the sea had drawn in. Ternia breathed in the chill.

–Nearly got a wet wake-up call. Her father worked fast to untie the canvas and pull the kayak out from under the shelter and tie it to a bush. Ternia collected the bedding and their damp clothes, eyes swollen from lack of sleep. She followed her father, hugging the sheets to her chest. Round the back of the bushes the ground rose to a clearing, high enough to escape the incoming tide and surrounded by sufficient undergrowth to conceal them and their gear.

–We'll be okay here. We're well hidden.

They carried up the rest of their gear. Settled once more, they ate dried fruit, watching the tide flood the ground where they'd slept. As the water rose, the kayak floated, tugging at the bush to which it was moored.

–Will the plants drown?

–No. Not these ones. Arnal spoke between mouthfuls. *I reckon this is mangrove.*

–Mangrove?

–Plants that live in salt water.

–Like fish.

–Kind of.

–How?

–I don't know. But they survive, somehow. Arnal stood up and scanned the horizon and the beach.

–Listen Tern, I'm going to collect the rest of the food. I'll paddle round, save me the walk up the hill.

Ternia's shook her head, eyebrows raised.

–There won't be enough room for us both. It was a risk, to both, but a calculated one. The annex troubled him, but he had to go back. The food was precious. If there were other people he reckoned he could deal with them better alone. Ternia was safer hidden in these bushes. That was his thinking, but not Ternia's.

–I don't want to be alone. Her face crumpling into a sob.

–Tern, just rest. I'll be back soon. His hand brushed against his daughter's face, the skin taut around her jaw. Her cheeks wet with tears. Time and circumstances, he thought. That's all life was. His only reason for existence sat before him, trembling, and he could only do what time and circumstances allowed. Nothing more.

Arnal slipped back down the slope and pushed the kayak into deeper water. He climbed aboard, waved a paddle to Ternia and disappeared into the silver-grey bands of fog.

Ternia wiped her face with the sleeve of her jacket. She saw how dirty her clothes were and cried some more. The bites on her legs itched but she tried not to scratch, then she shut her eyes.

Sometime later, she woke, curled in her sheet, wet with sweat. The fog banks had cleared and the empty sea glistened like the skin of a snake. She saluted the sky, eyes narrowed into the yellow haze above, and gauged the time.

–Dad should be back.

She waited. Hungry but no appetite. Exhausted despite the sleep. Looking out to sea like the wife of a fisherman. To pass time, she thought back over the last few days, tried to remember where they'd camped, last eaten, found the kayak, washed, when something made her tense. Weeks on the road had sharpened her senses. She glanced around. Nothing. Nothing behind, just bushes and trees. In front, an empty bay raked free of surf. Below, the tide lapping mangrove. Nothing had changed but something was not right and Ternia didn't know what until she spotted someone emerging from the track that she and her father had taken last night.

The figure drew closer, splashing through the mangrove pools, creating ripples that circled the plants. Ternia scuttled backwards into the undergrowth and wasn't sure the visitor had spotted her until he reached the slope, looked up and spoke.

–Do you need help? No mask and a blurred tattoo on his neck. He stepped from foot to foot as if standing on hot coals and looked over his shoulder. Seeing no-one, he looked back.

Ternia didn't reply. She drew her knees to her chin and dug her toes into the earth.

–*Where is he, your companion?*

–*He's my dad.* Ternia's voice soft, like in a dream when a scream comes out a whisper.

–*You're new here.* A crooked smile hung from his lips and his front teeth were gone.

Ternia shook her head. She had no idea what to do, what to say. This was a robbery, Ternia thought. Robberies were common and Arnal had told her several times to run if approached by strangers. But she had nowhere to run to and no energy to fuel an escape. Out on the bay her father was nowhere to be seen.

–*He fishing, your dad?* The man took two steps forward and hauled himself up the slope and squatted in front of Ternia, close enough she caught his body odour, sour like fat gone bad.

–*Fishing's good here. Sea's cleaning up. Fish are coming back.* A cold sore protruded from the corner of his mouth and the skin on his lips had cracked.

Ternia didn't move, her dilemma older than the rocks: friend or foe?

–*Why that look? I'm not going to hurt you.* The man again glanced over his shoulder, grinning, then the smile fell away and he grabbed Ternia's legs, pulled her towards him. Her head fell back and she felt hands pulling at her clothes. She struggled, winded, and like a netted fish lost her breath and went still.

Foe, she thought.

As the man pushed into her, Ternia entered another place, feeling nothing, just wanting it to end. She turned her head to one side, felt detached, an observer. She looked at the shrubs encircling her and noticed how the leaves were different shades of green, not just one colour. She thought about the mangrove plants below and imagined the submerged roots had gills and could breathe underwater.

They survive, somehow. Her father's words.

What seemed to last forever did not take long at all. When finished, the intruder wiped himself and stood.

–Consider that payment. He helped himself to Ternia's supplies, cramming tins into a cloth bag he pulled from inside his jacket. Then left.

Ternia tried to sit but felt as though the weight of the man were still upon her. The wound between her legs throbbed and then she remembered the soap in her pocket. She took it out and held it to her mouth. Something fresh, from long ago. The scent reminded Ternia of her mother and took away the man's sour smell.

She curled up and waited. This was no time to give up. Not yet. They'd come so far. There was still some food. And her dad would be back soon.

In the pool below, the branches of the mangrove swayed in the wash of the tide.

City Chant
Elbert Siu Ping Lee

Computations go on and on ...
day and night
like aimless souls wandering
so aimlessly
according to schedule
on highways and telephone lines
and

the clockwork has been strengthened
by the dictation of a more-and-more perfect formula
so comparably impeccably neat
and relatively justifiable that
only flip-flop souls can inhabit

to produce ever-better results
to almost satisfy the appetite
of the changing needs
of a grander building
or the evolving demands
of a project of seeming excellence
requiring thousands more aimless souls
with flip-flop minds
and millions and trillions of computations
to go on and on ...
day and night
like aimless souls wandering

Untitled
Hatrick Lee Pui-tin

A toothless lady
was breathing her memories
at Kwong Choi Market

The toothless lady
was reminiscing about
dead cigarette ends

The withered lady
was carefully watering
the blooming roses

An innocent lad
was silently witnessing
the secular life

All gone! All those scenes
foreshadowing my future
have gone with my past

Kwong Choi Market is a wet market in Tuen Mun

Providence
John Wu

A crowd of people wanders in the city square
Carrying armful of shopping bags, they aimlessly wander
  from one shop to another
Blank looks fill their faces as they descend into money
  grabbing lairs
Without a second thought, credit cards are smoothly
  swiped like butter

The vision of paradise fades
A violin playing an endless waltz, reflects the endless
  struggle
Why has Eden become so consumed with materialistic
  values?
Is this our Providence?

Alarmed by the charm of our own ruin
Andrew Barker

Alarmed by the charm of our own ruin
We kept clear of ever being tempted.
Now, we bear the burden of the craven,

To fear that treason in human union,
Where by mere tears, to blood we are scalded.
Alarmed by the charm of our own ruin

We fear this season of wounds and lesions
May fool the surgeon. Uncut, but sculpted
Now we bear the burden of the craven,

And appraise ourselves cheapened by caution.
Funded by fields to which we have yielded
Alarmed by the charm of our own ruin.

Being bludgeoned by commerce is common
But the bargain can still leave us twisted.
Now we bear the burden of the craven.

With our heads down our ears out for action,
Ambition blunted. Blighted, we wait and
Alarmed by the charm of our own ruin
Now we bear the burden of the craven.

Checkboxes
Nicole Wong

We thought they would be back on after the tenth anniversary, but they weren't, not even after our President and Premier had gone. The police did a good job: a dozen websites were wiped out overnight; search engines and forums were disabled the next day. What happened to our favourite girls in Hong Kong, spilling out of their see-through nightgowns, stretching their legs on leather swings?

"Everything had to be nice and rosy around the anniversary. The new police head liked to put up a show," Dave, a regular, wrote on one of the few surviving forums. Everybody joined the discussion; we wanted to know what to believe and what to expect.

"Fucking idiot. Did he think our country's leaders would click away at girls' profiles in their hotel rooms? There'd be hookers knocking on their doors."

"The cops knew those classifieds through and through. They're looking for something to hand over to the state security."

"Maybe some mainland officials have been spying on us."

"*Diu*! What if the web sites never come back?"

We remember the disappearance but we've given up hope. Night after night I hit the links to what used to be the most popular sites, to be reminded ("The page you requested no longer exists") or told off ("Access denied"). Some of the babes—like the model chicks and the Hunan girls—have moved to the only website that is still fully functional, which got a facelift in July. There are rumours about a change of hosts. It has anti-drug and AIDS testing banners popping up.

Monopoly or not, it beats not having anywhere to look. There's not much for me to do after I get off work at midnight, when most people have wined and dined their friends or snuggled up with their sweethearts in bed. I used to get high and crash clubs with my high-school friend Ted, before he got jailed two years ago for selling cocaine. I always told him to switch to something more profitable, like smuggling.

"The kids are getting high in discos in Shenzhen nowadays. Or they get cheap supplies from there," I said. "If you're a smuggler, you can work with some mainland gangs."

"I've been in the same business for years. How the hell would I get into a smuggling ring?" Ted said.

I didn't know the right people either, not after Ted got locked away and the rest of us went our separate ways. I was a fake anyway: I squirted the stuff in, jerked about for a few minutes on the dance floor, before Ted or somebody else dragged me into a room. When the other guys were lifting asses and thrusting their way in, I clung onto a girl's knees and drooled.

It didn't take long for me to clean myself up. With all the talk about the quality improvement going on in Hong Kong—indoor and outdoor air, fresh and frozen food, import tea and export figurines—I got a job at a university-run quality evaluation centre. They were hiring in large numbers and I had years of cold calling experience. Then I got a part-time night job and moved out of home.

You'd want to cop and squeeze a few good sets at night, if your day job is to check boxes—"Excellent", "Good", "Fair", "Poor", "I don't know" —in a call centre. Most people who take the time to answer are students, housewives and middle-aged men with singsong voices. Every now and then you get a guy who mutters. "I don't know," the guy breathes into the receiver as if he's stroking himself.

I lose track of all the checkboxes on questionnaires and on my screen when I go home to browse the day's new profiles and user reports. Age, measurement, price, location; hand job, blowjob, anal sex, overnight stay. We search for girls who pass for dreams for people like us, "brothers" who boast and buzz in their concise sex scenes. "Her pussy ran like a river." "I got a whole lot of cum on her face." We look for wisdom from one another's encounters. "Three stars for figure; four stars for service. Recommended for small-tit lovers."

These user reports are a big deal, since the host's comments on the girls' profiles are paid advertisements. Many of the pictures are studio shots or touched up. There are few pictures of streets or buildings.

"It's too hard to find the right alley. They all look the same in Mong Kok," Sexero, a premium member, complained.

"The prices of these new girls are a bit steep. I wouldn't pay $700 for this dark-skinned chick."

"To each his own. Every babe who's on here must have her fans."

"I doubt it," Dave wrote. "Some of these girls must work for the host."

"This website is fishy. It lacks transparency."

It used to be easy to find the gems when there were multiple sources. A lot more white thighs and pink nipples danced before our eyes. The girls' moans were louder, closer, more diversified. On weekends, at four in the morning, I sat listening to the echoes and read the latest posts. Hundreds of Hong Kong men, young and old, were surfing the pages and swapping notes. "Thanks for your detailed report. I'll give her a shot." "She sounds yummy but I don't like tall girls." "I'm new to this. Which girl do you recommend?"

I watched the ups and downs of the visitor numbers at the bottom corner of the web page. It carried me through the night, made me feel connected to the world out there. Some of our "brothers" must have left their homes and walked into a dark alley in Mong Kok, the neon lights along Temple Street, or the quiet of Observatory Road, to enjoy a new Korean girl on the market or some comfortology from an older whore. The rest of us, invisible companions for one another, wailed and bragged in our own rooms.

We still ask about the old websites but there isn't any news. There will be others, or the current one will have to do. Everything's cool as long as we have fun.

Except for some of us who've lost contact with our favourite girls. Cindy never gave me her mobile phone number. I never asked. She had a place in Sheung Wan when I met her last summer. Early this year she moved to Tsim Sha Tsui on a short-term lease. On her voice mail she read out her services and fees, and the security code to her building in a sweet and hesitant voice, as if she was reading somebody else's script.

When she opened the door to me for the first time, she was in a dark-blue satin slip. There was just a touch of blush to her cheeks. She told me she was twenty.

"I used to do part-time sex at a karaoke pub when I was at school."

"You look like a regular girl."

"Thank you," she smiled, brushing back her freshly washed hair.

I visited Cindy once every couple months, until her profile got wiped out along with the classifieds. Her land-line didn't work. I asked around the forums, but nobody had her contacts. When I last saw her in June, the police were clamping down on prostitutes in Kowloon.

"They won't let us stand around the streets, or they come up to our flats and send away customers. Our landlords have been talking about rent hikes," Cindy said. "You want a smoke before you go?"

"Have we got time?"

"You can stay a bit longer."

I lay beside Cindy and studied her tits, the familiar way they slinked and gathered at her top ribs. She wouldn't let me nibble, but I liked her just the same. Cindy has a petite figure, a round face and lovely toes. The other guys didn't like her service as much. "Not very professional," they wrote. "Jerked me off too hard. She looked annoyed."

Cindy would blow me for as long as I lasted. Unlike most guys who boss their whores around, I let Cindy do the work most of the time and watched us in the wall mirror. The flush of us was up-and-down and hot and wet. She swung her ass from side to side. I didn't always feel much when she did that, but the view was exciting. I cupped her tits or held her waist, waiting for her to scream. It sounded abrupt, almost severe, a far cry from the careful delivery of most other girls. Her face was impatient and eager. Her lipstick was smeared.

We kissed a few times. I always gave her tips.

I finished my cigarette.

"What're you going to do if you get kicked out?"

"What're you going to do?"

I stuck my fingers in her mouth, pried it open.

She pushed my hand away.

"What about a second shot?"

"Any discount?"

"Fifty bucks off."

"I'm buying."

Maybe she stopped being a slave to the checkboxes.

Ambivalent philosophies

I Grew Mushrooms
Agnes S. L. Lam

One afternoon I was walking
among the crowds
on Pedder Street in Central
and felt a sharp pain
on the calf of my right leg.
Something had hit me accidentally.

I turned around to see a man,
possibly South American,
carrying a short bamboo pole,
chipped at one end.
'I'm so sorry,' he said
with fear on his face.

I looked at my leg—a tiny cut.
'Never mind. It's just a scratch.'

'No, this is very serious.
The pole was dipped in
a culture that will not die.
You must see a doctor
right away, please.'

FIFTY-FIFTY

So I did. In a clinic
on the eighth floor of a Central building,
I waited quietly for my turn.
The wound became itchy. I continued to wait.

An hour or so later,
when the doctor examined my wound,
it had sprouted tiny
mushrooms.
The doctor was taken by surprise but kept her calm.
'Let's cut them off,' she said.
And so she did.

But the mushrooms continued to grow
on the surgical steel tray where they were placed,
even after they were cut off from my blood.

While the doctor turned her head,
roses sprang up from the wound instead.
'Let's cut them off,' she said.
And so she did.
But the roses trimmed off from my leg became
larger and larger, taller and taller,
till they had to bend their heads against the ceiling.

Meanwhile, some orange tiger lilies had appeared
from the same wound. They too were snipped off
but continued to blossom on the doctor's desk, sprawling
onto her shelves,
covering the glass of her windows.

Then hibiscuses shot up, enormous petals spreading over
the doctor's certificates, dusting pollen over the silver
plaques from her grateful patients. After hibiscuses came
tulips, gladioli, peonies, sunflowers, orchids, African

violets (not the small potted species) ... One giant
flower after another bloomed from my small cut, until
the doctor's office became thick with greenery growing
around us, through to the waiting area, into the elevators,
crawling on the landings of each floor, spilling from the
lobby of the building onto the streets of Central

as passengers got into red taxis with their bags of
shopping
and green trams went past with their ding-ding bells
from a hundred years ago ...

Hotel New Hankyu, Osaka, 24 December 2002

the chemistry of fireworks
Viki Holmes

the chemistry of fireworks is based on the simple theory of combustion. the composition inside the firework must, however, contain six vital ingredients:

I: charcoal provides fuel for a massive burst of energy

it seemed like all my friends were points of light as we sat twilit and conversational. her sequins gleamed and the fans whirled, we were careful with one another, our words traced the air and hung about us moments after their dissipation.

II: oxidising agents allow the mixture to ignite

i am loving how they shine. we retain our own skins. later there will be a man who traces orion in the freckles of her arm. like we are all cave paintings. or is that fiction? ideas catalyse somewhere behind our eyes—dream residues.

III: reducing agents burn the oxygen

we would all dance, if we weren't so tired, if talking hadn't been enough. some of us will dance tomorrow, or the next day. some of us will paint our caves and faces with that same bright flame. sleep reduces; raises high.

IV: regulators control the speed of the reaction

days later the impact is still written on us all. dazed from neons, smiling at how far away we are, how very close. words do nothing for any of this. sparkle! crash! begin!

V: the incandescence from the elements occurs when solid particles are heated in the flame

strontium, copper, barium, iron, gold. colours beyond language. stronger in their transience. we clutch at beauty in our words, our songs, our other selves. blue is hardest: for sky, for peace. we need to heat it more.

VI: the binders do not actually begin to work until the firework has been lit as they are too unstable for storage within the firework and are hence potentially dangerous

combustion is never perfect, or complete. residues can scar, burn on for days. exchange is not easy, but it is necessary. watch us glow, all of us, above the scattered plates, the purpling sky. fizzing, coruscating points of light.

Fish Fillet with Tomato Sauce
Cecilia Ying-chai Chan

In the Fairwood Cafe, people are preoccupied with finding seats, ordering food, waiting in the queue, engorging themselves, and clearing their plates.

A girl has been lowering her head. In front of her is a plate of fish with tomato sauce. The golden fried fillet has a shape resembling her home country. She carefully cuts it up, forks a cubic piece, dips it into the tomato sauce, juicy red. A tear drops as she begins to sob, mourning for the ill-fated country, a home she can never return to.

A young expatriate ordered the same dish, which he is now skinning. He separates the white, supple fillet from the golden crust with precision. As he looks up chewing the fish, a child stares at him with big, black longing eyes—eyeing the crispy crusts he'd put aside. The child's mother had ordered for him a dull heap of spaghetti bolognese.

The young man realises his deftness in skinning, and this conditioned habit marks the only Englishness that remains in him. In his eighth year living in Hong Kong, he can only feed his nostalgic appetite in this hardly Western fast-food restaurant. He recalls what he would have done as a child: eaten up the crust, discarding the wholesome meat. Does a child care more for sheer taste or obscure identity?

Two friends are meeting after school. One is fasting for Ramadan. She is well aware that the first day is always the toughest. How can she fight hunger, and worst, thirst? At the brink of being overcome by desire, she keeps on praying. It gives her strength to stay out of temptation—barely.

Across the table sits her friend, clutching a glass of water. She is on a diet. Her dinner is this glass of water. But at 4:05 pm, already, she is distracted by the thought of desserts: Sara Lee pound cake, Ben and Jerry's scoops, berry crumble ... she holds herself back with a tedious calorie count and a mental picture of extra workouts.

Having her loose thoughts shunned, she collects herself. She looks at her smiling friend, and looks back at her glass of water, which she is now too ashamed to drink.

An impatient office worker anxiously fiddles his thumbs, taps the table, and glances at the number on his receipt. He only has thirty minutes left on his lunch break, including time for running errands. He takes out a book, *The Culture of Slow Dining*, to distract his impatience, and sighs.

"When will I have a long lunch at an al fresco cafe under the Mediterranean sun?"

The Philosophy of Smoking by an Amateur Smoker
Nicholas Y. B. Wong

I started smoking to catch the sublime of
the moment. There are no reasons, so don't
ask me why. Reasons only entertained tactics
in lawsuits, not habits. This was what happened
then: the moments propelled themselves and I
moved forward with them unwillingly. Since
the first inhaling, the concept of moments
changed. Time didn't freeze; I did. I suddenly
refused to proceed but welcomed a pause
in life. Motionlessness turned into self-deceit.
My mind rumbled, but I detected an
order within the chaos. Non-smokers got
along with their time easily; I had a
problem with mine. I wanted a break and I
wanted nothing. Nothing to lose. Smoking is
always a part-time job, not a full-time career.
When the moments are too heavy to contain
themselves in the smoky air, I would undo the habit.

The Prophet Outside the Main Library
Christina Chan

The sun burns
a twisting pleasure
into her rusty young skin.

She sings a love song
in her head.

She sits
under the marble sun
with a 12-dollar Starbucks chicken pie in hand
and a plan to fly in mind.

Tien Pei-chun
draws a crowd
giving a speech about beliefs
he does not believe in.
The prophet has learnt,
through her philosophy
class, to be sick.

She sees
blindness. The sun burns.
She hears deafness. Chicken swims
down her throat.
She says nothing.

THE CONTRIBUTORS

MARTIN ALEXANDER

Martin Alexander is a member of the Hong Kong Writers' Circle and OutLoud, the poetry group. He is poetry editor of The *Asia Literary Review*. A collection of his poems, *Clearing Ground*, was published by Chameleon Press in March 2004. Martin won the SCMP Short Story Competition in 1999. He has had poetry and short stories published in *Dimsum*, *The OutLoud Anthology*, *CityPoetry* and *Poetry Live!* (Hong Kong), in *The Vientiane Times* (Laos), and in *Akhbar* (Egypt). Martin has been a featured writer at international literary festivals in Hong Kong, Singapore, Cairo and Guangzhou. The Kassia Women's Choir performed his work, *Survive the Night*, with music composed by Phil Tudor, in the Concert Hall of the Hong Kong Cultural Centre in June 2005. He has a motorbike, a macaw, a murderous appetite for meat and a dream come true: reading with Seamus Heaney (at the 2006 Man Hong Kong International Literary Festival).

VIONA AU YEUNG

Viona Au Yeung was born and grew up in Hong Kong. Her family's decision not to move to California gave her the chance to keep track of how people have lived and how Hong Kong has changed/remained the same after its Handover. This also allowed her to study in the Chinese University of Hong Kong for three years, during which she wrote her poems *The Best Comfort* and *Thirteen Ways of Looking at a Poem* collected in *CU Writing in English Volume V* (2005), and her short story *Mirror* published in *Volume VI* (2006). She completed her MA in Romantic and Sentimental Literature in 2007 at the University of York, UK, where she also did some travelling and writing.

ANDREW BARKER

Andrew Barker lives and works in Hong Kong. He holds a first degree in English literature, a Master of Arts in Anglo-Irish literature and a Ph.D. in American Literature. He has been published in journals in Asia. The poem here is part of an inter-connecting sequence of 36 villanelles.

SUSAN BLUMBERG-KASON

Susan Blumberg-Kason is a freelance writer and editor based in the United States. She spent most of the 1990s in Hong Kong, studying Mandarin and political science at the Chinese University of Hong Kong. As luck would have it, she got into writing and editing a few years before the Handover and hasn't looked back since. She recently wrote the first guidebook to drinking tea in Chicago. Susan lives with her husband and two children in a quiet suburb of Chicago.

CECILIA YING-CHAI CHAN

Cecilia Ying-chai Chan was born and raised in Hong Kong. She started creative writing as an escape from school work. She loves the sound of English and enjoys the process of writing, literally, on a page. She believes that spending time on writing something irrelevant is better than trying to work while thoughts keep bubbling out. She is currently an English major at the Chinese University of Hong Kong.

CHRISTINA CHAN

Christina Chan is a young writer who likes to write most of her stuff while on the toilet. She sees purple people all the time but she can cope with it pretty well, since she can always hide behind her 6-foot-tall rabbit friend Frank when the purple people start to eat the bones in her fingers. She is a student at the University of Hong Kong (and was put on the Dean's List this year for academic achievement!) and her greatest aspiration is to have her application for social welfare accepted when she graduates so she can get money without working and use it to buy bread loaves to feed the penguins in South Africa.

MONICA CHAN

Monica Chan was born and bred in Hong Kong. She was educated under the British colonial influence, and has developed her sense towards the English language in a Catholic school. Possessing a passion for Chinese dance, she intended to study performance arts after Form 7, but her parents urged her to go to Lingnan University for a "proper" degree instead. She completed two degrees in English Studies there, but is still dancing. Monica has taken up teaching and is constantly amazed by her students for the inspiration they spark off in their writing.

JENNIFER S. CHENG

Jennifer S. Cheng is an MFA candidate in the Nonfiction Writing Program at the University of Iowa. She received her BA from Brown University and currently lives in a place where spiders fall from the ceiling and the air smells like nearby farmland.

CHING YUET MAY

Ching Yuet May, associate professor of English at the Chinese University of Hong Kong, is particularly interested in Anglo-American modernist poetry. She also enjoys reading Chinese poetry.

STUART CHRISTIE

Stuart Christie was born in dry, grassy country off the eastern headlands of San Francisco Bay. He spent summers as a child along the lake that waters the cherry, peach, and apricot orchards of the Okanagan country. He studied for a long time and paid for it by landing boats and pumping fuel for Native and Anglo-European fishermen cornering salmon herds running northward to die in the arms of the Fraser. He lived in Portland, Santa Cruz, Paris, and Philadelphia before coming to Hong Kong where his greatest joys are those he has found and made here.

DAVID CLARKE

David Clarke was born in South West England. He studied at University College London and the Courtauld Institute of Art (where he gained his Ph.D. in 1983). He has lived in Hong Kong since 1986, and is currently Professor in the Department of Fine Arts of the University of Hong Kong. Clarke has published extensively in the field of art history, and is also active as a photographer. His most recent books are *Reclaimed Land: Hong Kong in Transition* (2002) and *Hong Kong x 24 x 365: A Year in the Life of a City* (2007).

EDWARD RODNEY DAVEY

Edward Rodney Davey was born and educated in England. He spent several years in Spain, France, Italy and Germany before taking up a teaching post at Hong Kong University. His creative writing has appeared in various literary journals, including *Ambit*, and a translation of his short prose pieces has recently been published in Germany. He presently lives in England.

MICHAEL GIBB

Michael Gibb is a long-term Hong Kong resident. He is currently working for a South Korean newspaper in Seoul. He grew up in the UK and has been working in Asia since 1992. He has published several short stories through the Hong Kong Writers' Circle. His email is mjcgibb@yahoo.com.

LAWRENCE GRAY

Lawrence Gray is the chairman of the Hong Kong Writers' Circle and a screenwriter with credits in British and Singaporean TV drama. His screenplay "Fat Englishmen" is in production in Hollywood and his production company, Idol Films Ltd, is developing numerous TV and film projects for local and international markets.

PETER GREGOIRE

Peter Gregoire came out to live and work in Hong Kong in May 2003, making the same journey his father, Anthony Gregoire, did in 1967. *Painting Statues Red and Blue* is dedicated to Anthony's memory. His email is pgregoire123@yahoo.com.

JUSTIN HILL

Justin Hill has been likened to a George Orwell, a boxer, and Leo Tolstoy. He attended the same school as Guy Fawkes and his internationally acclaimed first novel, *The Drink and Dream Teahouse* (chosen by the *Washington Post* as one of the Top Novels of 2001) won the 2003 Geoffrey Faber Memorial Prize, a 2002 Betty Trask Award, and was banned by the government in China. His second novel, *Passing Under Heaven*, won the 2005 Somerset Maugham Award and was shortlisted for the Encore Award. *Ciao Asmara*, a factual account of his time in Eritrea, was shortlisted for the 2003 Thomas Cook Travel Book Award. Inexplicably, in the winter of 1994, he was once mistaken for a Chinese Mainlander.

LOUISE HO

Louise Ho's poetry has appeared in two books, in literary journals in Hong Kong and internationally, and has been included in various anthologies in Hong Kong and elsewhere.

TAMMY HO LAI-MING

Tammy Ho Lai-ming, aka Sighming, is a Hong Kong-born and -based writer. She is the editor of *HKU Writing: An Anthology* (March, 2006), a co-editor of *Word Salad Poetry* magazine and a co-founder of *Cha: An Asian Literary Journal*. More at www.sighming.com.

VIKI HOLMES

Viki Holmes lived and wrote in Cardiff, Wales, for seven years. Her poetry has been widely anthologised and she has had publications in Wales, England, Tasmania, Hong Kong, Singapore and in online journals such as *Retort* and *Getunderground*. She was twice a finalist in the John Tripp awards for spoken poetry, and was runner up in Hong Kong's inaugural poetry slam. She has studied Egyptology, Welsh language and English literature. She currently lives in Hong Kong where she teaches in a Buddhist kindergarten and regularly performs her poetry.

AKIN JEJE

Akin Jeje has been writing multicultural experience since the age of eighteen. Born in the United States of Nigerian and Kenyan parents, raised in Canada and now a Canadian expatriate living and working in Hong Kong, Akin Jeje has seen much of the world, having lived in various countries from Nigeria to Japan. Jeje's works have been printed in various Canadian poetry publications such as *filling station*, *housepress*, and *carousel*. Jeje is currently working on a poetry collection entitled *Smoked Pearl*, which chronicle his various observations and experiences in Hong Kong.

ALAN JEFFERIES

Alan Jefferies is an Australian born poet and children's author who lived in Hong Kong between 1998 and 2007. He has published five books of poems but is probably best known for his children's book *The Crocodile Who Wanted to be Famous* (Sixth Finger Press, 2004) which is based on the life of Hong Kong's celebrity crocodile, Pui Pui.

AGNES S. L. LAM

Agnes S. L. Lam was born in Hong Kong and was later educated in Singapore and America. A linguist by training, she is now an Associate Professor at the University of Hong Kong. She has published two poetry collections and her work has been included in several anthologies.

AMY LEE

Amy Lee was born in Hong Kong. She studied Comparative Literature at Hong Kong University and the University of Warwick. She has taught professional writing and communication courses and creative writing. Her creative work has been published in various literary journals, and she is also working to incorporate creative practices into teaching at different levels. At present she is Assistant Professor in the Humanities Programme and the Department of English Language and Literature of Hong Kong Baptist University.

ELBERT SIU PING LEE
Elbert Siu Ping Lee holds a Ph.D. in psychology. As a freelance writer, he contributes to local magazines and he writes poetry on occasion. Some of his recent poems can be found in *Hong Kong Poems*, an English-German anthology, published by Stauffenburgs, 2007. He lives on an outlying island in Hong Kong with his two dogs.

HATRICK LEE PUI-TIN
Hatrick Lee Pui-tin is a secondary school teacher in Hong Kong. Hatrick experienced hardship in his young years. He regrets seeing the hollow eyes of children, hoping to light a fire in children's hearts. He is furious with the gutter media and the corrupt politicians who have a vested interest in seeing Hong Kong governed by eunuchs. In the prime of his life, Hatrick is not optimistic about seeing democracy in Hong Kong before he dies. Hatrick believes in the Lord.

SHIRLEY LEE
Shirley Lee, a composer and musician, is currently studying Classics at Oxford whilst reading poetry and other interesting things. Korean by mother-tongue, birth and nationality, Hong Kong and English have long been home; she is not sure where her next home will be but she is thinking that it might be a house. Another of her poems appeared in the *Asia Literary Review*.

ARTHUR LEUNG
Arthur Leung was first trained as a concert pianist. He received degrees from the University of Cambridge and the University of Hong Kong, and completed a postgraduate programme in creative writing (with distinction). His poems have been published in print in *Hong Kong U Writing Anthology*, *Existere* (Canada), *Crannog Literary Magazine* (Ireland), *Taj Mahal Review* (India), *Paper Wasp* (Australia), *Southern Ocean Review* (New Zealand), *Cha* (online literary journal) and are forthcoming in *Smartish Pace* (USA) and *Pulsar Poetry* magazine (UK). He was a Finalist for the 2007 Erskine

J. Poetry Prize (USA) and short-listed for the 2007 Margaret Reid Prize for Traditional Verse (USA). Contact: leung_arthur@hotmail.com.

KAREN SHUI-WAN LEUNG

Karen Shui-wan Leung was born and raised in Hong Kong. She earned a B.A. in Contemporary English Studies from Lingnan University, where she first began writing non-academic English poems and contributing to the annual English literary journal published by the university's English Department. In her spare time Karen, as an art lover and a keen traveler, often marks her footsteps around the globe where she immerses herself in art and culture, which add color to her poems.

KWAI-CHEUNG LO

Kwai-Cheung Lo received his Ph.D. in Comparative Literature from Stanford University. Currently he is teaching at Hong Kong Baptist University. His publications include English work "Chinese Face/Off: The Transnational Popular Culture of Hong Kong" (criticism) and Chinese works *Desiring Belly Button* (short stories), "Mass Culture and Hong Kong: The Revenge of Electrical Appliances" (criticism), "Colors of Hong Kong: Racial Minorities in the Local Community" (criticism and interview).

CHRISTINE LOH

Christine Loh, OBE, is the Founder and CEO of the Hong Kong-based non-profit policy think tank, Civic Exchange. She is a lawyer by training, a commodities trader by profession and a former legislator of the Hong Kong Legislative Council 1992-97 and 1998-2000. She chose not to stand for re-election in 2000 in order to focus on policy research. Loh is also a director of the Hong Kong stock and futures exchange, an adviser to the G8+8 Climate Change Dialogue, and Senior Policy Adviser to C40 Cities Climate Leadership Project. She writes extensively, is a published author and a sought-after speaker locally and internationally. She was named a "Hero of the Environment" by *Time* in 2007.

DAVID MCKIRDY

David McKirdy was born in Scotland and raised and educated in Hong Kong. He is one of the organisers of local poetry group OutLoud and a director of the Man Hong Kong International Literary Festival. His work has appeared in anthologies and literary journals and his collection of poetry *Accidental Occidental* was published in 2005. McKirdy currently repairs and rebuilds vintage cars for a living.

DORIS LAU PARRY

Doris Lau Parry, a native of Hong Kong, started writing as a journalist in the *Hongkong Standard* in the early 1970s. She wrote extensively, as a columnist and interviewer, for a wide range of Chinese-language publications, including *Ming Pao Magazine* and *Music Today*. Lau was also a founding member of the *Thumb Weekly*. Educated in Hong Kong, Taiwan, France and the US, she holds a Master of Liberal Arts from the University of Chicago. For the last thirty years Lau worked in corporate communications, specializing in media and crisis training, and public affairs, in Hong Kong, China and Singapore. She currently lives and writes in Chicago, Illinois.

MANI RAO

Mani Rao (b.1965 India) moved to Hong Kong in 1993. She is the author of seven poetry books, two of which are bilingual with Chinese translations. She has published in journals including *Wasafiri*, *Meanjin*, *Fulcrum* and *WestCoastLine*, and her poetry is featured in anthologies including W.W. Norton's *Language for a New Century* (2008), *City Voices: Hong Kong Writing in English, 1945 to Present* and forthcoming anthologies by Penguin India and BloodAxe. Mani was Visiting Fellow at the 2005 Iowa International Writing Program, and won the 2006 University of Iowa IP writer-in-residence fellowship. In Hong Kong, she was the co-founder of the OutLoud poetry readings, and contributed a weekly poetry segment to Radio 4 RTHK. She lives in Las Vegas for an MFA in poetry at UNLV. Her website is www.manirao.com.

KATE ROGERS

Kate Rogers has had poetry, essays and reviews published in anthologies and literary magazines in Hong Kong, Taiwan, Canada and the UK. The publications include the *Asia Literary Review*, *Dimsum*, *Pressed*, *The New Quarterly*, *Contemporary Verse II*, *Canadian Women's Studies*, *The Mad Woman in the Academy* and *Orbis International*. Originally from Toronto, Kate has been teaching writing, literature and ESL for colleges and universities in Canada, China, Hong Kong and Taiwan for the past seventeen years. She has traveled extensively in Asia and in Southern Africa. A bilingual collection of her essays about Taiwan, *The Swallows' Return,* was published in June 2006. Her first collection of poetry, *Painting the Borrowed House*, will debut in Hong Kong with Proverse press in 2008. Kate Rogers teaches English and writing for City University Community College.

KEANE SHUM

Keane Shum is a law student in Washington, DC. He wants to be a writer when he grows up. Or Batman. He also loves his mother very much.

MADELEINE MARIE SLAVICK

Madeleine Marie Slavick (思樂維) contributed the poem "Finger, Flower" as well as the 50-50 photograph. Her books of poetry and non-fiction include *Round: Poems and Photographs of Asia*, *Delicate Access* (微妙之途) and *My Favourite Thing* (我最寶貴的). She has lived in Hong Kong since 1988.

JESSE WONG

Jesse Wong is a former journalist with *The Asian Wall Street Journal,* and also has written for *Fortune, Institutional Investor* and the *Economist Intelligence Unit.* He wrote this essay for the anthology drawing on research he has done for a book about 1960s Hong Kong.

NICHOLAS Y. B. WONG
Nicholas Y. B. Wong is a Teaching Fellow at the Department of English of the Hong Kong Institute of Education. He has just completed his M.Phil. thesis on the relationship between body parts, desire and fetishism in contemporary films and literary texts. Besides academic research, Wong is also interested in creative writing and has published poems and short stories both locally and internationally. Contact: bishonennich@hotmail.com.

NICOLE WONG
Nicole Wong's fiction has been published in Hong Kong, the US, UK and Australia. She is currently a journalist for an English-language newspaper in Hong Kong. Contact: nicolettew@gmail.com.

WOO SEE-KOW
Woo See-Kow spent his childhood to teenage years growing up in Shamshuipo, Hong Kong. His poetry and writing mostly reflect a sense of place, a feeling of belonging, and his sentiments for the people he has met at various times and places from his boyhood to present in Hong Kong, a city he often mocks but always loves. He was educated and received his degree in the US.

JOHN WU
John Wu is currently a third-year student at the University of Hong Kong, with a major in English Studies and minor in Comparative Literature. Prior to studying in Hong Kong, he lived in Vancouver for ten years. He was a member of the 2006-2007 HKU Creative Writing class and is interested in writing poetry and short fiction covering a range of different topics and genres. Besides poetry, he also enjoys directing and creating short films inspired by others' stories and poetry. He is very enthusiastic about music, and being able to play both the violin and the guitar.

YUEN SIU FUNG PHOENIX

Yuen Siu Fung Phoenix was born and educated in Hong Kong. She received her bachelor degree of Arts in English and a M.Phil. degree in Literary Studies from the Chinese University of Hong Kong. This is her statement: "During my childhood, I lived in a village in the New Territories where I was close to nature and had a carefree life that was essential to foster my interest in imagination. In school, I found the informal writing exercise one of best ways to put my imagination in ink. After being admitted to the University, I had opportunities to incorporate my imagination into my study. *Petal Beauty* is one of the products and shows that I am only a beginner in writing."

XU XI, EDITOR

Xu Xi is the author of six books of fiction and essays, most recently a collection, *Overleaf Hong Kong: Stories and Essays of the Chinese, Overseas*, and the novel *The Unwalled City*. She also co-edited *City Stage* and *City Voices*, the first comprehensive anthologies of Hong Kong literature in English. Her essay collection *Evanescent Isles: From My City Village* will be published in 2008.

Her fiction and essays are published in numerous anthologies, literary journals and magazines worldwide. New work appears or is forthcoming in *Silk Road, Manhattan Noir, Muse, N Exposant Nouvelle, Ploughshares, The Writer's Chronicle, Asian Literary Review, Carve Magazine, Time Asia, Imagining Globalization, Now Write!, Saying the Unsayable*. Literary awards and honors include the shortlist of the inaugural Man Asian Literary Award, an O. Henry Prize Story, a *South China Morning Post* Story Contest winner, a New York Arts Foundation fiction fellowship, among several others, and residencies at the Chateau de Lavigny in Switzerland, the Jack Kerouac Project of Florida, and Kulturhuset USF in Bergen. In 2008, she was named the first English language Writer-In-Residence at Lingnan University, and will be the 2009 Bedell Distinguished Visiting Writer at the University of Iowa's Nonfiction Writing Program.

The author is on the faculty at the Vermont College of Fine Arts MFA in Writing, and holds an MFA in fiction from the University of Massachusetts, Amherst. She teaches writing internationally, as a visiting lecturer at several universities, and also lectures and writes regularly on globalized culture. A Chinese-Indonesian native of Hong Kong, she left an eighteen-year international marketing and management career in favor of the writing life. She now splits her time between New York, Hong Kong and the South Island of New Zealand. Visit www.xuxiwriter.com.